AM I DOING THIS RIGHT?

Kit Farrell

ISBN: 0692377026
ISBN-13 9780692377024

DEDICATION

To all the girls with big heads full of even bigger dreams-
Don't ever let anyone tell you that what you have to say doesn't matter.

To my parents-
Your heart is my favorite home.

ACKNOWLEDGMENTS

There are so many people who played a role in the creation of this book and some don't even know it.

My parents, Joe and Carol, for above all else, thank you for making sure I grew up listening to good music. And of course your endless love and support. And for letting me move home after college. Joe and Ryan, thank you for making sure I grew up tough. I love you both. My family, thank you for loving my brand of weird and always celebrating it, even if you don't always get it. To every teacher I ever had who let me skip class to hide away in the library, thank you for trusting it would pay off. Bridget Woznica, your friendship and advice is something I'll treasure forever. Thank you for the hard work you put in with me on this book and in school. Donna Steiner and Eileen Gilligan, your classes in college gave me wings. I was lucky to have such great college experiences with powerful female educators. Alyssa McClenaghan, you brought my book to life with the cover. Thank you for your art and your beautiful soul. The staff at Amazon and Create Space, thank you for giving more authors the chance to be heard. For my friends who read countless passages and stories, thank you for keeping me grounded. I'm hashtag blessed you even like me. To the editors and agents who wanted me to change the heart of my story to make it more marketable and main stream, thank you for teaching me that what I want is worth fighting for.

1

$272.76

"Do you think she's okay?" I could hear Dad's deep voice outside my bedroom door.

"She's fine," Mom chimed in.

"Are you sure? She's been wearing that same purple shirt for the last four days."

"She's fine Jim."

"Is it menstrual?"

I let a soft laugh out and seconds later my door was pushed open and my parents came hurtling through.

I was hungover. Four bottles of water next to my bed, hungover. Making deals with the devil to take away my throbbing pain, hungover.

"Good. You're awake," Mom said as she threw open the curtains and I felt like my body had been set on fire.

"Barely." I rolled away from their voices, but in a twin-sized bed, I could only roll so far.

"Okay, this isn't an intervention," Dad began as he sat on the edge of my bed. "But you could say this was the pre-intervention. You know like the staff meeting they have before the intervention goes down."

"She gets it," my mom interjected. "Quinn we're just worried about you, I mean it's been two weeks and you really haven't done much but lay in your bed and drink wine right from the box since you've graduated."

"Not true." I pointed to the pile of mostly dirty clothes in the corner of the room. "I unpacked."

"Right," Dad patted my knee. "Of course you did."

"We're trying to be patient, but it's getting a little pathetic," she said.

"Listen, I know I've been a little off lately." I caught my mom glancing to the empty boxes of wine scattered in between my 'N Sync dolls, "But I've just graduated. Doesn't that buy me a few minutes of nothing?" I eyed the way Joey and Chris were lined up behind Justin, JC and Lance.

I used to think I was a Justin, or at worse at JC, the natural leaders and main players of the boy band. But now, with my post graduation slump, I'm starting to believe maybe I'm a Joey Fatone, just dropping a couple of deep voice notes from the background every four or five songs so people remember I'm still in the band.

"Hon, a couple of days of adjusting we understand, but this," Mom gestured around the room, "this is the opposite of adjusting."

"Rejecting," Dad added, quietly.

"Yes. This more rejecting."

"You guys, I'll be fine. I promise." I tried to sound confident in my delivery, but even I noticed how forced and stiff it came off.

"It smells in here." Mom was now inspecting various cups on my windowsill. "This isn't normal."

"Right, well that was a good talk." Dad stood up and walked towards the door, sliding his body out the room one foot at a time to avoid Mom's line of vision.

"Uh," Mom was annoyed. "Didn't you forget to tell her something?"

Dad shook his head confidently. "No, I'm all set." He smiled at me.

"Fine." Mom gave Dad a look as she started for the door. "Oh and Quinn," she turned around as she held onto the door. "Let's try to put some pants on today, okay?"

I just really didn't see the point in wearing pants. I've weighed the pros and cons more times than I care to admit and to me there are more benefits to a life without pants. Your laundry pile is cut in half, as is your time spent going to the bathroom. Nobody expects anything from a person who's really only dressed from the waist up. That's the beauty of it. It also allowed me to have an illustrious collection of underwear.

I've been logging a lot of pants-less hours as of late. My roommates don't agree with my wardrobe choice, but then again they've seen me naked hundreds of times, sure most of them when I was shitting my pants as a baby, but still. Referring to my parents, Jim and Mary, as my roommates often softened the blow of living at home, if only slightly.

"I can't make any promises." I tipped my fingers to her in a salute.

I rolled over, trying to fall back asleep, but the throbbing ache in my body from too much Pinot told me otherwise. I got up slowly as to not disturb the two pounds of alcoholic waste sloshing around in my stomach.

I get their concern. Really, I do. I'd only been graduated from college for two weeks. That's it. Summer hadn't even started and I was fourteen days removed from my college education. I wasn't starting my new job or traveling abroad, here I was-- back home, getting comfortable in my twin-sized bed. My only plans for after graduation centered upon how early I could go to bed and how late I could wake up. You could say that I was absolutely crushing it in the life department.

When my cousin John moved back in with his parents after graduating college last year, he told me that the key to living at home was to blend. Don't do anything that makes you stick out, try to limit the rash behavior and always make sure to hide the evidence of any college style binges. I think what he meant was don't do stupid stuff that further hammered home the point that I was not yet an adult, mostly a child who could buy alcohol. The pre-intervention in my bedroom was not blending. The amount of boxed wine in my bedroom didn't seem like blending either.

I managed to take a shower, in hopes the nausea would subside if I no longer smelled like wine. I let the hot water dance down my body and convinced myself that this and this alone would make me whole again.

Afterwards I still felt like shit, but at least the scent of desperation on my skin dissipated slightly.

"I'm worried for her Jim," Mom was referring to me as if I wasn't in the kitchen next to them. "The other two didn't go to college and they both have jobs and moved out of our house. And then this one…" she paused. "Goes to a four year school for what, to take five years to graduate and then move home and prance around in her underwear?"

"I guess." He conceded. Dad is a stoic man who doesn't give into Mom's dramatic antics half as much as she'd like him to. He avoids confrontation at all costs. Maybe that's why they're still married.

"She would have been fine with her business degree, but all of a sudden she decides she wants to be the next Picasso. Who gets art degrees? It's the twenty-first century, not the Renaissance."

"I don't know."

"And that's why nobody has a job."

Mom gave my dad a look and after a forceful cough, he began talking. "Q we do need to talk about you working at the bar tonight," Dad concluded as he poured a cup of coffee and sat down next to Mom at the counter. "Your mother and I can't be there and…" he paused, rubbing his temples.

Kelly s was our family bar downtown and it had been a community staple for almost 25 years. After my parents got pregnant with my older sister Delaney as teenagers they did the quickie marriage thing and tried their hardest to keep their heads above water. After a string of crappy apartments and many meals eaten from the microwave they saved up enough money to buy a piece of property in the middle of town. Mom wanted to make it a café, but Dad wanted a bar. Why ruin the Irish stereotype? He said something about the people in this town not being sophisticated enough for a café. Right after they bought the place Mom got pregnant with my brother Patrick and Dad took over the majority of work with the building. He figured if he was doing all the work, it would be a bar.

As kids we spent a lot of time running around the bar and when we turned 18 each of us began to bartend. Fortunately I only had to for a little while before I left for college, but Delaney spent six years bartending before finally taking a couple classes on bookkeeping. She now runs the bar's finances and strictly works during the day. Pat worked there for a couple years but he got himself into the fire academy and now just sticks to helping out and drinking there on weekends with his high school friends.

"You don't have to explain it to her," Mom said, harshly. "Quinn we need you to work and as long as you're living here you will work." I shot her a dirty look, which she returned with equal disdain.

"I mean if you had a job then that'd be one thing, but you don't - and you don't show any signs of wanting one." Dad was choosing his words carefully.

"I do have a job." I wildly defended. "Who do you think keeps these streets safe during the day while everyone is off at work?" I used air-quotes to describe work. "I'm the neighborhood watch. It's a thankless job and the hours are horrible, but these residents have never felt safer."

Dad tried his best not to smile, mostly in fear of Mom. "Seriously Quinn," he pleaded.

"Dad, no offense, but I don't really see how working at the bar is going to help me."

"It's not," he replied. "It's going to help me."

"I'm not going to be here long. I'm going to get a call for a job any day, I can feel it."

"Okay, well until that happens you're going to need a job."

"This feels like oppression."

"This is life, sweetheart. Get used to it."

"Okay." I sighed. I knew that I was not going to win this argument, so I walked away before they could say anything else.

At times I thought my parents didn't believe I even wanted a job. That however was not the case. I had a plan. I was going to graduate and move to Chicago, where the art was appreciated and the pickup trucks were minimal. I was going to work in an art gallery and I was going to sell other people's paintings. Two years into my job, I would meet my future husband when I sold him a rare Jackson Pollock painting that I found after proving my worth to my mean boss with phenomenally sculpted cheekbones. We would then fall in love over dim sum and I would laugh at his witty puns and enormous checking account.

Sike! I'm home with mom and dad instead.

It was the perfect plan, until I found out that Chicago didn't have nearly as many art galleries as I planned and I hadn't gotten any of the jobs I applied for. I couldn't move anywhere if I didn't have the money and I would never have the money if I didn't get a job. I was stuck and the only option was to come home.

It was hard enough to get a job with a real degree, but my degree from Millstadt University just says I'm pretentious. MU is a moderate sized liberal arts college set in the Berkshires. I'm more likely to get hired at a ski resort than I am an office. I wasn't exactly living in a thriving metropolis built on setting trends either. My town was built on broken dreams, prescription drugs and forgotten promises. Springhaven, New York is known for many things, but being on the cutting edge of culture was not one of them.

My skill set wasn't screaming ideal job candidate either. Every employer believed that fine art degrees meant that the graduate had a healthy supply of tie-dye tee shirts and a thirst for existentialism. My job experience wasn't much and the one internship I had when I was a business major was a joke. I spent the summer trying to learn restaurant operations, but it was actually just me shucking oysters for eight hours a day in Cape Cod. Consider me qualified to run a business.

I walked back into my room. I longed for my bed and the infinite joy it brought me. Before I could climb in, I saw a lump move underneath the covers. Moments later, our family dog, Marlowe, popped her head out at the foot of my bed. Marlowe was a French bulldog who grunted almost as much as she farted, but she was who I'd been spending most of my time with recently, so I was happy to see her. I picked her up and settled her next to me.

My life was easier to manage from the comfort of my bed and by manage I certainly mean avoid. The world doesn't seem so bad when you completely ignore everything around you.

They don't tell you that this was what happened after college. Instead they fill our heads with big ideas and dreams and never bother to check back and tell us that our college diploma doesn't automatically come with a job offer and apartment lease taped to the back.

Nobody prepares you for what to do when everyone says *no* because where's the fun in that? I know what people say about my generation. Our blatant laziness cupped with a wild sense of entitlement to equal a generation of whiny sissies. But it's not like that. We were raised on the idea that pursuing a dream was enough to get us what we wanted -- even if we didn't deserve it. Hard work - not us. Struggle - wrong generation. We are the children of the Internet, where everything is a mere click away. We were pacified to the point of madness. Now I'm 23 with the emotional coddling of an eight year-old. An entire group of people with the same thought, "Now what?"

I grabbed my laptop from my nightstand and opened it, readying myself for the onslaught on post collegiate boasting that was to follow from various social media websites. My personal research, also known as Facebook stalking, showed me there were several different post college paths that people usually took. There are those who go on to graduate school either because their ideal career requires 17 degrees or they aren't ready to assimilate into being a real person so they'll squander another $40K down the tube to pretend they're still undergraduates. There are people who turn in their bachelor's degrees for Mrs. degrees, marrying their college sweetheart and giving up all hope of a career in exchange for an apron and a baby. Then, still, there are those who uproot themselves from their homes and travel to a city unknown in hopes of stumbling upon their dream. I would say that I fall into a fourth, and perhaps most popular, category: the ones who graduate from college and have no idea what they want to do. Call it naïve, dumb, irresponsible, whatever you want, but here I stand, age 23, still unsure of where my future lay.

I applied for exactly 117 jobs in the month before graduation, spanning three major cities and four different industries. Of the 117 jobs I applied for I received only 12 emails in response. Eight of which stated I was not right for the position, two offered me a subscription for their art publication, one letting me know that I spelled the hiring manager's name wrong, and finally one email asking for an interview. However, upon further research into the company, I learned that I would actually be receiving stolen artwork from a man in Australia via mail that I would then distribute among dealers. All I had to do was give him my social security number and checking account information. Serves me right for applying for jobs on Craigslist.

"Quinn," Mom called up the stairs to me. "What are your plans for the day?" I knew she wanted me to tell her that I would clean or apply for jobs or do anything, but I didn't want to lie.

"Uh," I shifted on my bed. "I was going to do some research on a couple things" I always found it best to be extremely vague with my parents when describing any of my daily activities.

"You know, I've been thinking, you should start one of those Twatter accounts and become a blogger."

"Twitter." I screamed back.

"God bless you."

"No Mom. It's called Twitter."

"Sure, sure. Alright, we're heading down to open the bar." Seconds later I heard the front door shut.

I grabbed the remote and began my endless search for a show on Netflix. Besides Marlowe, this entertainment-streaming device was the best thing I had going at the moment. Sometimes when I feel my life slipping off the rails I start a new show on Netflix and convince myself that binge watching three seasons in 34 hours is stable behavior.

It's not.

But at least then I can watch other people wig out about their fictional lives instead of planning my real one. More often than not I spend twenty minutes trying to find a show and then get so frustrated I turn the TV off entirely. It is this exact reason that at precisely 2:00 p.m. everyday I run out of things to do with myself. I can only watch so much daytime television without feeling like a stay at home mom. When I was home on breaks during college my best friend Maggie was home too so we would always commiserate together, but she moved to Houston after she graduated last year and took a job event planning for Houston's best event planning company.

Luckily for me her little brother is still around to sell me weed because I was the one who taught him how to properly roll a joint when he was in 8th grade. I considered it a valuable skill that would get him a lot of friends in high school.

In order for this all to make sense, this whole misery thing, I need you to understand something. I've never considered myself to be ordinary. Lack of self-confidence was never my adolescent issue. In fact many would say I was overflowing with it, the big fish in a small pond mentality at it's best. I always believed with every ounce of my being that I was meant for a life so much bigger than what this town had to offer. I thought I would have completely rewired the world by the time I was 23 and when that didn't happen, I lost it. I just completely and wholeheartedly lost my shit and I guess myself in the process.

"Hey Dillon, are you around?" I never bother with small talk because people get a false sense of friendship during a drug deal. Let's think about it, if this person who I am contacting for drugs didn't have drugs, would I still contact them just to see how they are? ... Probably not.

"Yeah, I just re-upped, picked up some fire."

"Alright mind if I just stop by and grab some?"

"Yeah, no problem, come through." Dillon spoke to me like I was one of his 16-year-old cronies who actually believed he had an ounce of street credibility. Dillon pissed his pants until he was eight and used to watch The Babysitter's Club with Maggie and I. He will never, ever have street credibility.

It took me a couple minutes to get ready for sunlight and vitamin D. I spent four minutes putting lotion on my hands and another three wiping it off after I used too much. Then I had to take Marlowe out. At least I had already showered for the day.

My jeep was parked in the usual spot in the driveway - closest to the house. It didn't get much use because there weren't a lot of places I was driving to. The car had been passed down from Delaney, to Patrick and finally, me. A 2003, white, Jeep with a removable roof that had me looking like Cher from Clueless, minus the plaid, every time I drove it. There was no sneaking around my town when you were driving that car. It was infamous.

I could drive the five minutes to their house with my eyes closed. I drove it so often. I knew which turns I could accelerate and which curves to brake on. Muscle memory. Left at the end of the development, straight for two miles, right on Crenshaw, left on Cooper and it's the third house on the right. My car probably expects to go there when I start the engine from my driveway. Only now instead of seeing my best friend, I'm buying drugs from her little brother. Isn't it ironic? (I really do think)

The expanse of windows as their house comes into view always bothered me. It makes their house look vulnerable and exposed with everyone being able to see into their windows as they drive by. The Jacobs' house is too big for just Dillon and his dad to live there. Their mother died when Maggie and I were 18, three weeks before high school graduation. That had everything to do with Maggie not wanting to be back in this town. The thought of living with just her dad and brother in a place she remembers her mother so strongly was too much for her.

Dillon was shooting a basketball in the driveway as I pulled up. His dorky body moved back and forth in the same three-foot space as he tried over and over to put the ball through the net. "Damn." He echoed loud enough for me to look up and see the ball soar halfway across the driveway when I got out of the car.

"Hey Dillon."

"What's up Q?" he bellowed through heavy breaths. His small body continued to flail recklessly across the asphalt.

"Not much. Working on your hoop game I see."

"Yeah, I'm trying to get my weight up for my new job." He pushed his snapback further up on his forehead and bunched his jersey shorts in his fist before pulling them up hastily.

"Oh really?" I was surprised because Dillon's interests were reserved for weed and the game show network.

"Yeah I'm interning to be the new night DJ on BeReal94.7."

I can't tell if he's serious or not because BeReal94.7 is the local rap station. "Cool," I finally managed to say after an awkward pause.

"Yeah I'm going to be working the graveyard shift at first, but I'm hoping to make the jump to morning radio. They're going to hook me up with classes at the local radio and television school too." He beamed with pride as he spoke, sticking his chest out. Although that didn't explain why he was trying to 'get his weight up' if he was taking a job where nobody saw him. With Dillon, I never asked questions because he has pot and I don't question the guy with pot.

"Do you want to hear some of the beats I've been mixing?"

Drug deals are how false friendships are started. Whoever holds the bag, holds the power. Everyone knows this. The longer he holds the bag in his hand, the longer I have to pretend to be interested in what he's saying. Any other day I'd be glad to listen to whatever scratches he was making, but today I needed to get home and back to my strict schedule of sleep, wine and no pants.

"Ugh," I rolled my eyes, "my parents need me to dust all the ceiling fans in the house today, but I would love to another time."

"Oh." The smile fell from his face.

Damn. "Okay. I have time for one song."

"Sweet." He smiled once more and I followed Dillon in the house and downstairs to his *studio.* His studio was actually a portion of the finished basement sectioned off with a sheet hung up to separate his turntables and computer from the couch and foosball table. He had posters of rap artists I didn't recognize taped to the wall and a collection of snap back hats tacked above the posters. "I've been mixing a bunch of new tracks."

"Wait, sorry," I interrupted him. "I need to smoke something immediately or the ache in my head will only get worse once you turn this on."

"Yeah, sure. Just blow into this will ya?" Dillon handed me a paper towel roll with a dryer sheet stuffed inside the tube.

"A sploof. Creative."

Dillon hit play on his track and I took the eight-minute mix as an invitation to sift through my wallet for my evaporating stack of graduation money. I was living on borrowed time. It was only a matter of drug deals before I ran out of the money I'd gotten from graduating, and then…then I'm fucked. Like, cashing in my stocks and savings bonds that I'd had since birth, kind of fucked. On multiple occasions I'd given serious thought to auctioning off my complete set of 'N Sync dolls still in the boxes, but I really didn't want to part with ramen noodle haired Justin Timberlake if it wasn't a life or death situation.

Dillon passed me a bong. I lit the mossy weed and lifted the slide after a few seconds. Water slurped at the bottom and I inhaled sharply before holding the smoke in and blowing the cloud into the sploof. By my fourth hit of the stuff, his music didn't sound too bad.

An hour and two joints later I was ready to go home. Quite frankly, I needed a nap. That was a big day out for me. I was going to need to recuperate if I was to finish that box of wine in my bed tonight.

Dillon's tracks sucked, but his pot was dynamite. It should feel wrong, but I greatly benefited from his need to impress me. Dillon was always heavy on the bags because he wanted my approval. We had a beautiful relationship.

I was envisioning the sandwich I would make myself when I pulled onto my street and saw that not only were my parents home, but both Patrick and Delaney's cars were in the driveway as well, because sometimes it's not enough to get interrogated by just two people.

I lowered my body further in the car and kept driving past the house. I'd made it two neighborhoods past my house before my phone rang.

"I saw you drive by the house you little brat," Delaney spoke into the phone when I picked it up.

"Hello Delaney."

"You're high, aren't you?" she pressed.

"Not even a mom yet and those maternal instincts to nag are already in high gear."

"Ha. Ha." She let out a forced chuckle. "We all just left so you're safe to go home."

"Thank you." I said, grateful to her for looking out for me.

"I'll talk to you later."

"Bye." I hung up and swung back around to the house.

I pulled back in the now empty driveway. That's typical behavior for my family. At any given point in the day there can be between two and five members of the Kelly family together, always going on about some awful catastrophe that will be fixed by the end of the day. One day it was the foundation of the bar needing to be jacked up. Another time it was the dishwasher who stole $200 from the drawer. My parents, sister and brother all have a part in the family business so I understood their need for constant communication, but in the past few weeks most of the time they stood around talking about me.

"I can't believe that even your brother has a plan in life." I paused to inhale the milky smoke emitting from the joint. "And I'm sitting here smoking joints on my parent's patio furniture with my thumb up my ass." I exhaled directly into the phone screen in my hands. Maggie laughed. She was in her office on a 'conference call' AKA a weekly hour-long video chat session we have. It made us feel like we weren't an entire country apart from each other.

"My little brother wanting to live out his rap video fantasies is not a life plan," she declared while pinning her blonde hair on top of her head. "Besides who is going to take him seriously?"

I took a bite of my sandwich before answering. "Obviously the listeners of BeReal94.7 are if these guys are willing to put him through school." I took another bite. "Shit."

"Hey, don't get down about it. Not everyone knows what they want to do right after they graduate."

"No. That's not it. This sandwich is delicious. The perfect peanut butter to jelly ratio."

"Right." I can tell she's trying to be supportive, but it's hard to understand my struggle when she's literally landed her dream job.

"Most of the people who don't know what they want to do with their life can figure it out in their own place." I panned the camera around to show Maggie the backyard. "I'm living with my parents."

"And not wearing pants I see." She points towards the bottom of the screen quizzically. "What's going on with that, huh? It's almost 4:00."

"I'm on a pants strike."

"And from the looks of your legs, a razor strike too." She smiled after the last comment. "But really Q, what's up? You're looking a little glum."

"I'm not…I'm just high." I stepped on the joint and threw it across the yard.

"If you say so. I've gotta go, I have a planning meeting in ten and I still have to prepare my notes. I'll see you soon when I'm home for Dillon's graduation."

"You sound so sophisticated when you make office talk."

"Screw you. Love you. Shave those legs. Bye"

"Love you too. Bye."

After talking with Maggie I either felt really happy because she's doing so well or really sad because she's not here. Today I felt sad. My legion of friends at home wasn't too big, not because of any crazy dramatic story where I slept with the homecoming queen's boyfriend, but simply for the fact that I didn't do a very good job of keeping in touch with people after I went to college. Distance puts relationships to the test. As I got older, I began to understand how relationships grew. As a kid, I believed relationships were simple. They grew straight up and down like bean stalks - but the older I got, the more I began to understand that relationships grew like vines of ivy that twisted and wrapped around objects so tightly that sometimes the only option was to cut them down and let them go.

High school friends are weird. Sure there are a always few people that you'll keep in touch with, but for the most part you lose the friends you had in high school. You'll always share the emotional awakening of your youth with them and you'll nod in acknowledgement when you see them at the Kelly's during winter break but there's an understanding that the relationship you once shared is gone.

I remember one party I went to the summer after my sophomore year of college at Nick Coffey's house in the woods by the lake. It must have been 100 degrees that day because even the night air felt like it had been set on fire. There were so many people there. I saw people I hadn't seen since graduation and even then I could feel something had shifted. Relationships had already changed. I stood by the keg, drinking plastic solo cup after plastic solo cup of flat beer because I didn't have anything worthwhile to talk about with these people. It seemed most of us were only friends because we spent four years in the same soulless building.

Suddenly all of the inside jokes and mutual interests that kept us as friends back in high school seemed trivial and no longer relevant. All of those interactions were such bullshit. I wasn't going to force a relationship with someone I had nothing in common with simply for the sake of it. From that night on I didn't go to parties or nights at the bar with people from high school. And since I didn't have any missed phone calls or messages from them, I don't think they missed me much either.

It also didn't help that all of my friends from college were spread out over the country. Sure we had emails and group text messages, but it wasn't the same as being with each other, knowing they were going through the same post-college separation anxiety I was.

I needed to get ready for work. I was supposed to be there in an hour and I still had to take a shower. After my conversation with Maggie, an email from my college roommate Lizzie distracted me and the next thing I knew it was an hour later and I had three separate tabs open on my laptop, all videos of dogs reuniting with soldiers. I was a mess.

2

$232.76

Pulling into the gravel parking lot of Kelly's I was shocked to see a dozen or so cars already there, it was barely 6:00. As soon as I opened the double doors I wanted to turn around. The bar was filled with people.

Since moving home I've been trying to spend as little time as possible there. The chance of running into too many people I've been trying to avoid is too risky. After you graduate college people ask you the same vague questions so they can look like they care, but not have to actually remember anything about you. You're now classified into categories: single, dating, engaged, married, kids. Checked off like a box on the census. What are your plans? Do you have a boyfriend? Are you happy to be home? The trifecta of uncomfortable conversations.

I can tell you that my original plan did not include me having this dumb conversation with you. If by boyfriend you mean Jack, Jim and Jose than yes, I'm in a committed polyamorous relationship. My happiness is in direct correlation with the amount of alcohol currently floating through my bloodstream.

Dad looked up from behind the bar, "Quinn," he waved and a few people turned around to see me. I returned a stiff wave and made my way behind the bar, making sure to keep my head down just in case anyone wanted to talk.

The place was just how I remembered it. Not that I expected anything drastic to change since I'd been here last. The oak wood of the bar that ran the length of the room divided the space almost evenly. It was the same bar that was here when it opened. High top tables were strategically placed throughout the open floor with bench seating along the wall in the back where the dartboards and two billiard tables sat. There were local newspaper articles and frayed Polaroid pictures splashed along the green and white backsplash behind the bar, most highlighting local sports stars and a few of us as kids. Kelly's was the same as I always remembered.

"Hi," I greeted him and put my purse under the bar.

"Thanks for doing this, Q." He handed me a clipboard. "I just checked all the inventory, Nora's in the back with Sam and they'll be here all night too."

Nora was a year ahead of me in high school and had been working at the bar since she was 18. She was in a permanent daze from too much acid, but she was nice enough to work with and it was better than being here by myself. Sam washed dishes and did general bitch work at the bar, but he couldn't have been happier about the position. He was one of Pat's friends from high school and he really didn't have a lot in terms of career choice due to a brief stint in jail when he turned 18.

"I'll be back later to close up." He walked to the back to grab Mom from the office.

"Also the guys from the bowling league usually come in tonight. Make sure they take a table in the back and be sure the bathroom toilet paper is stocked in the men's room before they get here."

"Ew."

"Well bowling alley fries will do that to a man."

"Gross, Dad."

The bowling league is compromised of a dozen men in their late 60s who still bowl once a month and then come to the bar to complain about the lack of respect in America's youth along with a faulty immigration system. We're all a little confused as to how these dudes are still hauling 12-pound bowling balls down a lane with no bumpers, but we can't tell them that.

"Don't serve Mo anything else," my Dad pointed to the elderly man slumped over in the corner. "His cab is on the way."

Great. Not even here ten minutes and already the first casualty has been amassed. I turned to look at the crowd and see if I could spot anyone I knew. Melanie Gorman's now husband Mike was at a high top in the corner talking closely with two other guys, one I recognized as Craig Frasier who was in Patrick's grade and the other as Sal Pinella, a kid who used to sell me pot. Solid.

I glanced at the drink specials board written in bright chalk. Happy hour draft specials were $2 off and we were running $3 shots of Jameson until 8:00. When did we become a happy hour bar?

"Can I grab three drafts?" I looked up and Mike standing in front of me. "Oh shit. Quinn, what's up?"

I plastered a wide, semi-psychotic, smile on my face before answering. "Hey Mike what's going on?"

"Nothing, just having a couple beers after work. What's up with you, college graduate?" He pointed to the most recent picture on the wall, a not so subtle 8x10 of me on my graduation day in full cap and gown. Jesus.

"Oh you know," I began pouring the beer, "just killing it in all aspects of life." Mike laughed. "That'll be $6," I said, all business. Mike handed me a $10 bill.

"Keep it," he nodded at the money. Awesome. The only thing worse than serving people you went to school with is getting good tips from people you went to school with. I could never figure out if I was getting a good tip because I just made the best drink since Tom Cruise in Cocktail or because they thought the extra money would pad my body when I hurled myself into oncoming traffic because I was back home working at the bar. "Charlie should be here in a little bit," he said before walking back to his table.

"Great," I muttered under my breath. I saw my parents walking out of the office towards the door, holding hands like a couple of teenagers. "DAD!" I yelled and he turned around immediately.

"What's wrong?"

"Charlie's coming." At the mention of Charlie's name Mom's face lit up like a Christmas tree, like for the first time since I've been home she had hope for my future.

"Okay," he started before Mom broke in.

"That's great Quinn." Her wide eyes and excitement genuinely scared me. Sometimes I believed she wanted me to find a husband before I found a job.

Charlie Dwyer, my high school boyfriend and the boy that everyone in this town, including Mom, wanted me to spend the rest of my life with.

"Well, what do I do?" I said, panicked. The last thing I wanted was to be the beer maid for my high school class's happy hour.

"You serve him what he wants to drink," Dad said.

"You tell him you're single and living back home," Mom chimed in.

"Mar," Dad gave her a pleading look. "Give it a rest." He looked back at me. "You'll be fine. Have a drink, lighten up." He placed his hand on mine and gave it a reassuring squeeze. "You'll be fine. We've got to get to Mickey's."

"Tell him I said hi."

I did have a drink.

In fact, I had four.

The burning taste in my throat lessened after each drink and after my fourth whiskey I felt more relaxed than I should. I'm not sure this is what he had in mind when he told me to have a drink. Oops.

The crowd in the bar lessened significantly. Mostly younger people lingered around, a few regulars sprinkled in between them. Mike and the guys were in the corner, still nursing their second round of beers. Mo's cab came and I had the pleasure of slinging his arm over my shoulder as I brought him outside. I handed the cab driver a $20 bill and gave him Mo's address. Mo had been a regular since the bar opened, coming in most days and not leaving until he had offended someone so badly he got kicked out or he passed out. Luckily it was usually the latter, but when he did offend someone, I almost always laughed.

I was wiping down the bar when I heard a high-pitched squeal. "Oh. My. God." *Fuck.* "Quinn. Kelly."

I looked up and there she was in all her caked on make-up faced-glory. Melanie Gorman, in the flesh. Her outfit was utterly ridiculous. She was wearing a fedora with a cheetah print maxi dress and platform sandals. *Relax, girl. You're at Kelly's, on a Wednesday.*

"Hi Melanie," I pursed my lips evenly; as close to a smile as I could manage.

"Shut up bitch," she slapped my arm. "How are you?"

"I'm good. How are-,"

"I'm so freaking fabulous." Melanie cut me off. She stuck her hand out so I could see the huge rock on her ring finger. "Mike and I are married." I looked over at Mike who was deep in conversation with Sal.

"Wow." My eyes grew wide. "That is," I paused trying to match Melanie's demeanor, "super great." Of course I knew Melanie had gotten married because Melanie is the type of person to make sure everyone knew she got married… and I stalked her on Facebook and saw all the pictures she posted. "Do you want something to drink?"

"Vodka with club soda," she spat. She would order that. It screams 'I want to drink, but not add too many calories to my day.' "So what are you up to now?" One. She tapped her fake nails along the bar. "You must be so excited to be home." Two. "Are you seeing anyone?" The trifecta. The only three questions I've been asked since I've been home.

Luckily two more people came up to the bar and I avoided answering. When I came back Melanie had placed a $5 bill on the counter and joined Mike, sliding close to him and he wrapped his arm around her.

"Fucking Gorman." Nora said from behind me. I laughed. Nora got it. She dreaded seeing these people just as much as I did and she had to do it year round.

"Can you watch the bar for a minute? I'm going to stock the toilet paper in the men's room and go outside quick."

"Mmhmm." Nora didn't look up from the text she was reading on her cell phone.

I wished I still smoked cigarettes. Nothing made me crave nicotine more than being at this bar. I used to sneak out back and smoke on the loading dock. Afterwards I always put 800 pieces of gum in my mouth before I went back inside. It's a disgusting habit, but I missed the soothing compulsiveness of bringing a cigarette to my lips and then flicking the ash away. Instead I settled for burning the rest of a clip I had in my car.

I made it back just in time to change the toilet paper before a man with a Korean War mesh hat waddled into the men's room. *Woof.*

The final Jeopardy question on the flat screen had my attention when Charlie walked in. He still walked like he had cement deodorant on with his arms jacked out to the side of his body at what could only be an extremely uncomfortable angle. It made him look like such a tool. I tried to remember the last time I had seen him. When I was home for Christmas and Maggie had a party? I couldn't remember.

He looked good. I'll give him that. His skin was already slightly tan and his shirt was hugging his body in all the right places. When did he get those biceps? His face had a two-day scruff that would have looked gross on anyone else, but he wore it well. His brown hair had grown out a little, and the ends tickled the bottom of his neck in an endearing way.

But it's not like I was just going to jump back into his arms because he looked decent in the shitty bar lighting. When Charlie and I dated it was because we were 17 and people thought we looked good together. Your first love is all knees and elbows. It's awkward, passionate and dramatic because you're 17 and think that forever only stretches to next Sunday. You don't look before you leap because you haven't been burned yet.

Besides, I was only going to be home for two months tops. Why bother? It could make for interesting sex. I could see if he had gotten past the awkward phase of teenage sex where you're still figuring out the whole two bodies in motion thing.

Maybe.

I quickly checked my reflection in the mirror that hung behind the bar. My face was oily and what little make-up I'd put on had rubbed off. My hair was limply hanging on either side of my face and I could already feel a nest of it clumping on the back of my head. I had mastered the art of making myself look exactly how I felt: a hot mess. I wiped my hands on my shorts before turning back around. I wasn't expecting him to be standing right there. "Hey stranger." His voice was quiet. I smiled, a genuine smile, before responding.

"Hi," I managed to get out before my voice broke. "How are you?"

"I'm alright. You look good."

"So do you." I pointed to his arms, "Where did you find those things?"

"I've been working construction." I poured his beer without even asking because he always drank the same thing.

"Here." I handed him the draft. "It's on the house." He stared back at me, not saying anything, but looking at me like he was trying to figure something out. I poured myself a whiskey and raised my glass to tap his.

"Still whiskey." He nodded knowingly at my glass when I took a sip.

"Still whiskey." I repeated, curtly.

An awkward silence took over.

"I'll be back." He nodded quickly before walking over to his group of friends.

Okay, perhaps there was a tiny piece of me that was excited about seeing him. Maybe it made me feel better to know that even though I couldn't get a job, I could still get my high school boyfriend back if

I wanted. I'm not sure it would work though. Our deepest conversation during the three years we dated was probably about the emotional trauma that would happen to you if you ever walked in on your parents having sex.

He's a simple guy, someone who knows what he likes and isn't chomping at the bit to try something new. He's dependable and really loyal, but so are dogs.

A part of me wished that Charlie had gained 50 pounds and developed a stutter. No such luck. Now I was going to have to see him all the time knowing that I broke up with him because I thought I was moving to a big city after college to start this crazy life in my 20's. I thought that was the next step because all those reality TV shows make it seem a lot more glamorous. Shouldn't I be living in some posh flat with my gay roommate sipping mimosas and using words like brunch and filibuster and worrying about the important issues, like shrinking my pore size? It sure seems like every 20-something is doing that. Wrong. Some of us are slinging drinks at the same place we've been since high school, using our college diploma to roll joints on.

I took the rest of my whiskey with one sip.

"Hey boozy," I looked up and saw my older brother Patrick walking behind the bar. "I'll take over. You're drunk." He gave me a disapproving look.

"How can you even tell?"

"I know you spend all daylight hours resting indoors so the red on your cheeks isn't from sunshine."

"I'm actually fine," I shot him a death glare, "but I will gladly hand this over to you." I stepped out of the way. I might have been a little drunk, but I certainly wasn't going to tell him that.

"What's wrong?" He cast a worried glance at me. "Did something happen?"

"No. I just really don't feel like being around all these people. It's weird."

"What are you all freaked out by? Charlie being here?" He looked across the bar and waved at Charlie who nodded and raised his beer in return. "You are, aren't you? Oh this is going to be great. Mom is going to love this." He chuckled to himself.

"Shut-up." I reached out to slap him across his chest, but he dodged me easily. "You don't have to say anything to mom because there's nothing to tell her." I exhaled dramatically. "Now if you'll excuse me, I'm leaving."

"You're going to walk home, tough guy?" He replied with a smug look on his face.

"Yup." I walked towards the door, "Bye."

Patrick had the uncanny ability to make me seethe with rage in under a minute. He's been like that since the day I was born, always pushing my buttons, knowing what to say to make me snap. I pushed the door open and started angrily down the block.

I'd say my first day at work was a success.

I only walked two blocks before I heard Charlie call out behind me. "Do you want a ride?" I turned and saw him walking towards me. "Your house is on my way."

"No that's okay. I don't mind walking, but thank you."

"You're still this stubborn, huh?" He shook his head. "Just let me give you a ride." He stopped in front of me. "Your brother would be pissed if I let you walk home."

"Fine." I crossed my arms as we walked back towards the bar in silence.

His car was the same one he had in high school, a red pick up truck that his father bought him his senior year. I opened the door and climbed in hastily.

The car was silent as we drove through town, the radio softly playing some country anthem about a shotgun and an ice-cold beer. "You cut your hair." Charlie finally spoke.

"I did." I ran a hand through my now chin length cut, catching my fingers on the snarl's in the back of my head. I had long hair all through college. Right before I graduated I decided to cut it off in hopes of appearing more professional. "You still drive this truck." I pointed out as I ran my finger across the dashboard.

"I do." He replied in a serious tone. "So you're home."

"I am." I smiled at him. It felt like he was driving me home after a date in high school. I sat in this front seat so many times. "Home sweet home." I added, sarcastically.

"What are your plans?" Jesus Christ. It was like I was listening to a scratched CD that just kept playing the same three chords over and over again.

"I have a plan. Wait for my phone call for a job and then move to Chicago. I'm keeping my job options open."

"That's cool." He kept his eyes on the road. "It's good to have options. There are always new jobs opening up around town." I knew he was just trying to be helpful. He probably felt bad for me. "Mrs. Piez is looking for help at the bakery." Charlie added, speaking of the local bakery.

"Yeah. Maybe. So what are you up to?"

"I'm still at Langley Construction," he began, his voice full of pride. "I got a promotion last year. I'm a site supervisor." He was trying to brag without trying to brag, something he'd always done.

"That's great." I choked out.

"Yeah. I close on my house next month."

I was thankful the car was dark so he couldn't see when I picked my jaw up from the floor. He was about to buy a house and I couldn't even afford the toilet paper to vandalize it with. My self-esteem and general will to carry on with life was dropping by the minute.

"You're like a real person. Holy shit." I hiccupped.

"It's pretty crazy," he agreed as he drove by the line of sugar maple trees that surrounded the entrance to my neighborhood. "Are you going to be around this summer?"

"Just waiting for my phone call."

"Well maybe we can hang out sometime, when you're not behind the bar sneaking too much whiskey."

"Ha." I finally coughed. Humor was never his strong point. Charlie pulled into my driveway. "Definitely, we can hang out with all the old gang." I added with fake enthusiasm.

"I'll give you a call later this week." He said when I opened the door. I turned to thank him for the ride and he leaned in awkwardly. I tried to plant a chaste kiss on his cheek, but my mouth skimmed the top corner of his lip by mistake. I pulled away quickly, but the smile on his face told me I had given him false hope.

"Goodnight Charlie." I stepped out of the car. "Thanks for the ride."

"Anytime." He nodded before reversing his truck.

I walked up the path to my front door quickly, needing to put some distance between that awkward exchange and myself. I reached in my bag for my keys. They were nowhere to be seen. Shit. I gave them to Pat at the bar.

I walked around the back of my house through the gate and onto the patio. I had two choices, hope the screen door was open or try to get on to the roof and into my bedroom window. I tried to claw the patio door open even after I saw the lock in place.

I snuck in and out of my house all the time when I was in high school, mostly for dumb reasons. Sometimes Maggie and I would drive around and smoke joints, other times we would go to senior parties when we were freshmen. Ya know, cool girl stuff. I had only gotten caught one time. It was actually the first time I hung out with Charlie and that night he kept me out past my curfew. We were at the apple orchards and I stayed out late because I wanted him to kiss me but refused to make the first move. My plan was to sneak into my bedroom and somehow convince my parents I had been there the whole time when Mom heard me banging around on top of the garbage cans. She thought I was a raccoon. She yelled for Dad to grab the shotgun. I had to reveal myself to her when she turned the light on, seeing my body halfway hoisted onto the roof, my feet still dangling over the trashcans. I still remember the entire conversation that followed.

"What the hell are you doing up there?" She screamed.

"I was grabbing that tree branch." I dropped down and my feet hit the ground with a hard thud. "You know they can damage your roofs if left unattended."

"Where were you?" She didn't wait for an answer. "I swear to God if you ever want to see the outside again you will answer me right now." Mom was dramatic most times, but I knew not to push her right now.

"I was with Charlie Dwyer." I braced myself for her to start yelling but a strange look of relief poured over her face.

"Oh thank God," she brought her hand to her chest. "He's Dean and Lucy's son, right?"

"Yes, mother."

"Oh, he's going to be such a handsome man. You two will be perfect together."

From that day forward Charlie Dwyer was the only person I was allowed to date, ever, according to Mom. She had the wedding stemware picked out after our third date. In her eyes I would graduate high school, go to junior college and be married to Charlie by the time I was 24.

In reality, after high school I went away to college and Charlie spent two years at the local junior college before taking a job in construction. We tried staying together freshman year, but we grew into two separate people. I had tasted the freedom of what life beyond this town had to offer and Charlie would probably die in this town. We broke up when I came home for summer break after my freshman year. I told him it was because I didn't want to hold him back. It was a lie. What would I hold him back from, driving over the town line?

Luckily tonight I was able to pull myself on the roof after I stepped up off the high top table. I scraped my forearms along the roof shingles and hoisted my legs over. I rolled further back on the roof and shook the pebbles that were embedded in my palms off on my shirt. It wasn't graceful, but I was up.

I tiptoed around the side of the roof across the front, hoping nobody would see me and think I was a burglar. But let's be honest, a burglar would have a better plan. I turned the corner, relieved to see my window open. I lifted the screen and slid in one leg at a time. Dropping down to my bed, I exhaled deeply and caught sight of the clock on bedside table. Barely 11:00. My parents wouldn't be home for another hour. I stood up and took my sticky-beer smelling clothes off. I changed into an old soccer sweatshirt and grabbed my jar of weed from the back of my sock drawer. I rolled myself a joint and hurried down the stairs to the backyard, pausing in the kitchen to pour myself one last whiskey.

I sat outside and thoroughly enjoyed my nightcap like a respectable human being. My body had become so used to drinking alcohol in a horizontal position that it was a nice change to be sitting up.

Tonight wasn't that bad. I had to be seen by people eventually. This town is only so big. Only now that I had been spotted in public, news that I was home and working at the bar would spread like a rash on a wrestling team. I'm sure everyone would just eat that right up.

By the time I stubbed the joint out, my whiskey was gone and so was I. Nothing like a solo night of binge drinking to really bring you down to your knees. I stood up and immediately sat back down, the rush in my head being too much. I was going to fall asleep in this chair, but I made no attempt to move, even as my eyes began to close.

3

$232.76

Perhaps the only thing worse than waking up and having no idea where you are is waking up and knowing exactly where you are.

I felt the sun beat down mercilessly on my face and when I opened my eyes I was met with the chilly fog of early morning. I passed out on the wicker love seat in the backyard. A new personal best…or worst, depending on which way you looked at it.

On one hand, I already felt a closer bond with nature, but then again I didn't have pants on and it was still May so I was pretty cold. I looked down and saw a piece of paper taped to my big toe. *We need to talk* was written out in Mom's best passive aggressive cursive.

Yahtzee.

Shit was about to get real. The only thing better than your parents having a pre-intervention with you, is later on that same day, having your parents come home to you passed out drunk in the backyard when you should have been at work.

I debated bolting right there, but when I stood up and my bare legs were exposed, I realized that wasn't an option. I walked slowly towards the door, knowing the lady upstairs already sealed my fate.

The first thing I saw was the whiskey glass on the kitchen counter, one of my mom's subtle ways of letting me know that she knows. Total mom power move.

I didn't dare go upstairs and risk waking the sleeping lion. It was best to wait my future downstairs. I quickly made a pot of coffee to ease her stone heart just the slightest. I organized a stack of papers on the counter and put the silverware in the dishwasher away. I was getting eggs out of the refrigerator to scramble when I shut the door and she was calmly standing on the other side, still in her nightgown. Her face was unreadable.

"Ah." I let out.

"You're not going to talk for the next five minutes," she began, her voice barely above a whisper. "You are going to nod and you are going to do nothing else. Sit," she demanded as she pointed to the stool on the other side of the counter. I nodded and sat down. Mom took a breath. "If you think for one minute that you are going to come home and pretend that this is your house at college with all of your friends, you are mistaken." I nodded. "If you ever pull a stunt like you did last night again you will not be living here." She cracked the eggs into a metal bowl. "Your father and I don't have to let you live here, rent free, without a job." I continued nodding. "I don't comment much on your life because let's face it, you don't listen to a word I say anyway, but you will not run around this town binge drinking and smoking your pot every night. You will not get drunk while you're at work and you will not leave when your brother is trying to take care of you." I bit my lip to keep from butting in. "Quinn, it's time for you to get it together. When I was your age I was married with two children and a third on the way."

I hated when she said things like this, like I was somehow less of a person because I wasn't walking directly in her footsteps. Weren't parents supposed to want better for their children? Shouldn't she want me to go off and get a great job?

"Frankly the only good thing to come of this mess is that Charlie was there to take you home safely, but apparently you were too drunk to make it to your bed." She quieted for a moment. I took this as my cue to speak.

"Okay, two quick things," I started tentatively, "one is that I'm sorry about last night but I just don't think I can work at the bar." I paused waiting for her reaction. "I mean look at me mom, I can't work there if I want to get it together. I would end up drinking every night and sleeping every day."

"Different than your current schedule?"

"Besides, I don't really want to see everyone all the time and be the one serving them shots." Her cheeks were starting to flush and I knew she was going to explode. "And secondly," I quickly continued, "is that Charlie taking me home really made me rethink my feelings for him and if I want to spend time with him, I can't be at the bar in front of all those other guys." I added in a serious tone.

Mom furrowed her brow and drew in a harsh breath. I had her hook line and sinker. "You could still be married by 24. You wouldn't have to have a long engagement because you've dated before and I mean technically we could plan now and just wait for the official go ahead."

"By official go ahead did you mean proposal?"

"All a mother wants is to be able to plan her daughter's wedding."

I winced. "Okay, but I'm nowhere near that step yet so let's just worry about him calling me back after I was so drunk last night." I winked at her.

"Oh he's going to call," Mom said, confidently. "He went back to the bar to see your brother after he dropped you off and your father and I just got there. Mom's smile was eerie. "He said he looks forward to seeing us more often."

I worry about her obsession with marrying her children off. She thinks we'll wither and die if we don't settle down by the time we're 30. I couldn't argue with her about it right now. Compared to how things could have gone, this was a walk in the park.

I turned around and headed for my room. "Oh hon, before I forget," Mom called out. "You have two weeks to find a job, or you will be scrubbing every inch of that bar with a toothbrush for $5 an hour and no breaks." She added a close-mouthed smile. I gave her two thumbs up and walked down the hall. I paused to open the front door and reached down for the paper, grabbing the classified section from the pile before going upstairs.

I didn't want to get a job here. That meant that a part of me believed I wouldn't get one anywhere else. I didn't want to begin throwing away my idea of a dream job, but the reality was: I needed money. Moving to Chicago had to happen immediately. I wouldn't wait for a job. $3,000 is enough to move there and start with. I could make that in a summer.

Looking at the paper, it was clear my options were limited. *Adult Caregiver.* No. *Overnight Manager.* Creepy. And no. *Dog walker.* Possibly. These jobs weren't what I was expecting to find, but then again it was the twenty-first century and I was looking in the classifieds section of a newspaper. I scanned further down the page. Bingo.

America's premier display food center is looking for a recent college graduate to contribute to our growing company. Art degrees preferable. Contact Wade Diamond at 704-245-8541 for more information.

The ad was vague, but I couldn't be choosey if I wanted to avoid another summer slinging beer for locals who were trying to avoid their own life problems. It was still early, I could wait an hour or two before calling.

Marlowe walked into my room and whined dramatically while dragging her ass on the carpet. She had to go out and knowing my parents would ask me anyway, I'll take some initiative. Blend.

I stood up and she followed diligently behind me downstairs and through the hallway and kitchen where my parents sat reading the paper. We walked quickly out the back screen door. Marlowe circled around the backyard, sniffing and grunting but not going to the bathroom for a few minutes and I stood watching her like an overprotective parent. She continued sniffing. I didn't have the patience to wait all day and I was ready to go back inside when she darted towards the neighbor's yard. "Marlowe!" She was wedging her portly body through the one piece of missing fence between the yards and just before she flung her body through, I ran towards her and grabbed her by the stomach. I tried pulling her back to our side of the fence, but she insisted on trying to squeeze through.

"Hey girl." A voice came from the other side of the fence. Shit. Our next-door neighbor, Mr. Lanigan, was in his backyard probably tending to his vegetable garden like he spent all day doing.

"I've got her Mr. Lanigan, but thank you." I pulled Marlowe back over and suddenly his head appeared in the hole.

"Ah, Quinn. How are you?" His morning breath hit me square in the face. Then I realized I still hadn't put pants on. I froze. I couldn't move because the further away from the fence I got, the more of my body you could see.

"I'm good, how are you?" I put my head further in the fence hole so we were merely inches apart. Startled, he backed up to reveal a shirtless stomach and generous beer belly that smelled like it was already covered in baby oil for a day of outdoor tanning.

"Great, just checking on the crop this year, it's going to be a big haul," he nudged towards his garden where three rows of sprouts were growing.

"That's great Mr. Lanigan, sorry about Marlowe, she's just excited." I was trying to say anything to take away from the fact if you put both our clothes together we formed a complete outfit.

"Oh she's fine, probably just smells Roscoe," he noted, speaking of his Basset Hound. "Well have a good day Quinn, and sorry to hear about Chicago, but I bet you're real glad to be home for a little bit, huh?" I didn't even have the energy to respond so I just smiled and waited for him to turn around before standing up and running back into the house.

"See, that's why you need to wear pants." Mom pointed at my bare legs. "So I don't have look out my kitchen window and see your head in the fence and your keester raised in the air."

"Better my ass in the air during the day than at night like a call girl." Mom shot me a disapproving look but didn't say anything.

I needed to call Wade Diamond immediately.

A dull voice greeted me. "Flashy Foods, this is Megan."

"Hi. May I please speak with Wade Diamond?"

"May I please ask who's calling?"

"My name is Quinn Kelly."

"One moment." As soon as the hold music came on I regretted making this phone call. This is a food display company. My interview process will probably be correctly identifying fruit shapes and labeling them based on their harvest season. After two verses of some Jamaican reggae a raspy voice spoke.

"Wade Diamond, no relation to Neil." He laughed at his own joke, which he had obviously told a million times before.

"Hello Wade, my name is Quinn Kelly and I'm inquiring about the position you advertised for a recent college graduate."

"Yes, we're looking for someone with art experience to come in and help revitalize our production efforts."

"Well I recently graduated from Millstadt University with a fine arts degree if that's any benefit."

"Really?" He sounded skeptical.

"Yes sir."

"Alright, well let's set up an interview. MEGAN!" He yelled directly into the phone, "Get this girls information and set up an interview as soon as possible."

Wade Diamond had no patience when it came to new hires. My interview was scheduled for the next day. After Megan got back on the phone, she told me more about the position. I'd actually be the one painting the fake food they make. That didn't sound that bad, it sounded a lot better than scrubbing caked on vomit with a toothbrush.

I wandered back into the kitchen to tell my mom but she had disappeared from her judgment perch. She had probably gone down to the bar.

Marlowe's hostile barking let me know that someone was at the front door. Before I got the chance to open it, Delaney came bouncing in, her baby bump leading the way. "Hey," she greeted. She rested her hand on her growing belly. Delaney was the spitting image of my mother, all blonde hair, hips and boobs where Patrick and I both inherited our father's gangly figure and fine dark hair.

"Hey."

"Did Mom and Dad already leave?" I nodded. We walked down the hall into the kitchen and she opened the refrigerator. "I had to ask them a question," she added from behind the refrigerator door.

When she emerged she had a bowl of leftover spaghetti in one hand and the milk in her other. "I have a job interview tomorrow." I boasted proudly.

"No shit. Where?"

"Ummm, I would be doing some consulting on artistic visions for a big company." I didn't want to go in to details and the more vague the job sounded, the better. She didn't seem to notice.

"That's cool, have you talked to Pat lately? I haven't been able to get a hold of him and I need him to take care of some paperwork."

"No. So that means he didn't tell you about last night?" That's surprising because the only thing my family loves more than arguing with one another is telling everyone else in the family about the arguing.

Delaney shook her head and I told her about everything from the first drink of whiskey to me scaling the roof to the deal I made with Mom.

"Why didn't you just come over and get the key?" She asked plainly.

"That is all you have to take from this?" She shrugged, indifferent. "It was late and I was drunk. I didn't think that was an option?"

Delaney and her husband lived right up the street. If she could, she would have just built an addition onto my parent's house and lived with them forever. She's scary close with my parents. Not like Pat, who when he moved out two years ago, refused to live within a two-block radius of any family members. He bought a condo on the other side of town. He lives with two of his best friends from high school. A real bachelor pad. I can't make fun of him too much for it. After high school Pat kind of jerked around for a couple years until he got his shit together and went to the firefighting academy.

"Mr. Lanigan saw my butt today," I brought up casually as I dug a fork into her pasta.

"Still boycotting pants I see."

"Yup."

She took one more bite of spaghetti. "Alright I've really got to go talk to Mom and Dad about some financial stuff. I'd invite you, but I already know your feelings on going there." She smirked before walking out of the kitchen. "If you're bored later come over to the house I've got some new baby stuff to show you for the nursery."

"If you keep buying stuff there's going to be nothing left to buy for the baby shower," I called but she had already shut the front door.

Delaney freaked out about every little thing during this pregnancy and while most would say its just her hormones and whatever else happens when there's another life growing inside you, anyone who actually knew her would agree that it's just how she is. She's always anxious about one thing or another, whether it was planning her wedding, some reunion, even a family party. She obsesses over tiny details to the brink of insanity, and every time it turns out perfect. Why would this baby be any different? If nothing else her and Corliss would make a gorgeous kid with their light hair and good facial structures.

The two of them are the love story you hate to hear about. Country artists make millions off stories like Delaney and Corliss. It's cute, if you're into that shit. High school sweethearts who stayed together and got married and lived happily ever after in the house down the street from her parents. Better her than me.

I spent the rest of the day preparing for the interview. Even though I had no real desire for this job, it was still a job and even though most of my time is spent not taking things seriously, I valued myself too much to fuck it up.

I spent two hours meticulously typing out my resume, which had exactly two jobs listed. Neither of those jobs makes me qualified to work with art, but I'm hoping Wade Diamond doesn't notice. I even drove to the office supplies store and bought a fancy dossier so I looked professional. It was not so professional when I used Dad's credit card to pay for it and the cashier noticed that I was in fact not Jim Kelly.

After I finished my resume I rewarded myself with a glass of wine and a joint on the patio because carpe diem. I took out my phone intending to call Lizzie but I got sidetracked. The next thing I knew, I was on Facebook.

It doesn't help my plummeting self-esteem when I sign on to social networking websites and see just how fucking happy Jenny Lowenstein is because she got a gallery job in San Diego and her boyfriend, soul-patch-wearing Jonah, proposed to her at her first show.

If Melissa Gorman was the ever-present annoyance in my life in high school, Jenny Lowenstein was that girl in college. She popped up everywhere, in my classes, random parties, even the dining hall. It used to make me feel good when I would see her status updates about her cat and shit but I might have to de-friend her after this. Aw, how cute Jenny, please post the same fucking engagement ring picture on all 20 social media sites, just in case I missed the first 19.

I'm not bitter.

Okay, maybe I'm a little bitter.

It's not like I would ever want to marry Jonah, but its just another reality check that life is moving on. People are moving on. I'm moving on too. I mean, until recently I was moving from one side of my bed to the other to avoid bedsores, but now I'm fucking booking it.

The next morning I woke up early, ready for a new opportunity.

That's a lie.

I woke up late and was left with a half hour to get ready. I didn't even shower. I ironed my button up dress shirt and skirt and put on my most professional blazer like millions of other Americans did each day. It didn't feel all that satisfying.

"Do you want a cup of coffee?" Mom asked.

I told my parents about the interview last night and I made sure to make the position sound more important than it was. I told them I would be an assistant creative director. They sounded impressed.

"Yes. Thank you." I grabbed the cup. "Alright, see you later." I grabbed my keys off the counter and headed for the front door.

"Good luck," Dad shouted from upstairs. "Knock 'em dead, girl!" I laughed. Anytime Dad said girl he was just trying to talk like he thought people my age did.

After only fifteen minutes of driving, my GPS told me I arrived at my destination, and holy shit did I ever. I pulled into the sketchy parking lot. It was the kind of sketchy parking lot used as a location for fight scenes in movies and network television. Tons of graffiti and empty truck cabs were scattered throughout the empty space.

The building had character - I'll admit that. The awning careened away from the brick structure and set underneath was an elaborate farmer's market filled with baskets and picnic tables of fake food. There were bushels of berries and ears of corn stacked next to each other on top of red-checkered tablecloths. There was even an antique cash register next to the display. It was borderline creepy how perfect everything fit together in a realistic way. If this was the outside, I could only imagine what was inside.

I opened my car door, but didn't step out. I needed a minute.

Did I really go into this place or did I bail? Sure I said all that stuff about taking my job seriously, but could I take this place seriously? What was this place?

I now had one foot firmly on the pavement, the other still hovering close to the gas pedal.

"Excuse me?" A voice called from outside. I looked up at a mess of arms and legs belonging to a guy around my age standing outside my car. "Is everything okay?" The guy asked.

"Yes, I'm fine."

"Are you sure because I've been watching you sit with the door open for about five minutes now."

"Yes. I'm fine." I repeated, this time more forcefully. I rolled up the window and turned the car off. Stepping out, I tried to step around him, but he stayed rooted in front of me. I tried to move around him again and he stepped in front of me again, blocking my path.

"Hey, you have a box of wine in your backseat." Like I had no idea.

"I know."

"That's weird."

"Actually, you're weird."

"Are you sure you want to go inside?" It wasn't so much of a question as a warning.

"Well I'm as sure as I'm ever going to be. Excuse me." I walked by him and picked up my pace as I headed towards the front door.

I felt the sweat start to wind up in my armpits. It was hot out. I was just experiencing heat sweat, not nervous sweat. I pushed open the front door.

If I thought the exterior of the building had shocked me then the interior knocked me right on my ass. Just inside the door lay an entire shop of fake food. There was a Thanksgiving meal set up in the center of the room on an old door that had been converted to a dining room table. The table was set with place settings. There was even fake wine in stem glasses. On either side of the table, shelves of food were set up like tiny pantries. It was surreal. The colors spilled over into one another and the room looked like something taken out of a southern living magazine. Every last detail was carefully picked and placed within the room.

"Freaky shit, right?" The voice from behind startled me and I jumped a little. The guy from outside was standing behind me tossing a plastic roll in the air and catching it repeatedly.

"I don't think it's freaky, I think it's..." I paused trying to find the right word, "fresh."

"You don't have to pretend to like this stuff, you'll get the job."

"How do you know I'm here for a job and not here to buy some food?"

He blinked. "Because nobody comes here for the food and then opens and shuts their car door a million times wearing a stuffy blazer." He pointed this out as if it was the most obvious thing in the world. He put the roll down and stepped closer to me. "Besides you're the only person who responded to the ad Quinn Kelly. The job is yours." He brushed by me and walked through a double set of doors. Who was that douche?

I didn't have too long to think about it because no sooner had he swung the doors shut did they swing open again. I knew the man walking towards me was Wade Diamond immediately. His small body carried him gracefully through the display room. His hair, although receding, was slicked back on his head and he had a pair of designer sunglasses pushed on the front of his forehead. He was wearing a pair of khaki cargo shorts and a Hawaiian barbeque shirt. His skin was tan, but in the leathery sense, like he had spent too many summers in the sun without SPF.

"Quinn I presume." His voice was loud, but not in an angry way, he just seemed excited.

"Yes, it's nice to meet you Mr. Diamond."

"Please, call me Wade. I see you met my stepson, Simon." He pointed behind us to the doors he just walked through. "He's a bit of a nut."

So that was his name. "Yes, I did." I wasn't sure what to say next. "I have a copy of my resume for you to look at sir."

He put his hands up in protest. "Please, save all that stuff for human resources. Let me show you around the place." He chuckled at himself.

Wade led me through the main showroom that extended back into a second room with more fake food. This room was set up like a grocery store. Food was displayed on metal shelves to resemble store aisles. There was even a checkout line that had fake candy bars and real magazines.

It was equal parts creepy and mesmerizing.

"See." He stopped walking. "Look at this bag of flour," Wade pointed to a particularly large bag in the baking aisle. "Simon drew the design, sketched the dimensions and carved the polymer clay, but the coloring is all wrong. Flour should be white with maybe one or two other colors on the labeling." I nodded in agreement. " Enough of this." He led me away. "Let's take you to the back room and show you where the magic happens." I cringed slightly.

We walked through the double doors into a large, brightly lit production room. The room was quiet except for the sound of talk radio coming out of an old set of speakers. There were only two people working in the corner of the room.

Simon and an older woman sat huddled together around a long table and as we got closer I saw they were molding the food. He held a tool that looked like the same thing my dentist used to clean my teeth and was digging at the clay at a rapid pace, the discarded pieces slipping to the ground. Simon placed the finished piece on the table between them and I saw it was a banana.

"Quinn, you've met Simon," Wade pointed to Simon who nodded briefly at his name before continuing, "And this is Gloria."

Next to Simon the older woman was rolling a foam cylinder over the clay until it was smooth. She stood up to shake my hand, pushing her eyeglasses off the bridge of her nose and wiping her hands on her smock. "Nice to meet you hon," She sat back down and continued rolling out the clay.

"Gloria's been with us for years, " Wade said after we walked away. "Simon does the bulk of the sculpting and Gloria does the details. You'll be doing the painting."

We walked across the room to an L shaped desk with an enormous shelf of acrylic paint to the right of it. There were dozens of brushes laid neatly on the desk and a retractable magnifying mirror attached to the wall. "So once the clay comes out of the kiln, you'll paint in layers. Do I have to explain it? You get it, right? Ha. Of course you do. " He seemed hurried, like he needed to be somewhere else and I was the one taking up his time.

"Yes. Painting was my concentration in college. I know the shading and tinting that's involved when working with clay and I have a good understanding of the curing process and how that effects the type of paint that can be used." Sometimes I amazed myself at how well I could bullshit any situation.

"Sounds great. How about starting tomorrow?" I smiled on the off chance he was joking, but the incessant tapping of his foot told me he was waiting for my answer.

"I have the job?"

"Yes, you've got to be better than the last guy we hired. So tomorrow it is?"

"Sure."

"Great, Megan from HR will set you up with everything. You're going to love it here, good environment. Great creativity. Ha. The best." He walked away, talking quietly to himself.

I stared down at my new desk. It didn't have much on it, but I guess I wouldn't need much if I were going to be painting fruit all day. There was a small panel of windows behind the desk that looked out to the rest of the mostly rundown warehouses on the lot. A dying fern sat on the windowsill and there were some old scrap pieces of paper with patches on paint on them on the floor. Other than that the space was completely bare.

"Enjoying the prestigious corner office with the nice view?" Simon appeared out of nowhere behind me. He was annoying, but at least he would be nice to stare at for eight hours a day. He was tall with messy hair and wide set shoulders. He had an unpolished look that screamed he worked with his hands and not behind a desk. I could dig it.

"I'm not sure *Simon*. I was told I was the only one who possessed the skills needed for the job. I think that deserves the corner office."

"Well it's a pretty important job," he spoke, stepping closer to me. "The hours are long, the pay isn't that good and the coworkers are even worse."

"I think I can manage," I took a step back.

"I hope so," he lowered his voice and leaned in, "Quinn Kelly." I shifted nervously with the way my name rolled off his tongue. I wanted to find something witty to say back to him but my mouth was paralyzed. He smiled slightly, a crooked grin, and walked away.

Megan from HR turned out to be Wade's 19-year-old niece who worked two days a week while she was home from college over the summer. She seemed more interested in texting on her cell phone than figuring out my paperwork when I stood in front of her desk.

"Is there a dress code for work?"

"Don't wear nice clothes unless you want them to get ruined," she said, not looking up from her phone.

"Okay, what are my hours?"

"9:00 am until whenever you finish your work."

"How much am I getting paid?"

"Seventeen dollars an hour because you have a college degree."

"Oh. Okay. Sounds good." I forced a smile, took my paperwork and walked back through the showroom. Two customers were in a serious debate over whether or not asparagus was universally understood and appropriate for their display.

What the fuck was I about to do with my life?

Mom was both surprised and disappointed when I told my parents I got the job over dinner that night.

"Are you going to be one of those artist's who wears the little hat with the clitoris on top?" I almost spit out my drink at Mom's question.

"Probably not Mom."

"Are you going to get an easel and one of those trays with the thumb hole?"

"Did you actually look up these stereotypes before you started this conversation?"

"No."

I knew it bothered Mom that I went to such lengths to avoid working at the bar. In her mind it meant I was looking down on them, I overheard her talking to my dad about it one night when I first moved home. It's not true.

Okay, it's not entirely true.

"I think it's good babe, something different." Dad finally offered in support as he swirled his potatoes.

I felt the room growing more tense and I knew exactly what would happen if we continued talking. I was doing an awful job of blending right now so I gave Mom the only thing that would calm her down and get her away from me for a little bit.

"I might call Charlie and see if he wants to go out this weekend." Her face lit up like a fireworks display.

"Oh that's great!" She slapped Dad on the arm. "Isn't that great Jim?" Dad relaxed his shoulders.

"That's great Q."

Blend. Blend. Blend.

4

$213.32

First days at new jobs are like the first week of college classes each semester. You basically show up and do nothing but go over instructions. The hard stuff never comes the first week. That's how my first day should have gone. A quiet day spent at my desk reading a syllabus.

No.

My first day of work brought constant noise in the form of Simon.

"I didn't peg you as a black coffee girl." He pointed at the cup of black liquid on my desk. "I figured you would drink chai lattes with kitten's faces drawn in foam."

"Well, now you know so you can buy me a cup tomorrow morning." I didn't look away from the human resources manual I was reading.

"Oh. You're actually reading that? You're already way better than the last guy that worked here." He pulled a metal stool next to my desk and sat down. "He was an anglomaniac. A real freak." I looked up, confused. "You know, a person who is obsessed with the English." He continued like we were old friends. "He had this weird Spice Girls calendar from 1997 hung up on his desk and a Mr. Bean bobble head. It was some strange stuff."

"Are you always this talkative?"

"Depends on if you're always this miserable." I whipped my head up. "I'm joking," he added, quickly. "But this job gets pretty boring. It's nice to have someone to talk to. Gloria," he pointed across the room to the elderly lady, "doesn't talk much."

"Right."

I looked beyond Simon to the pushcart of food he had behind him. "What's going on with all that?"

"This is your job." He pulled the cart next to me. "Somewhere in your desk there should be a stapled set of papers. Within those papers is a spreadsheet that will give you certain numbers for each food. The numbers correlate with the paint that is stored on those shelves," he paused to make sure I was following "You paint the foods only by the numbers they correlate to."

"Paint by numbers. I'm supposed to paint by numbers?"

"Yes."

"Seriously? I thought I was hired to make things *fresh*."

"Seriously. Wade just put that in the ad to make it sound better. I brought you some strawberries. They're pretty easy to work with because they're small. You can get a lot of them done. You should be good with this for a while, but let me know if you need anything."

"Great." I grabbed the stapled set of sheets and looked for strawberries, seven and nine. Shockingly enough, those numbers were green and red. How original. Even though some strawberries had small white patches near the stem and yellowish seeds all over them.

The production room was pretty sparse. It looked like someone had robbed the place years ago and Wade just decided to roll with it. Besides my desk, there was the long table that Simon and Gloria worked at, a small supply closet next to their table that kept the clay cool, a kiln that was placed next to a shelf of drying pieces, and a rolling cart filled with odd tools used to carve the clay into shapes. On the other side of the space there was a small kitchenette, housing only a small refrigerator, coffee maker and another closet. The front of the room had two doors, one leading to the showroom and the other to the hall where Wade had his office and his niece had a desk to take phone calls from.

Wade disappeared quickly this morning, probably to go talk to himself in the mirror and chuckle incessantly at the sound of his own voice. I looked at Gloria who was nodding along diligently to talk radio, like some member of a cult hearing their leader speak and Simon was leaned back in his chair with his feet on the table shaving down what looked like a chicken wing. It was a motley crew at best.

If nothing else this job would motivate me to apply for more jobs in Chicago.

"What's the latest you've ever had to stay at work?" I asked Simon when I finally noticed it was 4:30. He came over to check on me or so he said. He was probably just making sure I wasn't planning on walking out. That option hadn't been ruled out.

"I've spent many nights sleeping on the couch in Wade's office." He seemed proud of the fact. "Anything for the art."

"Whoa." I lowered my voice. "Do we get paid overtime?"

Simon flashed a grin. "You think I have to stay late," he pointed at me, "you have to wait for me to finish the clay before you can even do your job." He laughed picking up a strawberry. "You're going to need to buy a cot and put it next to your desk. And yes, we do."

"Honestly I don't think I would mind. I need a break from my roommates."

"Are your roommates crazy?"

"Ha. No, they're just the sort of roommates who are always in my face about what's going on in my life."

Simon nodded. "How many roommates do you have?"

"Just two," I continued painting, "but they come with a lot of baggage."

"That's good. At least you have your own place. I live in Wade's basement." He confessed. "I mean it's cool because he doesn't really bother me, but still."

"That sucks."

"It could be worse."

I couldn't let him continue feeling like he had some sort of communicable disease because he still lived with his parents.

"My roommates are my parents." I finally announced like a member at an Alcoholics Anonymous meeting. "I call them my roommates because it makes me sound cooler." I felt my cheeks flush.

Simon let out a deep laugh. "It does make you sound cooler. I'm going to have to start using that."

We worked for another hour or so before my last strawberry was painted. I washed out my brushes and set them on the windowsill to dry overnight. "I'm going to head out." I grabbed my purse.

"Sounds good. See you tomorrow." He waved slightly.

"See ya."

Today could have been worse. It definitely could have been worse. Don't get me wrong, I was still going to apply for more jobs in Chicago, but for now, I have something. Something is always better than nothing.

My first week at Flashy Foods showed me that Simon wasn't as annoying as I first thought. He was easy to talk to and time passed quicker when we talked. Though he did suffer from diarrhea of the mouth from time to time. There was no sensor in between his brain and mouth, like when he told me that his dream job was to narrate Discovery Channel documentaries on mating in the wild. "How cool would it be just to go into a room and get paid to talk about sex all the time."

"Probably cooler if it wasn't animals," I responded, creeped out by his confession.

"I mean yeah, but you can't narrate porn."

Our conversations weren't limited either. We talked about everything from why he didn't trust packaged deli meats (because there should never be that much slime on any type of meat) to why I still thought I was going to attend Hogwarts. "I can be an adult learner," I argued Friday while I painted white onto a head of iceberg lettuce.

"You'd look pretty weird hanging around a bunch of 13 year olds. That's all I'm saying."

Simon continued to work next to me. He crafted a makeshift table out of a milk crate and covered it with newspaper. He was currently shaving excess clay off a honey-baked ham that was needed for a television commercial next week.

It was nice having someone at work around my own age to interact with. I logged enough hours around my parents that I missed nonsensical conversations that have no real meaning. You can't have with those types of conversations with your parents. They just grow more concerned about your mental state.

Even though I call them my roommates, lately my relationship with my parents had taken on the distinct stench of tenant and landlord, minus the whole paying rent part. I couldn't remember the last time I had talked to them about anything that wasn't related to the house. It was always a grocery list or a note about WD-40 for the sliding door.

It was an effort to stay awake when I got home from work Friday night and that annoyed me. I wasn't ready to be one of those people who fell asleep at 9:00 PM on a Friday night, but I definitely wouldn't be making it past midnight.

As usual nobody was home, but Mom had left a note of the table for me to call Charlie. Okay. I'll bite. What would be the harm? It wasn't like seeing him once would change the way I feel. Plus, if calling Charlie would make Mom even a little less worried that I was going to die alone with thirty cats, calling him was the least I could do. When he picked up on the third ring, though, I blanked on what to say.

"Hello?"

"Hey Charlie," I choked out.

"Quinn?"

"You bet it is." I cringed with embarrassment.

"Quinn, I was going to call you."

"Trying to dodge me already?" I joked.

"No, not at all."

"Relax, I'm kidding." I paused. "So we should do something soon."

"We should get together for drinks and catch up." He suggested.

"Yeah we should."

"What do you have planned this weekend?"

"Nothing too much, just settling in to my new job." I made sure to drop that line.

"That's awesome, you'll have to tell me about it."

After five minutes of conversation we would most likely repeat the next time we saw each other, we decided to meet up for drinks tomorrow.

There would be a two drink maximum.

Marlowe grunted enthusiastically next to me and I knew she had to go out. I didn't want her in the backyard after what happened last time, but I didn't want to walk her around the neighborhood either. As usual I wasn't wearing pants. "Come on girl," I called to her. I grabbed my car keys and as soon as she heard the keys jingle she was by my side waiting for my next move. We walked out the front door to my car and as soon as I opened the driver's side door Marlowe wagged her tail in anticipation.

We drove around the neighborhood for a while. Marlowe stuck her head out of the passenger's side window and took in all the smells the night had to offer. She was in complete ecstasy. All she needed was the sunglasses. My parents would never let it go if they found out that instead of walking, I drove the dog to go to the bathroom, but Marlowe loved it and I was feeling lazy. I pulled the car flush against the trees, under the one working streetlight on the dead end two streets over. The door was barely opened when she flew past me. She sniffed a few dandelions on the ground before she peed. I followed behind her and lit a joint. My phone vibrated. I didn't recognize the number, but the area code was local so I picked up.

"I might have violated a bunch of privacy laws, but I took your phone number off your resume." Simon's voice came through the phone.

"I'll have to take this up with HR."

"No, but seriously, I hope this is okay."

"It's fine, you're not interrupting anything except my dog's hunt for the perfect bathroom spot." I took a drag of the joint.

"Well I wanted to let you know that this weekend there is a Harry Potter marathon on TV and since you'll never go there in real life, I figured you could at least enjoy the theatrical version."

"Oh really?" I took another long inhale.

"Are you smoking a cigarette? Cigarettes are bad for you."

I exhaled into the receiver. "I'm not smoking a cigarette Simon."

"You're smoking something." He probed.

"A joint." I said finally. "I'm smoking a joint. Don't tell Wade."

"Don't tell Wade. I'm offended you never offer me any."

"I don't smoke at work Simon."

"Right." He paused. "That's good."

"What are you doing?" I asked.

"Well if you ever know where to get some, could you let me know? I'm asking for a friend." Simon ignored my question.

"Simon, if you want me to get you weed, just say so." I watched Marlowe finally settle on a spot in front of a tree.

"Quinn, would you get me weed?" He asked, innocently.

"Yes Simon."

"He wants to fuck you." Maggie screamed into the screen when I told her about Simon. Whenever Maggie heard stories about anything dealing with the opposite sex, she ran straight to sex. Everything was sex.

"No he doesn't."

"He. Wants. To. Fuck. You."

"Maggie, two people of the opposite sex can be just friends. I just met the dude like a week ago."

"Do you believe anything you're saying?"

"Yes. I do." I went on. "See, this is why I never tell you anything. You turn it into something completely different."

"Well it could be something more. I'm just saying, take it where you can get it."

It was Saturday morning and for once I actually had something positive to tell Maggie during our weekly talk. Maggie was the one always going on about her latest escapade. Whether it was a weekend fling with an investment banker from New York or a month long tryst with a rodeo clown, she always had a bizarre story to share.

"I want to meet him. What are you going to do about Charlie?" She changed gears quickly.

"There's nothing to do, I'm just going to have two drinks and see how he's been the past four years."

"Two drinks can lead to more."

"Not when your father's the bartender."

"I don't know Quinn."

"I do and I wish that you would stop acting like Charlie and I were this great couple. We were kids."

"You guys were hot together."

"What happens when we become not hot?"

"You'll figure it out. Just don't go there already trying to leave. You always do that," she urged. "Are you sitting in your bathroom?" She leaned further into the screen.

"Yes." I panned my phone out so she could see me sitting cross-legged on the toilet. "I'm hiding from my parents."

"Why?"

"Because wherever I turn, there they are. I haven't spent this much time so close to them since I was in Mom's stomach. I'm suffocating."

"Well you should get out more, hang out with people your own age, like Simon." She made a kissy face. "Or Charlie. Either will do. You just need some good sex."

"You're insane."

"I've got to go, I have an event this afternoon and I need to do a million things."

"Oh you're so important." I teased before hanging up.

"Quinn," Mom's voice rang outside the bathroom door. "Who are you talking to?"

"Myself." I turned on the shower to muffle her voice. "I'll be out in a little."

"Quinn!" Dad exclaimed when I walked into Kelly's later that day. I was meeting Charlie for drinks at 5:00. I wanted there to be no confusion that this was not a date and therefore would not take place during routine dating hours.

"Hey Dad." I walked towards him, noticing that the usual degenerate crowd of day drinkers had thinned out. Only two people sat at the bar.

"What are you doing down here?"

"Taking Mom's subtle advice." I rolled my eyes.

"Meeting Charlie?"

"Yeah, can I grab two beers?"

Dad poured two light drafts and passed them to me, his eyes sympathetic to my situation. I think he knew this was mostly to appease Mom.

I went outside and sat on the patio facing the road. The patio offered a million-dollar view of Saturday afternoon traffic in Springhaven.

I took my phone out and saw a message from Dillon. He took care of fulfilling Simon's wish. Quickly scrolling through my contacts for the number, I called Simon.

"Hey I got that thing you needed," I said when he picked up.

"You did?" He paused. "I'm in the middle of the fifth movie." He confessed.

"Are you watching all of them?"

"Of course." He said, casually. "And I was completely wrong about your goals of going to Hogwarts. I think that's where I'm destined to be."

"I told you. I'll be at Kelly's Bar for a little bit. Stop by and I'll take you to grab it. If you can tear yourself away."

"I will. I'll text you when this is over. Thanks Quinn."

"You're welcome." I looked up just in time to see Charlie's familiar red pick-up truck pull into the parking lot. "I've got to go, I'll see you soon."

"Hi," he greeted when he walked up the stairs. I stood and gave him a hug and quick kiss on the cheek, this time making sure I missed the corner of his mouth.

"How are you?"

"I'm good, busy now with the new job." I needed to sell this point early and often.

"That's awesome, what are you doing?"

I could either tell him the truth- that I painted fake food for a living, or I could take creative liberty with my profession. After all I am in the arts and the arts are nothing without creativity.

"I am," I paused for dramatic effect, "the assistant to a successful designer." It wasn't a total lie, I mean Simon carved the food and I painted it. That's assisting. We also have national accounts, so I'd say we're pretty successful as well.

"Wow." Charlie seemed surprised. "That's really cool."

"Yeah, I started this week. It's good, something different." I took a long sip of my beer and thought of the pies I had to paint Monday.

"Look at that," he put his hand on my arm. "Just a few weeks and you've already got a job."

I bit down on my lip. "Yup, really something." He was talking to me like I was a baby learning to potty train.

"I remember you painted a lot in high school." He shifted. "You were really good, actually." He sounded surprised.

We grew quiet and I drank the rest of my beer out of boredom. .

"Do you want another one?" I asked pointing at his still half filled glass. "I'll go grab two more." I walked away before he had a chance to answer. Inside I motioned for two more beers and Dad saw a worried look on my face.

"What's wrong?" He asked, concerned.

"I'm dying out there. We've already run out of things to talk about."

"You'll be fine. I've got to go stock the bar before tonight, but your brother should be here soon if you need anything and Nora's in the back somewhere." He said and walked away.

I was going to need a lot more alcohol to continue sitting in an uncomfortable silence with Charlie. Forget a two drink maximum, it was going to be a two drink minimum. I reached behind the bar for the bottle of whisky, and poured two shots worth into a glass before shooting it quickly.

"I was wondering if you were coming back," Charlie spoke when I walked back outside.

"Yeah, just talking to my dad for a second."

"You know I'm going to be honest, I was surprised you called." Charlie said after I sat back down.

"I know. I was surprised I called you too." Did I mean to sound that honest? "Now that I'm home I just wanted to make a better effort to get in touch with everyone. "I mean there's no reason we can't all hang out." Yes there she is, the liar I was quickly becoming.

"That's great." Charlie reached for my hand. I pulled it back instantly. He pretended to pick at a splinter on the table to lessen the embarrassment. "So tell me about college."

I could talk about college forever and I did. We each had two more beers and I snuck another shot of whiskey in between rounds of me waxing poetically about my time spent living in an easily condemnable house with my three friends. The place was an absolute shack, but we didn't care. We were drunk on the feeling of being young and on our own.

"I fell in love with the freedom I had at college."

"You don't think you have the same freedom here?"

"Not that I don't have freedom here, but here I'm someone's daughter, sister, niece, everyone knows me. At college I was whoever I wanted to be. Nobody knew my parents, Pat, or Delaney. None of their drama followed me." "I get it." He said.

"So what's going on with you? Any girlfriends on the radar I should know about?" I shouldn't have asked that question, it wasn't my business and it would only lead him on, but I couldn't keep talking about myself.

"I've dated on and off, but nobody really serious." He looked at me, "What about you?"

"Having a boyfriend in college would have ruined my fun." The words actually left my mouth. "I didn't mean that how it sounded." *Yes I did.* I backpedaled a bit. "It's just after we broke up, I didn't want to whole relationship thing."

"Yeah, I get it."

"Hey." Pat called out, walking towards us. "Give me your car keys." He held out his hand out and I handed my keys over before grabbing the house key off the chain. "What's up Charlie?" He nodded across the table at Charlie who busied himself studying his beer.

Pat loved any time he could play the overbearing brother. He was good at it. In high school he always seemed to magically appear right when I was about to start having fun. I'll never forget one party when he was a senior and I was a sophomore. I had a couple drinks and thought I was cooler than I was. I tried to play quarters with a bunch of Pat's friend and right before it was my turn Pat appeared out of nowhere, grabbed me by my wrist and brought me home. "You're too young to be hanging out with those kids," he lectured. "My friends are idiots."

Now I'm 23 and he's still the same. "Let me know when you want to go home, I'm going to be here for a bit," Pat said. He walked away, turning back around just before the door. "Someone called the bar for you, by the way"

"Who?"

"He didn't say him name. It sounded like he was crying. He kept saying something about Sirius radio." Pat shook his head. "I hung up."

"Probably a prank call." I shook my head. "Fucking kids." I added. I looked down at my phone and saw two missed calls and a text message from Simon. I completely forgot I was supposed to take him to pick his weed up.

"Pat!" I called out to him. "I don't need a ride. I forgot my boss is coming into town to take me to an exhibit for work."

"Whatever. Just don't drive."

"Whoa. Work on the weekend?" Charlie's voice caught me off guard. I forgot he was even here.

"I know, it's messed up, right? I just don't want to get on his bad side."

"I'll head out of here then. This was fun. We should hang out next weekend."

"Maybe." I hugged him for good measure. "Great to see you."

"You too."

"What's up with that," Pat nodded towards the door when I went inside to wait for Simon.

"Just meeting an old friend."

"Jesus." He shook his head. "You want a beer?"

"Yes."

"I won't charge you for the beer, but I'm charging you for all the whiskey you drank tonight." Pat smirked.

"Fine, fine. I'm a working woman now, I can afford it."

"Yeah," Pat reached across the bar to squish my cheeks. "I forgot to say congratulations. Good for you Q." He poured two shots. "I'll get your drinks, but take it easy on the whiskey." We clinked glasses and the amber liquid was instant fire in my throat as it traveled down and settled in my stomach.

That was the one.

That was the drink that sent me over the edge from someone who's sporting a mild buzz to someone who's legally drunk. I nursed my last beer for a few minutes before I heard his car. The obnoxious screech of his engine, like a hundred dying cats, could easily be heard for a half-mile radius. He warned me about it on my first day of work. I waved to Pat who was at the other end of the bar talking to his friends and stepped outside to the warm evening. Being outside made me more alert, but I was definitely drunk when I watched the sun dip low in the sky.

"There she is." He walked towards me.

"Turn around. We're taking your car."

"Are you drunk?"

"Aren't you picking me up at a bar?" I questioned when we reached his car.

"Touché." He opened the passenger door for me. I m not trying to be romantic, the door is jammed and I seem to be the only person who can open it.

"Noted."

The outside of his car was a piece of shit. The black compact car's doors were painted four different shades of blue and the muffler dragged heavy against the ground. The interior however, was spotless. The seats and floors were vacuumed and there was no garbage anywhere. It smelled faintly of new car scent and a clipped joint.

"This beast is pretty clean," I said once Simon was in the car.

"I try to keep her looking nice." He pulled out of the parking lot.

"Thanks for driving. I met a friend for a drink and well one drink leads to seven."

"You don't have to explain it to me."

"Did you call the bar?"

"I might have. Okay fine I did," he turned the radio down, "the end of the fifth movie really put me in a vulnerable place and you weren't answering my messages."

"You're converted."

"It's a good story."

"It's a great story." I pointed to the house. "Pull in here."

We pulled into the driveway. Simon killed the lights and Dillon walked out from the darkness of the garage.

He walked to the passenger's side. "What's up?"

"Hey." I said.

"You're faded." Dillon said.

I put my hands up in defeat. "I have no idea what that means." I said. "Dillon, this is Simon." I pointed at Simon. "Simon is my boss."

"Oh shit." Dillon backed up. "Is this weird?" He pointed at the bag of weed he was holding.

"No. The pot is for him. My usual?" I grabbed the bag and passed it to Simon. "Pay the man."

"Thanks bro," Simon said before handing me a wad of bills. I fished out a few bills and passed them to Dillon.

"Alright great. Bye Dillon."

"Peace." He tapped the car and disappeared back into the garage.

Simon pulled into the gas station. "Stay here, I'll be right back." He directed, before getting out and locking me in the car. I watched as Simon went in and grabbed two bottles of water and some rolling papers before paying the cashier. He stopped and picked a coin off the floor on the way out.

"So why am I your boss?" He asked when he got back in the car and handed me a bottle of water. "Here, you look like you could use some of this."

I twisted the cap off and took a long sip immediately. "Thank you."

"You're welcome, but why am I your boss?"

"Do you want the long version or the short version?"

"The long version." He pulled out into traffic. "Where do you want to smoke?"

"We can go to my house." I offered.

"Aren't your roommates home?" He said, teasingly.

"Ha. No. They're out."

"Alright. How do I get there?"

Before long Simon pulled into my driveway and turned the car off. We walked in to a dark house and a frantic Marlowe shaking because she believed that every time we left the house we were never coming back. I picked her up and cradled her into my arms, pulling her close so she knew that I didn't forget her. She relaxed into my body immediately.

"Look at this dog," Simon reached forward to pat Marlowe on the head.

"Her name is Marlowe. She's my ride or die."

I put her down and walked further into the house. I turned the kitchen lights on and opened the sliding door to the patio. "You can sit out here, I'll be back in a minute." I led Simon to the patio before going upstairs to change.

When I made it back outside, Simon had Marlowe on his lap and two rolled joints on the table. "This dog is pretty cool. Little dogs normally freak me out." I sat down in the chair next to him. "The boss thing." He lit the joint.

"It's a ridiculous story."

"Try me."

"I met my high school boyfriend for drinks today and it was awkward. He thinks he's still in love with me. Hopefully he'll figure out soon enough that he's not." He passed me the joint and I took a hit. "He just bought a house. He's 23 and he has a house." I took another drag. "Our lives are in completely different places."

"So that's why you got drunk? That seems dumb. No offense."

"No I got drunk because it's easier to be around people when I'm multiple drinks in. He's my ex-boyfriend. Everyone wanted us to spend the rest of our lives together, but he's kind of a dud."

"That's a little harsh."

"Fine. It's like when you're waiting at the doctor's office and they have all those old magazines. You don't read them because they're good. You read them to pass time before the doctor calls you in."

Simon nodded, as if he was trying to understand.

"I wanted to make my life sound glamorous and important." I picked at the already chipped nail polish on my fingers. "I told him that I was an assistant for a successful designer."

Simon coughed and a milky cloud of smoke billowed out of his mouth. "Come again?"

"Technically it's not a lie." I sat up. "You do design stuff and I paint the stuff you design…you know, assisting you."

Simon sighed. "I mean technically that's true"

"And then I told him that I had to leave because my boss was coming to take me to an art exhibit for work."

Simon shook his head. "So not only are you an avid Harry Potter fan," he put the joint between his fingers, "but you're a lush, liar and pothead." I sounded like the total package when he said it like that.

"I really appreciate that you put HP first on the list of describing qualities." I paused, taking a sip of water. "Is that my identifier?"

"Could be worse."

"Enough about my lies. I want to hear about you."

I passed him the tiny joint and he squished the clip between his two fingers and let out a deep breath. "Do you want the long version or the short version?"

"Long."

"Of course you do." Simon lit the second joint, leaned back in his chair and began his story.

I learned Simon was actually his middle name. His first name was Paul, (Yes—like Paul Simon) but he thought Paul made him sound like an old man, so he started going by Simon when he was five. His mom married Wade Diamond when Simon was eight. He was originally from Georgia, but after his mom met Wade he moved to central New York. Simon's dad was never really in the picture. He played little league just because he liked the ice cream they served at the concession stand. He took a few classes at the local community college before declaring that school wouldn't teach him what he wanted to learn. He recently turned 25. He believed that anything could be accomplished if you had the right soundtrack and his real passion was building and restoring furniture.

"What about any ex-girlfriends you're still trying to impress?" I raised my eyebrows up and down. "Everyone's got at least one," I added, resting my head in my hand.

Simon looked down at his shoelaces. "There was one girl, Sara. I dated her for a couple years."

"See. I'm sure if Sara was around you'd want to make sure you weren't looking like a schmuck."

"A schmuck."

"Yes. So what happened with Sara?"

"Typical relationship shit." He spoke softly. "She wanted something I couldn't give her. I told her you can't change people, but she thought she could make me into her own version of me. What is it with you girls always trying to turn guys into their own personal project?"

"Whoa. Whoa. Whoa. Don't generalize us like that."

"Fine. What is it with some girls wanting that?"

"You think I have a clue? You're nuts."

"It's getting late." Simon looked down at his phone. "Almost midnight. I should go."

"Yeah. That's probably best." My parents would be home soon and I didn't want to try and explain this situation, especially after I my mom called me out on smoking too much pot. "This was fun, we should do this again." I said, genuinely.

"You're still drunk."

"I'm not drunk." My buzz had taken a nosedive and the joints had taken my headache away. I was now hovering in that thin space between chaos and clarity.

"Alright, I'll see you on Monday and I'll have a full report on all the movies." He announced diligently.

"That's good, but after that we'll move on to the books. Never judge a book by its movie. See you Monday." I offered a small wave.

Simon left and I grabbed Marlowe and went to my room. I needed a good sleep to end my long day. I was still awake when I heard my parents pull in to the driveway sometime before 1:00. I heard Mom's footsteps climb the stairs and I debated whether or not to close my eyes and feign sleep like I used to when I was little. It was too late. I heard the quiet turn of the doorknob and Mom's soft voice. "Q, you awake?"

I rolled over and looked at her. "Yeah."

"How was tonight? I didn't even see you."

"It was," I paused trying to find the right words, "eventful."

"That's good." She sat down on the edge of my bed. "Things are heading in a good direction?"

"Don't get crazy on me, it was one date."

"Alright" she smoothed my comforter, "but I just want you to be happy."

"Goodnight, Mom."

5

$145.19

"I thought that as American citizens we were bound by this great nation to have today off?" Simon said when he carried over more hotdogs for me to paint. Today was the first nice day in over a week and we were inside getting thirty pounds of clay meat ready for a barbeque display.

"Well Wade is offering time and a half today. It's not that bad." Working at Flashy Foods beat having to sling drinks to all the old people while they waited for the Memorial Day Parade to go through town. By Memorial Day Parade I actually mean 30 different types of fire trucks and two trolleys carrying veterans who lip sync the same patriotic songs year after year.

One year Mr. Harris kicked a speaker off the trolley into the crowd. The speaker took a bunch of wires with it and the same song was on repeat for the rest of the parade. After that day everyone knew the jig was up, yet year after year they still lip sync - only now with surround sound speakers so Mr. Harris can't powerhouse kick anything else.

I inspected a finished hot dog. "How did you get so good at this?" I asked Simon.

He stared at the real hotdog on my desk. He eyed it a few seconds longer and finally took a huge bite. He finished the hot dog in two more bites and immediately began carving an identical hotdog out of the brick of clay in front of us.

"When my mom was a waitress in Georgia I spent a lot of time being babysat. My sitters would always run out of things to keep me busy until one time my babysitter took me to the Savannah College of Art and Design because she had to drop a project off and it was like someone turned a switch. I knew that I wanted to build stuff with my hands. That's actually how my mom met Wade. He was in town for some summit trying to convince these art students to give up their dreams and get into food making. She took me to an exhibit on campus and yeah, you get the rest." He shook his head, chuckling at the memory. "When we moved up here I spent a lot of time watching the guy whose job I took, Leon, sculpt. It's just like second nature. Some people are good at math and I'm good at this." He shrugged his shoulders. "I think the better question is how did you end up here?"

I rolled my eyes and bit down on my lip. "Well I wish I could say it was my dream job, but it was either find a job or work at the bar."

"So you thought the classified ads were the best place to look for one?"

"I've been burned by Craigslist before."

"Right. Flashy Foods wasn't your plan."

"That would be correct."

"So what was your plan?"

"Don't worry about it."

"Come on, you can tell me."

"I'm waiting for a call." I spoke mysteriously.

"For what?" He pressed.

"To work in an art gallery. So far I haven't gotten any of the jobs I applied for and I spent all my savings paying for my fifth year of college because my parents wouldn't pay for me to get a fine arts degree after I switched my major from business. They said the arts aren't practical."

Simon let out a cough. "Oh."

"Yeah, not exactly a million dollar story."

Both my parents were sitting around the table when I got home from work late that night.

"Hey."

"Oh I see your boss you work for let you out of work early." Mom pursed her lips and looked at the clock. It was past 8:00. "I mean really, it's Memorial Day."

"I offered to work today, time and a half."

"I didn't know artists offered overtime pay."

"They do. How was the parade?"

"Mr. Harris got heat stroke by Medina Road." Dad said. "Good thing there were twelve ambulances n the parade."

I looked at him, not wanting to laugh out of respect, but still finding it funny. "Is he okay?"

"Oh yeah he'll be fine," Dad said.

"What are you guys doing home?"

"Nora's training a new bartender and your brother offered to hang around for a little while." Dad looked up. "How's work going?"

"It's actually going really well."

"That's good. Do you see yourself working this job for a while or is this just something for the summer?"

"I don't know. Guess I haven't really thought about it."

"Maybe you should."

"Who knows, I could get a call for a job tomorrow."

"Would you take it?" She asked.

"Yes."

"You're pretty quick to answer." She noted.

"Why would I stay?"

"Oh come on, Quinn."

I knew what was coming next, a guilt trip from Mom with a guest appearance by Dad because I didn't want to stay in Springhaven.

"I'm leaving." I walked away from them. "I'm not going to have this conversation with you guys." I picked up my keys. "So I'm going to leave before I say something that I don't really mean."

"Be home by 11:00." She called after me.

"I'm not 16." I slammed the front door.

There was no destination in mind when I started driving. I just needed to get out of there. Sometimes they were too much. I called Simon, not even thinking twice. "Can we do something?" I asked as soon as he answered.

"Like what?"

"I don't know, anything. My roommates are pissing me off."

"Mine too. Wade is going on about lead-based paint and it's effects on the brain."

"Sounds serious."

"Breaking news, serious. Come pick me up, my friends band is playing a show over in Denton." Denton was a town 20 miles away.

"I'm on my way, text me your address and don't tell Wade. I don't want him to think I'm a bad influence making you sneak out of your house on a week night."

"Fine. See you in a little bit."

Fifteen minutes later I pulled up outside of Simon's house. It was a colonial-style house with an electric blue front door that stood out against the red brick. He lived just outside of Springhaven in the even smaller town of Harris. I was going to call him but before I even had my phone out he popped up on the passenger side of my car.

"Christ!" I jumped. "Do you always creep up like that?"

"Not always," he said climbing in, "only when I'm sneaking out on a school night."

"Alright. Where am I going?"

"Get on the highway."

"So tell me about these friends of yours, I was getting worried you were anti-social."

"Actually it's the complete opposite. I'm a social butterfly," he said dryly. "My friends Miles and Tim are in this band called Rustling Foliage."

"Rustling Foliage?"

"Yeah it's a stupid name. They came up with it after they did peyote a couple years back. It was a weird time in their life."

"Are they hipsters?"

"They're like the product of a funk band and a hipster band hooking up after huffing too much computer duster."

"That's quite the comparison."

"It was either Rustling Foliage or The Deloreans, but they felt that would pigeon hold them to only cover music from Back to the Future."

"Right. They're hipsters."

"I'm personally a big fan of old music but I get their reasoning." Simon leaned back in the seat.

"I am also a big fan of old music." I said after a moment.

"Really?"

"Yeah, I mean my parents were like the original gangsters of teenage parents, so they made a rule that everything else would be about the kids, but they got to keep control of the radio. I grew up listening to a lot of hair bands."

"Interesting."

We walked into the place and the band was already on stage covering an old Bob Dylan song. "That's Miles," Simon pointed to the lead singer, a short guy with black-framed glasses. "And that's Tim," I looked at the stocky kid playing the bass.

"They really do sound like the result of duster-fueled love making," I tried to talk over the bass as Miles stretched out the last note of the song in an off-key. Simon laughed and we shuffled through the cluster of people towards the bar. It was moderately crowded but we were able to grab a booth towards the front of the makeshift stage.

The song ended and Miles announced that they were taking five. Immediately the band dispersed into the crowd and Miles and Tim headed towards our booth.

"Paulie. What's going on man?" Miles asked when he slid in next to Simon.

"Not much man." Simon said.

Tim stood awkwardly on the outside of the booth. "You can sit down," I gestured to the spot next to me, "you're freaking me out standing there like that." Tim looked painfully uncomfortable but took a seat next to me anyways.

"Guys this is Quinn, she works with me." Simon said. I offered a limp wave. "She's the one who got me that weed we smoked." Miles and Tim both grinned at me.

"Nice to meet you Quinn," Miles reached down to kiss my hand, "and thank you for that pot."

Tim still said nothing. "You're the strong silent type aren't you?"

"He still gets nervous around girls," Miles added and stood up. "I'm going to grab a drink quick. It was nice to meet you Quinn." Tim got up and silently followed.

"They don't strike me as the peyote type." I said to Simon once they left.

"I know, right."

We drank a few beers and listened to a full set. Their music was interesting, better than the shit Dillon was making on his laptop, but still not the music I preferred. They sang a lot of songs about riding bicycles and searching for the perfect sunrise. They were about to begin their last set when Simon caught me covering up a yawn.

"Do you want to leave?"

"No. We can stay." I looked down at my watch. "It's not even midnight."

"Yeah, but I saw that yawn."

"Do you mind leaving?"

"Not at all. I wasn't even going to come out tonight until someone called me and convinced me to sneak out."

"Whoever she is, she sounds like bad news."

"She is," he responded, standing up. I followed behind him and we made our way through the smaller crowd by the bar and out into the hot night, the moon hung lazily over us.

"I wish I could drive anywhere else but home right now," I said when I started the engine.

"Why do you hate being back so much?" Simon asked.

"I don't fit in here." I said frankly. "It's always been this place that amplified how different I am from everyone else. Growing up, my dreams took me far away from home. I wasn't like any of the people who dreamed of growing up and living here all their lives."

My town is built on the idea that you graduate high school (go to college—if you're lucky), marry the person you've been dating since you were 17, and have babies before you're grown up enough to know who you really are. It's been that way for years and it won't ever change and that was never my plan. I couldn't have that life. I still spend a majority of my time in my underwear. I'm still too selfish.

"So leave."

"It's not that easy." I defended.

"Yes it is. Stay or go. Seems pretty easy to me."

"Mom has been anticipating this moment. She couldn't wait for me to come home after college with my tail in between my legs." I seemed bitterer than I intended.

"I doubt your mother wants that for you."

"Well it's easier for her to control my life when I'm upstairs than when I'm across the country."

"Moms aren't like that."

"I feel like Mom will always be able to tell me what decisions to make with my life." I snapped. Simon shook his head. "What, you don't think that's true?"

"No."

"Why?" I looked over at him.

"Because no matter how badly you want someone to do something, there is absolutely nothing that can stand in their way once they've made up their mind."

"Why?" I pushed.

"Because."

"That's not a reason."

"Fine. I'll tell you why," he divulged. "Because no matter how bad I wanted my old man to stick around, he bailed. He already had his mind made up." The car grew quiet.

"Shit." I fumbled over my words. "I'm sorry. I shouldn't have."

"It's not a big deal, I stopped letting it make me upset years ago. But I also decided that you couldn't ever control someone else, because leaving the mother of your child and your kid, that's the ultimate fuck you."

I sounded like such a whiny bitch. Here I was complaining about my mom trying to fix me up with my high school boyfriend while Simon had his dad walk out on him. "I'm sorry."

"It's alright...we've all got our shit, right?" I expected the rest of the car ride to be awkward, but when I pulled up in front of Simon's house, he turned to me, "We should sneak out more often."

"Yeah. We should."

I should have never picked up the phone when I saw Charlie's name dance across the screen, but I've always had really shitty judgment.

"Hey Charlie." I greeted after the fourth ring.

"Hi Quinn. Do you have any plans tonight?" I looked at my parents who were both squinting at my mom's smart phone and laughing at a picture of a Great Dane dressed as a member of British Parliament.

"None at all."

"Do you want to go to a party at Taylor Danahy's house?"

"Sure." I answered before I could think it through and change my mind.

"Alright. Want me to pick you up?"

"No it's cool, he lives in the next neighborhood over." A close location meant for an easy escape when things inevitably got awkward.

"That's his parent's house."

Right. Of course most people my age don't live with their parents.

"Oh okay. Yeah could you pick me up?"

"No problem. I'll get you around 5:00."

"Sounds good."

Charlie started to say something else but I hung up.

"Did you just make plans?" Mom sounded surprised.

"Yes. A real live outing into the jungle of my high school classmates."

"That sounds like fun." She added.

"Balls. Now I'm going to have to record the ninety-minute special on Full House."

Yes, that came out of my mouth and I realize how pathetic and sad it made me sound.

I'm not entirely sure why I agreed to go to the party. It was partly out of curiosity and partly because I couldn't stand my parent's cackles at dogs in costumes for one more moment. I grabbed my box of wine from the refrigerator and fled for the safety of my room.

5:00 PM seemed a little early to start a party, but I wasn't in a position to complain and it gave me an excuse to have a drink at 3:00. Well it didn't, but it made me feel better when I justified having a drink. Drinking a cup of wine in the shower isn't blending, but screw it, it's Saturday.

Three glasses of wine and a failed attempt at a side braid later, I was ready as I could be for the impending fuck fest.

My phone buzzed on my nightstand. It was a text from Charlie. *Leaving my house. Be there soon.*

I opened the cardboard box and took the plastic bag of wine out. I twisted the spout open and pressed it my lips.

Bottoms up bitches.

Taylor and his brother lived in a two-family home on the edge of town that they rented from their uncle. It wasn't anything spectacular, but it was nice enough for two young guys to live in, like bunk beds for adults.

The small crowd that was already gathered turned and gawked at the sound of the gate being opened when Charlie and I walked into the yard. Okay maybe it wasn't a full gawk, but I felt the root of their stares burn into me the further I stepped into the yard.

"What's up?" I offered a small wave with my greeting.

A chorus of half-hearted hellos followed. Taylor walked over first, greeting me with a hug before turning to Charlie, "Did you remember the beer?"

"Yeah I left them in the truck." Charlie said.

Shit. Should I have brought a hostess gift? Are we at that age already? Instinctively I pulled the bag of wine from my purse and thrust it towards Taylor. "Here. I brought wine."

He stared at me for a moment before he thanking me and walking the wine over to the cooler. I instantly regretted parting with it.

"Should we get a--"

"Yes." I cut Charlie off. "We should get a drink."

"Okay then."

I recognized most of the people here. They were either from my grade or Taylor's brother's grade the year before us. Melanie and Mike were leading separate group conversations on either end of the yard, boys and girls on opposite sides like a middle school dance. I decided to change the game and stand by myself next to the cooler while Charlie went out to the truck.

Booze was number one on my list. It always is.

Cups. I needed one immediately. I scanned the yard for plastic cups, my heart beating wildly with anticipation for my reunion with my beloved. My wine and I had already been parted too long. The sun broke through the clouds and shone down on the plastic cups at the exact same time I made eye contact with them on the table directly behind Melanie Gorman's friendship circle.

I mustered up my best pageant smile and headed towards them. "Hi Melanie." I reached behind her for a cup.

"Quinn. Hi. What a surprise." If she thought I would take her greeting as a slight then she had no idea that I was already buzzed and could not care less.

"I know right. The gang's all here. I threw an arm around her shoulder for good measure. "Ladies." I nodded my head to the three girls surrounding her. "I see these parties are still a sausage fest." They forced a polite laugh. "Well, great seeing you all." I didn't wait for a response before walking away.

The other side of the middle school dance didn't fair much better. Charlie walked back from his truck and headed in the direction of the guy's circle jerk. I joined him.

"Oh man," Adam Clark clapped Charlie hard on the back. "That homecoming after party junior year was the stuff made for legends." I put my head down to hide my shit eating grin during this story. I remember that party and it was not the stuff legends are made of. Adam passed out with his head in Kara Weaver's lap after he drank vodka from a boot. A dozen people tee-peed Adam's house and Michelle McIntyre broke his television. His parents came home and had to get the pipes to their house drained because someone stuffed three tee shirts down the master bathroom's toilet. Griffin Hart stole his parent's grandfather clock. Who even steals a clock?

"Yeah man. Things got crazy." Charlie said.

Jesus. I wanted to believe that I could do this, just play the part, smile and laugh and the appropriate moments and eventually the stifling atmosphere of this party would be enough for me. My patience was wearing thin. I could only take so many stories about the glory days of high school.

Was that really the best it was ever going to be? The rest of their lives spent on one big *remember when* where everyone waxes poetic about how good things were back in the day? I don't believe my best days were when I was 17. I drank wine coolers in Maggie's closet and snuck out to parties I didn't even want to go to when I was 17. If that's getting top billing in my life, take me out back and shoot me 'Ol Yeller style.

By the third hour of remember when I needed to smoke something, badly. There was little for me to offer in terms of stories and I politely laughed at enough of them already. Nobody would notice if I slipped away for ten minutes.

I power-walked to back door. The kitchen was empty. It seemed as good of a place as any to roll a joint. I sat down and pulled my papers and weed out of my purse. I was breaking up a tiny nugget when I heard footsteps and intense sniffling coming down the back stairs. Shit. I tried to shove the weed back in my bag but it was too late, two guys that were both a year ahead of me in high school walked into the kitchen. They were equally as surprised to see someone.

"Whoa." The first one spoke before swiping his nose intensely. The second one added a dramatic sniffle. They were definitely upstairs blowing cocaine. "You probably shouldn't roll that in here." I think his name was Dave, pointed at the bag of weed in my hand.

Seriously. This motherfucker was calling me out for rolling a joint on the kitchen table. If we were sitting in California, this would be legal.

"Oh I'm sorry, did me rolling a joint get in the way of you two snorting coke upstairs?" My comment made their already pale faces turn even whiter and they shuffled out the back door without another word.

This barbeque was dismal.

I finished rolling my joint in peace and walked through the house to the front door. I sat down on the front step and sparked the joint, inhaling deeply and enjoying the silence.

I'm dumb if I actually thought the barbeque was going to end any other way but this. I never stood a chance at this party full of people excited to see me back home after I made such a big deal out of leaving. Nobody actually came out and said those words, but it was heavily implied in their attitude.

"Aha. This is where you've been hiding." Charlie appeared in the doorway

"Yeah, turns out, this party is not really my thing." He sat down next to me on the front steps and took a sip from beer in his hand. He gestured to the joint in my hand, "You still smoke?" It wasn't a question.

"You say that so disapprovingly." I took another drag.

"It's childish."

"So I should move on to adult drugs like cocaine?"

"No. You just shouldn't do drugs."

"Ah." I took another drag and exhaled. "Well we can't all be good little boys like you." I patted his knee.

"Why do you even smoke weed?"

What was this, the Spanish Inquisition? "Because I would be even more abrasive if I wasn't stoned all the time."

"Oh."

"I think I'm going to call a ride. I'm kind of all partied out."

"I'll drive you home."

"No, stay here. I'll be fine."

"Who will you call?" He asked.

"I'll figure something out." I patted his leg and stood up. "See you around, Charlie." I walked down the steps and into the glow of the streetlights.

"So did you have fun?"

"Not really mom."

"I'm glad you called me for a ride."

"A real banner moment for me too." I glanced at the dashboard. It wasn't even 10:00.

"You can hang out with your father and I tonight." She offered politely.

"I think I'm just going to go to bed."

"Fine."

Silence took over the car until she pulled into the driveway. She barely had the windows rolled up and I already fled the car, walking quickly up the driveway and into the house. I didn't even stop to say hi to my dad.

I opened the door to my room and grabbed my computer off the bed, opened a new search tab and typed. *Art gallery jobs, Chicago*

6

$1,354.32

June moved fast. Delaney continued to expand, now in her last trimester and she became even more obsessed with cleaning and reading the labels on everything.

"I didn't think nesting was a real thing," I whispered to Mom as we sat folding more baby clothes in Delaney's living room one afternoon.

"Oh it's real. I made your father scrub the baseboards for a week before you were born."

"I can hear you." Delaney squeaked from across the room. "I'm not nesting. I don't even have the nursery painted yet."

"Yeah but you've got this." I held up a breast pump. "So at least you'll be able to put those huge boobs to use."

"Stop," she whined. "Completely unnecessary."

"I'm sure your husband feels differently." I wiggled my eyebrows suggestively.

"Quinn," Mom barked. "Enough."

"Sorry." I held my hands up in surrender. "Just pointing out the obvious." I folded a pair of socks before speaking again. "Alright, this baby shower, we're having it at the bar, right?" They both nodded in agreement. "Because nothing says welcome to motherhood more than a bar full of alcohol you can't drink." They gave me an identical look of disapproval. "I'm just going to ask this up front: I'm allowed to drink? Like I don't have to abstain on your behalf, right?"

"Yes, you can drink." Delaney responded politely while she lifted herself out of the chair in a less than graceful fashion.

"But not if you plan on getting drunk like you do off boxed wine." Mom forcefully interjected.

"Hey!" I shouted. "Boxed wine is not the issue here, okay? It is better to drink boxed wine because it's in a cardboard box and you can't tell how much you've drank. You lift it up by the handle and if it still feels heavy, you haven't drunk much. It's basic physics." I pointed out. "Wine in bottles makes my alcoholism so much more visible. Besides boxed wine comes in plastic bags. It's useful because the bag can be transferred and carried around. It fits excellently in most purses." I took a breath. "It is bottled wine that's the enemy here. Okay. We're all on the same team. Team boxed wine. Remember that."

"I don't care. Your sister's baby shower is not the place."

"If you don't think alcohol played a part in the conception of your grandchild," I started before they both said my name. "Okay, I get it. Lock it up." I stood up. "I've got to go anyway. Have to stop by work and take care of some stuff."

That was a lie. I needed to pick up weed from Dillon, but the simple fact that I could mention work meant nobody would question it. Work, explosive diarrhea and your period are three excuses nobody will ever fight you on.

I called Dillon on the way to my car. "Hey Dillon can I pick up?"

"Whoa. Whoa. Not on the phone."

"Okay. How would you like me to do this? Send you a message by telekinesis?"

"Do you want a slice of pie?"

"What? No."

"I can get you a slice."

"Ooh." I understood what he was inferring. "Is the pie an 8-cut? Because I would like one eighth of the pie."

"Forget it. Just come over."

Something on the passenger's seat of Dillon's car caught my eye when I walked up the driveway into the house. I paused at the sight of a box of sandwich bags and a scale that looked like it belonged in the high school science department blatantly lying on his passenger's seat. I opened his car and grabbed both things.

I walked in the house and down to the basement where I knew the drug lord himself was stationed. I found Dillon blowing odd noises into some sort of voice modulator

"I'm sorry, I didn't know that you were being watched by the cops." I dropped down to the couch next to him.

"I'm not." He didn't look away from the machine.

"Then what was with the weird shit on the phone?"

"I'm trying to be more low key."

"Oh. Well you might want to give your customers a heads up on that next time. You're going to spook them. The last thing stoners need is more paranoia."

"How can I do that?" He asked in a serious tone.

"Get a feel for your regular customers. How often are they buying? How much are they buying? Then establish their patterns and then transition to a weekly drop off to diminish the sketchy phone calls. They'll appreciate the scheduled time and you'll appreciate not having to make a fuck ton of pies."

"That makes sense."

"How long have you been selling pot?"

"Three months."

"Fairly new to the game." I sat for a moment, weighing if I should say what came next. "I can help you out. Tutor you in the art of selling pot to teenagers if you want, just going to help you get started."

"How would you even know what you're doing?"

"I was a business major in college for a bit. I can increase your profits by 50% in a few weeks. Plus I smoke a lot of weed."

"Really?"

"Yes."

"Why would you help me?"

"Because."

"What does that mean?" Dillon asked.

"Don't make it a thing."

"Would I have to pay you?" He asked, skeptically.

"No. Just give me free weed."

"Okay."

"Perfect. Lesson number one, don't ever carry bags and a scale in your car." I put the items I found on his front seat in front of him. "Come on, stupid."

"Alright, chill I'll take it out."

"Good. Now, you shouldn't push nickel and dime bags. You want people who are going to buy in bulk. The faster you can move your product, the better. Plus there's no good money in pushing ten bags."

"Were you a business major or a drug dealer in college?"

"Actually, a little of both."

"Really?" He seemed impressed.

"Yes. Tell anyone who asks that I'm tutoring you in Spanish and if anyone comes to me saying otherwise I'll deny it until I die. We're not telling Maggie. She would kill me."

"Alright."

"Good."

He pulled out a ratty looking backpack from his other side. The initials S.A.N. stitched to the front.

"S.A.N. What does that mean?" I ran my hands over the stitches.

"Smoke anything necessary." He pulled out a freezer bag of bud.

"Okay. No."

"Why not?"

"Why not?" I scoffed. "Because smoke anything necessary infers that you wouldn't turn down a crack pipe. Acronyms are outdated. Just sell a good product and people won't need the other stuff." I started tearing at the stitches with a pair of scissors I pulled from the coffee table drawer.

"You're sure about this?" He sounded skeptical.

"I graduated college, of course I'm sure."

Family dinner tonight at 6:00. Tell your boss to loosen up. The text from Mom was the last thing I wanted to look at. The air conditioning had blown at work and I had swamp-everything. Wade couldn't even let us leave early because he needed four-dozen chili peppers shipped out tonight. Even poor Gloria had a sweat 'stache.

I found a binder in one of the drawers of my desk that had another Excel spreadsheet with food names and what color they should be painted. I flipped through the binder and decided the spreadsheets would be more useful to me as a fan than they would a guideline. You can't just paint an apple red because it says so. You have to paint it red with a tint of white and a splash of purple to offset the red hue. You can't measure out the amount of color you need; you have to mix it yourself and when the color is right, you'll know. Painting wasn't something you could instruct. It had to be a natural chemistry between colors.

"When you break the rules, you really break them," Simon sat down and pointed at the paper fans I had made out of the spreadsheets.

"I'm still shocked that someone actually typed this," I replied, still fanning my face.

"Megan. There's not really much else for her to do around here and she's Wade's niece so he has to give her hours."

I passed him a paper fan. "This should help."

"I was actually on my way out, but I couldn't leave you here alone to stink up the place, so put me to work painting these peppers."

"You don't have to stay and help. Go, be free in the land of air conditioning."

"It's cool, the only other thing I would be doing is going to Tim's apartment and listening to him and Miles complain about the absence of rock and roll on today's radio."

I raised my eyebrows. "Sounds amazing. I get to go home and have dinner with my whole family, including the girl that Patrick is sleeping with this month." I rolled my eyes. "He insists on bringing these trolls to family dinners. Always turns out to be a good time."

"Sounds like it."

"I mixed some color for the pepper." I passed him the ice cube tray that I've been using as a palette. "If it's easier, you can gloss them and I'll color them. There are some dry ones over there." I pointed to the windowsill.

"I know you spent all your savings," Simon spoke, quietly, "but I'm glad you changed your major to art history."

I smiled. "I was a horrible business major."

I walked into my house at 5:30 sweaty and exhausted. I wanted a drink and a shower immediately. I heard the shrill sound of Mom's voice in the kitchen, which meant that Patrick's flavor of the week must already be here. I didn't want to deal with that right now, but I also needed wine. The kitchen was necessary.

"Quinn," Mom sashayed over to me, putting on a good show. "Oh, hon," she paused checking my appearance, "you look a little butch right now." I caught my reflection in a hanging mirror. It was true, my hair was sweaty and matted on my head and my face had streaks of paint all over it. The old tee-shirt I had on was Patrick's and to top it off I had a pair of drawstring shorts on that I found in my car because the jeans I had on were too hot to wear in the heat.

"I forgot to tell you," I stated as I walked towards the refrigerator, "I'm a lesbian now."

"Those jokes aren't funny, Quinn." She looked across the room, "this is Nina."

"Hi Nina, how are you?" I greeted her in a flat tone. I knew Nina. She was a couple years ahead of me in high school and a huge slut. Figures she would know Patrick. Her dyed red hair was pulled back into a ponytail, exposing her roots and she had on hoop earrings that made her look like an extra in a rap video. You know what they always say, the bigger the hoop, the bigger the ho.

"Wow Quinn, I haven't seen you in so long. You're a grown up now."

"Yeah actually I was only three years behind you in high school." I opened the refrigerator and my mother reached over and pulled out a bottle of wine. It was a nice departure from the boxed stuff. "Remember you were in my math class your senior year? Did you ever get the hang of polynomials?"

"I went to hair school."

"Of course you did." I grabbed the bottle of wine and headed out of the room.

"Don't you want a glass?" Mom asked, rushing after me.

"No, I'll save you one less dish."

I was still in the bathroom when Delaney came in and sat down on the toilet. "So Nina seems nice." She said. I continued putting lotion on my face.

"Nice is one way to put it."

"Let me guess…you hate her?"

"No, I don't hate her. I just think she's kind of a slut. Don't you remember when she would always come in the bar, stick her boobs on the counter and wait for someone to buy her a drink?"

"OH!" Delaney's eyes lit up and she turned to me. "That's the same girl!?"

"Yup."

"Ew." She stood up and flushed the toilet. "So how's the job?"

"It's actually really good." I smiled. "It's the only part of my life that I like right now." I took a swig of wine from the bottle.

"God I can't wait to drink wine." She dried her hands and they went instinctively to rub her belly. "I mean, I love this baby, but I miss wine."

"Don't worry," I winked at her, "I'll drink enough for both of us."

When I arrived downstairs for dinner I was mildly buzzed, the table was set and Nina was helping my mom prepare the salad. Delaney was sitting at the counter looking bored and tearing at her cuticles. I sat next to her. We stared at each other for a moment and then over to Mom and

Nina who were both laughing at something Nina said. She was laying the charm on thick and Mom was lapping it up, none the wiser.

Okay so I don't like Nina. That much is obvious. However the more I make that fact apparent, the worse I am. It's always protective and endearing when brothers disapprove of who their sister is dating, but when a sister disapproves of her brother's choice in girlfriend, she's a bitch and jealous. For the record, I'm nowhere near jealous. I would say I'm hovering on the border of pity and concern at most. The more my mom laughed with Nina, the more I felt like taking my wine and peacing the fuck out. I couldn't understand why the same woman who pushed for me to date someone that was all wrong for me was kissing the ass cheeks of a girl who blew her way through high school.

Moments later the screen door opened and Dad, Patrick and Corliss walked in carrying a tray of meat.

"Quinn," Dad looked over at me. "When did you get home?"

"A little while ago, but I had to take a shower. The air conditioning broke at work and I was a mess." I paused. "Or as Mom likes to call it, butch."

"What a hard-working girl," Corliss joked as he walked by me to stand next to Delaney.

The dining room table was set for seven people, but was only built for six. I found myself crammed next to Nina because Delaney played the "I'm pregnant and need more space card." Lucky. We all sat around the table passing steak and potatoes in between passive aggressive comments. Okay mainly my comments were passive aggressive.

"So let's have a toast." Mom raised her glass and I was already embarrassed for what would soon come out of her mouth. "To Quinn, for finally getting a job and hopefully a husband." My eyes went wide.

"And to Mom," I let out a drunk giggle, "for becoming a grandmother before the age of 50. Cheers." I drank the rest of the wine bottle in one long sip.

"Whoa," Corliss exclaimed. "I haven't seen someone chug a drink like that since college." Delaney gave him a glare and he leaned back in his chair.

"Have you decided on a theme for the nursery yet?" Mom asked Delaney and Corliss, ignoring me entirely.

"We're still deciding, we're looking for someone to paint it. I'm awful at painting and Corliss will undoubtedly have a tantrum halfway through the process so it's just easier to get someone else."

Corliss nodded in agreement. "I don't have time for painter's tape and I always touch the walls when they're still wet," he broke in.

"You better find someone soon. Ready or not that baby's coming." Mom's words hung heavy in the air.

"So Nina," Dad spoke. "What do you do?"

"Hair," she divulged like she was spilling espionage secretes. "I work in Denton."

"That's nice." He smiled in the way that dad's smile when they're not sure of what else to do.

The mood at the table had shifted from awkward to uncomfortable. It wouldn't have been half as bad if Nina weren't sitting next to me eying the silverware like she would inherit it. "This is delicious," she said, breaking the silence.

"Isn't it?" I nodded at Nina, my lips pursed together.

Mom shot me a look from across the table, but I ignored her, feeling brazen.

"Just think what it will be like on holidays when we can cook all day together like real women." Patrick choked on his drink and Corliss and Delaney both let out a laugh that they tried to turn into a cough.

Nina just smiled.

"It was bad," I explained to Simon the next day when he asked how family dinner was. "I drank a bottle of wine and my mom was her usual overbearing self."

"Sometimes I'm glad to be an only child. Do you have any plans this weekend?" He continued framing unpainted chocolate chip cookies on a tray.

"I do. Maggie comes home on Friday. I asked Wade if I could take the next two Fridays off to help her with stuff for her brother's graduation party and pick her up from the airport. So I'll be around with her all weekend. You?"

"Oh I'll probably spend a lot of time with Rustling Foliage while they get ready for their tour." Simon said with mock enthusiasm.

"They're going on tour?" I asked, surprised. They were a decent band to listen to when you've had four or six drinks, but I wouldn't say they were tour-worthy.

"Yup." He said plainly. "They're going on a Western New York bar tour. They want to play every dive bar in the state before they go to other states."

"Well at least they're doing something they love," I offered up.

Simon looked back and forth in the empty warehouse before speaking. "Be careful, someone might hear you saying something optimistic." He smiled with his eyes.

I pursed my lips into a hard line before glaring at him. "I pick and choose my moments."

"Noted." Simon tapped a finger to his head and went back to the strategic placement of cookies on the tray.

"Simon." Wade's voice came over a loudspeaker I didn't know existed until that very moment. "Come here, will ya?" It wasn't so much a request. Simon looked at me and exhaled deeply. I offered him a weak smile as he pushed himself to his feet and trudged towards Wade's office.

He returned five minutes later, a menacing scowl etched onto his face. "He's gotta be fucking kidding me." Simon paced in front of my desk. "He wants me to drive an hour and a half to drop off the pig we did last week because Hector forgot it when he took the delivery this morning."

Hector, our delivery guy, was a nice enough guy, but to be honest-- he sucked at his job. He was constantly forgetting to load things and his driving left a lot to be desired. The worst part is he would just shrug his shoulders and kind of chuckle when Wade yelled at him. Wade wouldn't fire him though because apparently the guy's got a wife and three kids and Wade feels bad. He obviously feels less bad when he makes Simon fix the mistakes.

"Ouch." I kept painting a cinnamon bun. "Have fun with that."

"Well part of the deal is that I get gas money and I get to take someone with me so..."

"Let me grab Gloria for you." I stood up and started to walk over to where the older woman was sitting completely engulfed in a radio segment on online dating after age 50.

Simon narrowed his eyes down at me. "Cute." I smirked half-heartedly. "Do you want to come with me?"

I looked up at him and pondered for a moment. "Will that pig even fit in your car?" I was serious. "I painted that thing and it was ginormous."

Simon waved me off. He already turned my light off and grabbed my phone. "Yes it will. Come on, we've got to leave now."

"Alright, alright. Calm down." I followed behind him as he stomped through the warehouse. We passed through the showroom and out to his car. He jiggled the lock on the passenger side door and opened it before stepping aside.

"Not romantic." We both nodded. "Chivalrous at the very best," he added thoughtfully. I slunk down into the passenger seat admiring, yet again, how clean the interior of his car was. Not even for a boy's standards, for everyday life standards. I couldn't help but notice the faint traces of vacuum marks on the floor mats.

Simon climbed in hastily and started the engine before putting his seatbelt on. We almost left the parking lot, Simon driving far too dramatically, when I pointed out that we didn't have the pig.

"Fuck." He reversed back to the front door. "I'll be right back." He said and then added a huff of annoyance. He slammed the door shut.

This was the first time Simon had shown any negative emotion. It was funny to see Mr. Zen so worked up.

He reappeared outside with the pig under his arm and yanked open the back driver's side door. The pig was thrown roughly in the back seat before Simon slid into the driver's seat. I looked over at him, not to say a sarcastic comment or give him a strange look, but to really look at him. He clenched the steering wheel so hard I saw the veins in both his hands strain against his skin. I looked past his hands up his toned arms that clung tightly to the sleeves of his ratty white shirt. His skin had an olive tone that made me think his some of ancestors descended from Greece. His clean-shaven jaw and neatly trimmed sideburns and eyebrows highlighted the angles on his face. His coffee colored eyes narrowed on the road.

Am I sexually attracted to him? Maybe I am. I can be attracted to people. People like Simon, with his bouncy hair that crawls down the back of his head to feather whimsically below his ears. People like Simon with his long, nimble fingers that create things. He looked over at me and my head fell forward immediately. I felt the blush on my face.

"Do you have OCD?" I asked quickly.

"No. Why?"

I looked down at my feet again, noticing the lack of dirt anywhere in the car. "Well your car," I pointed out. "It's very clean. Almost borders on obsessive."

"Nah." He shook his head. "Occasionally I need to get out of my house. I just need a break from Wade and my mom—sometimes they're just too much," he added after a beat. "I go to the 24-hour car wash by my house a lot. Spend 20 minutes vacuuming my car, it calms me down." He ran a finger over his spotless dashboard. "The joints help with that too," he tacked on, thoughtfully.

"I walk my dog a lot."

"Yeah." He nodded. "You just need like 20 minutes..."

"...To not hear your parents." I finished for him.

"Exactly."

"Been there, done that. Sometimes you just want to be by yourself. I get way too excited to be home alone."

"Yeah, you almost feel bad for it, but then you remember that they're always around."

"And not only that," I added. "But you don't know if you've reached that relationship where you have to tell them where you're going or you have to call and let them know you'll be home at 10."

"Yeah. I always wonder if they expect me to tell them everywhere I go. Miles and Tim don't get it."

"Neither does Maggie."

He looked down at me with a smile that stretched so far across his face it reached his ears. I didn't know what to say so I just smiled back.

7

$1,700.16

I was late. Maggie's flight was supposed to land in ten minutes and I still hadn't left my house.

"I'll be back later, I'm going to pick up Maggie!" I screamed to my parents as I struggled to put my sandal on my foot. I ran out of the door not waiting for their response. I stopped at a coffee place and picked up Maggie's favorite coffee, knowing it would make up for my lateness, yet also make me later.

By the time I pulled up to the airport drop off she was standing on the curb tapping her toe incessantly - such a diva. She was overdressed. Maggie was always overdressed. She was the only person I know who would fly across the country in a peplum dress and four-inch stilettos.

She flagged her arms dramatically as I pulled up in front of her. "Helloooo." She pulled a strand of hair from her face.

"I'm late. I know." I got caught on my seatbelt when I tried to get out of the car. I ripped the seatbelt across my body. "I brought you a coffee." I ran around and pulled Maggie into a bone-crushing hug.

"I never thought I'd say this, but it's good to be home," she squealed as she pulled away. I put her bags in my trunk while she adjusted her dress.

"Jesus, I know everything is bigger in Texas, but let's talk about this hair." I pointed to the teased mess of blonde on top of her head.

She patted her hand on her hair. "Just tryin' to blend in with all them Southern belles," she replied in a Southern drawl.

"Please don't start talking like that," I pleaded as we pulled into traffic.

"Why?" She played aimlessly with the radio knob. "I kind of like it."

Sometimes I just had to laugh because we literally never agreed on anything. If Maggie and I hadn't been friends since we were five, I think we would hate each other. We had the exact opposite style and opinions on almost everything. That didn't matter though: Maggie knew everything about me.

"It's weird," I offered, thinking about the accent. "People obviously know you're from New York." I put my blinker on for the highway.

"I guess." She wasn't convinced and honestly, I didn't see the point in disagreeing. If it were anyone else, I would have continued to push but for some reason, that never worked with Maggie. "Am I going to meet Simon?" She quickly changed the topic.

"Ha, I don't think so." I hadn't told Maggie about how much I'd hung out with Simon, for fear of her overreaction, but she still insisted that Simon and I were on the track for sex.

"Come on. I'm home for a whole week," she whined. "There's not seven days worth of activities to do in this town." Maggie was right. There was maybe three days of activities, tops. The outlet mall an hour away will be the highlight of the trip. "Plus, now that you have a fucking job," she lit a cigarette, "I'll have to do all the boring shit during the day with Dillon."

"Tough life." I pouted my lip at her. "I took next Friday off to help you with Dillon's graduation party." I knew Maggie would be doing most of the work for the party anyway. Her dad wasn't good with this sort of thing.

"You just saved my life. But I'm still going to meet Simon." She flicked her ash out of the window. "Invite him out tonight, he'll be one less person there you hate." It was true, if Simon came out I wouldn't feel obligated to talk to all the people Maggie wanted to see.

"Fine, but, if he comes…" I paused, "IF, he comes - because he will probably have other plans—you are to tell everyone he is my boss. He is a successful designer and I am his assistant"

"That is a heaping load of bullshit," she coughed.

"Would you rather me tell everyone that I paint fake food for a living?"

"Good point," she nodded. "How did this lie come about?"

"Okay, I didn't tell you on the phone because I knew you would get weird, but I have hung out with him outside of work a few times." I found myself defending it, like I owed her an explanation. "One time I had to take him to your brother to get pot. And we went to see his friend's band play."

"Didn't you recently have drinks with Charlie?" Maggie asked, even though she already knew the answer.

"You are allowed to do more than one thing over the span of the entire weekend." I teased. "But yes, I did." I merged the car onto the off ramp.

She raised her eyebrows, but didn't say anything.

"Well," she finally said. "Are you going to tell me what happened or am I going to have to use my imagination?" She tapped her head with her index finger.

"There's nothing to tell. I was out with Charlie, it was weird and Simon needed pot. So I took him to get it. I had to make an excuse to ditch Charlie so I told him my boss was coming to take me to an art exhibition." Maggie nodded skeptically. "Why would I lie to you about it?"

"You wouldn't," she added, "but you also wouldn't tell me if you were starting to have feelings for Simon."

"I'm not." I said defensively. I gripped the steering wheel tighter. "We're friends." Were we friends? "We work together." I added.

"He's actually your boss," Maggie corrected me, a smug look on her face.

"Smart ass." I drove down Main Street.

"I want to take you out to drinks to celebrate your return to the big town." I laughed and Maggie rolled her eyes.

"No. You're broke and I'd be a bad friend if I made you pay for drinks."

"Don't worry these drinks won't cost a thing." I turned the car into the liquor store parking lot. "There's a vodka tasting today. Free booze." I put the car into park and turned it off.

"You have no shame."

"None."

We walked into the liquor store that was mostly lit by neon signs advertising wine that stopped being made in the 70's. The rattle of bottles when we walked unearthed a smell of must with every step. It would do in a pinch. We needed liquor more than we needed ambiance.

A middle-aged man stood behind the register reading the newspaper. "We're here for the vodka tasting." I boasted proudly. Maggie shook her head with what could only be described as embarrassment.

"Great. It seems you're the only ones so far." The man smiled.

"That's not surprising." Maggie whispered and I elbowed her in her side.

"Hey you're on townie turf now. You better lock it up."

"Sorry."

The man led us passed the cooking wine aisle into a back room. There was a single bottle of vodka chilling in an ice bucket and a stack of bathroom-sized paper cups on a folding table in an otherwise empty room.

This was either the sketchiest liquor tasting ever or someone was going to have to call Liam Neeson because we'd been taken.

"Well ladies this here is a new blend that's distilled seven times." The man launched into his presentation. "It preserves the flavor and gets rid of the burning after taste." He poured two cups and passed one to each of us before pouring a third for himself. "Cheers, ladies." He tipped his cup towards us in salute before he shot the cup back.

Maggie and I glanced at each other before doing the same. The liquor snaked its way down my throat with ease and even though I kept waiting for the harsh after taste, it never came.

"Wow. That was pretty good." Maggie said.

"I'm not sure," I spoke. "Maybe we should try it again."

The man smiled politely and poured two more Dixie cups of vodka. I glanced sideways at Maggie, silencing her with my eyes.

We needed to play our cards right, the only way we would be able to catch a quick buzz was if we disagreed with the initial reaction so we could try more. It was a mutually beneficial arrangement. The man was happy enough to have people actually show up to this tasting and we were happy because we didn't have to spend $15 per drink at the bar by the airport. Plus if worse came to worse we could leave my car and walk to Maggie's house.

The world was our oyster.

The man poured us another shot before the bell above the door rang. "I'll be right back, ladies." His emphasis on the word ladies was slightly off-putting. He turned and left the room, leaving the two of alone with the bottle of vodka. We each tipped back our shot before Maggie reached for the bottle and poured us another. "Let's call this friend of yours," she raised her eyebrow and drew the paper cup to her lips.

"I understand why you're an event coordinator," I chided, "You're kind of a bossy bitch." I tipped back my own shot.

"Thank you."

I picked up my phone and scrolled through to the contact that was becoming all too familiar. I knew Maggie would only annoy me until I called him anyway so we might as well get it over with.

It rang four times and I silently hoped it would go to voicemail. "Well look who it is."

"Hi Simon. What are you doing tonight?"

"Well Miles and Tim are pretty much useless, so I was going to work on some stuff at my house."

'Want more vodka?' Maggie mouthed the words to me and I nodded. She poured two more shots.

"Oh so you have plans," I said, hopeful he wouldn't want to go out. Not that I didn't want him there, but there was something nice about keeping Simon separate from everything else.

"Why?" He asked. I took the shot. "Do you know something better going on?"

"Yeah, I'm with Maggie and we're going to go to Kelly's tonight. Do you want to come?"

"It's not a school night," he said, innocently. "So I can stay out all night."

I laughed and noticed there was a nervous pitch to it, something Maggie noticed as well when she arched her eyebrows at me. "Okay that sounds good, meet us there at 10."

"See you then." I hung up the phone.

Maggie was staring at me. "Are you still going to tell me you don't like him? Because I know you've never worn blush a day in your life and your cheeks are pretty fucking rosy right now."

"I don't know if I like him. I just know that he's not like anyone else around here and it's nice having someone to talk about my shit with."

"What am I?" She pretended to be offended.

"You know what I mean. He's here. He also lives with his parents. He let's me complain about everyone and it doesn't matter because he doesn't know any of them."

Maggie shrugged. "Well I hope he brings a friend because I'm not third-wheeling it and the dress I'm going to wear is too cute to waste on townies."

"Watch it, I'm a townie now."

She drew in a breath. "Ooh yeah, you are." She crossed her fingers, "Hopefully not forever."

The man came back into the room. "Sorry about that girls. How about one more?"

"That sounds great." I said. I smiled politely and the man poured three more cupfuls of vodka. "Cheers." His voice rang through the empty room.

Maggie and I tipped back our shot quickly. "That was really great. We'll be back to buy some of that." Maggie walked towards the door.

"Thank you, sir." I followed behind her. "Really great vodka." The liquor on the shelves shook lightly when we half-ran out of the store, laughing all the way to my car. "Okay we have three minutes to get to your house before I'm no longer legally allowed to operate a vehicle." I grabbed the door handle.

"Let's go then."

We were both sporting a heavy buzz when we walked to the bar later that night. We made it back to Maggie's house safely and drank half a bottle of wine while we attempted to get ready. It was an awful plan. We reached that point where we were too drunk to be putting eyeliner on so we just drew a thick line above our lids and covered it up with eye shadow, hoping nobody would stand close enough to notice.

Pre-gaming in college was fun because what else is there to do four hours before a party but start drinking? Post college pre-gaming is a whole different game. It's necessary because the idea of facing too many people from your past sober is awful. Isn't that why you want to be drunk in the first place? Plus, being drunk will ensure that you'll be more tolerant of people. I'm generally a nicer person when I'm drunk.

We put the rest of our wine in a water bottle and drank it on our walk to the bar. We reached the point in our drunk where walking seemed like the best adventure and the summer evening matched our moods perfectly, just warm enough without feeling too hot. It wouldn't last long though. The long, drawn out days of summer were on their way.

Twenty minutes later we walked up to the door and I was surprised to see Dad sitting outside. "Big Friday crowd, I've got to start checking IDs." He smiled.

I couldn't imagine anyone being intimidated by Dad, his wiry frame made him perfect for a boxer, but it had been years since he threw a punch in the ring. He smiled past me when he saw Maggie. "Hey stranger," he stood up and pulled her into a hug. "Can I trust you girls to behave tonight?"

"Jim, what kind of girls would we be if we were well-behaved?" Maggie questioned. Dad shook his head and we walked inside. The bar was already crowded. A Blue Oyster Cult song finished playing from the jukebox and we did a quick scan to see if anyone we knew (needed to avoid) was there. I spotted a clusterfuck of kids from high school instantly and bee-lined in the opposite direction towards the bar.

"Hey," Nora came over instantly. "A real fuck fest tonight." Nora made even me seem like the most optimistic person in the world, but customers loved her sass. She poured two glasses of whiskey before handing me one, and taking the other for herself. "Cheers," she said grimly. She downed the drink and walked over to a customer who was waving a $20 bill at her. "Sir," she said calmly, "I can see that you need a drink, we all need a drink, that's why we're here, but if you keep waving that at me I will pretend that I can't see you all night." I turned around to see what Maggie wanted to drink but she had already been sucked into the tornado of people happy to see her. She glanced over at me quickly and I pointed to my glass. She nodded. I tried to make eye contact with Nora but she was still scolding the man who was now putting the $20 bill into the tip jar.

"Hey." A girl walked by behind the bar that I hadn't seen before. "You're the new girl right?" I questioned.

She had a confused look on her face. "Ooh you're Quinn?" I nodded. "I'm Hilary."

"Hi!" I said, too loudly. "Hilary can I please have a Jameson and a vodka and tonic?"

"Sure," she smiled and walked away. I stood with my back to the bar so there could be no chance of a sneak attack from anyone. Maggie was still balls deep in a love fest with April Nordstrom. April, I had learned from stalking online, had moved back home to go to graduate school, but already had a job in Albany lined up. She was always really nice, but only if it benefited her. Actually, she was kind of a twat.

I grew more and more impatient, checking my phone out of habit when someone bumped into me. I turned around, expecting to be mad.

"Quinn," I looked up.

"Elliot!" I laughed. Elliot was one of my closest friends in high school and one of the people I actually kept in contact with throughout college, but the last time we spoke he had taken a job in Seattle. He pulled me into a hug. "What are you doing here?"

"Michelle's shower is this weekend so I flew home with her and then rented a car to come here." I could have cried I was so happy to see him. "You're still coming to the wedding Labor Day Weekend, right?"

"Of course," I said, honestly. "I wouldn't miss it."

Normally exuding happiness for other people is something I lack, but in this case it's genuine. Elliot and Michelle met their freshman year of college and they are the cutest hippie-loving couple trying to save the planet one reusable shopping bag at a time. She grew up just outside of Albany, but their wedding is actually going to be in Springhaven, out by the apple orchards.

"Scared to throw yourself to the sharks?" He nodded at the group of people that had somehow doubled in size in the back corner of the bar.

"Ha, you know me all too well." I picked up the drinks. "Come with me, I'll feel much better using you as my human shield." Elliot laughed but led the way, keeping me behind him the whole time.

Maggie saw Elliot and let out the obligatory high-pitched squeal. I stepped out of their way.

"I don't see why you wouldn't want to work in the nightlife industry." I turned around and Simon was standing there awkwardly with Miles behind him.

"I'm so happy to see you right now, I could hug you," I cried.

"Have we not reached the hugging stage in our relationship?" Simon asked before pulling me against his body for a hug that lingered just a second too long.

"I guess we have." I looked passed him. "Hi Miles." Miles offered a wave. "Do you guys want to get some drinks?"

"Yes." They answered in unison. We walked through the crowd back to the bar.

"What do you guys like to drink?"

"Beer's fine." Simon said.

Nora walked over to us and I ordered their beers and two more drinks for Maggie and myself. "Oh so it's that kind of night," Simon noted when he saw my whiskey. He looked at Miles and they both drank their beers in two long gulps before ordering vodka. I gave them a quick nod of approval. They understood that survival required aggressive drinking.

"So this is Simon," Maggie said coming into the group and grabbing Miles' arm.

"No." I shook my head. "That's Miles."

"Oh. I'm an asshole." I handed Maggie her drink. "Well hello," she stared at Simon. "I'm Maggie."

"What's up?" Simon greeted her. "It's nice to meet you, Maggie."

"Maggie," I called out to her. "Miles," I turned my attention towards Miles who was swirling his vodka drink with his index finger, "is in a band that's going on tour."

Her eyes grew wide and a devilish grin appeared on her face. "Really?" She said in a hushed tone.

Miles shook his head, "I mean we're only-" I elbowed him sharply in the side before he could continue.

"It's a huge deal," I confessed.

"Let me grab my purse, I need a cigarette," she announced and walked away.

I looked at Miles. "Maggie has a fuckit list, like a bucket list, but…" I trailed off, "you get it. A touring musician is on it."

Miles' face lit up. "I think I need a cigarette as well." He started after Maggie.

"You're the worst," Simon laughed lightly.

"Or the best." I shrugged. Another song, one I didn't recognize, began to play.

"This is easily one of the best songs in a movie soundtrack, ever." He said before starting to nod his head to the rhythm. I couldn't make out the song until the chorus began playing: *I wish that I knew what I know now when I was younger.*

"This was a good movie," Simon commented, still nodding his head.

"What movie is this even from?"

"Aw come on. It's the end credit song to Rushmore," Simon cried.

"I've never seen it, but I like this song," I added.

"What would your end credit song be?"

"I don't even know what that means."

"Come on," he whined, playfully. "The song that would play as the credit's roll to the movie of your life." He said as if every other person on this planet knew about this game except me.

"I don't know," I scoffed.

"Fine. Mine is You can call me Al." He put his empty glass on the bar.

"Makes sense. You being named after Paul Simon and all." I laughed.

"Real funny," he shook his head, "at least I can think of one."

"You're right Paul. I should give this some more thought."

"I should have never told you that. Pretty soon you're going to know all my secrets."

"Consider me invested."

"Want to go smoke a joint or something?" Simon asked after a moment.

"Yes, you know I do, but my dad is the man that checked your ID on your way in so that would be weird."

"It would be, but there's got to be a side door or something and this is your bar."

"Who's the bad influence now?" I teased.

I pulled his arm and headed towards the back of the bar where the employee entrance was. We were almost to the door when Melanie Gorman appeared out of thin air because it wouldn't be a night out if Gorman weren't there to slam her velvet hammer of gloating upon us. "Quinn, you look so different when you're not behind the bar."

"Melanie!" I exclaimed, my eyes wide. "You look the same on both sides of the bar. How are you?"

"Forget about me, who is this?" She pointed at Simon.

Simon stepped in front of me partially, blocking me from Melanie's rapid-fire of questions. "Hello I'm Simon Andrews, you might have seen some of my visions at MOMA this past fall." He didn't wait for her response before adding, "Truly revolutionary work, I'm really cultivating and rehabbing modern art single-handedly." Simon had adopted a dignified accent that sounded like he was either from Wales, Scotland, or he had peanut butter stuck to the roof of his mouth. I hid my face in my shoulder to keep from laughing.

"Melanie, this is my boss, Simon," I said as I finally emerged from behind Simon's body.

"Nice to meet you, Simon, and Quinn I didn't know you got a job."

"Well I didn't exactly send out announcements," I smiled. "I was just showing Simon the back of the bar. He's thinking about using dishwashers in his next piece."

"Such magic how they take the plates from dirty to clean, no?" Simon's accent was fading.

"Nice seeing you, Melanie," I said, barely keeping a straight face until Simon and I disappeared through the employee only door. We walked down the hallway past the office and the dish area through the back door where the loading dock was for truck drop offs.

"We're going to need to work on your accent a little more," I said. I took a seat on the loading platform.

"I just kind of went for it." He grinned.

"I could tell."

Simon sat down next to me and pulled a joint out of nowhere. "Your parents' owning a bar is kind of cool."

I made a face. "It has its advantages." I leaned back and looked up at the sky. It was a clear night, the air still warm. It was the kind of summer night you remember vividly as a kid. Somehow the heat of summer made you lighter, younger. The warm nights reminded you of times of youth. Summer's spent playing neighborhood games of cops and robbers and late nights trying to catch lighting bugs in a jar. If I took a deep enough breath I could almost feel the anticipation for the summer freedom I felt as a kid.

The smell from the dumpster had wafted over and I took a deep breath and let out a cough as the distinct taste of hot garbage traveled down my throat. Simon passed me the joint.

"It gets pretty packed in there." Simon nodded at the building behind us.

"Springhaven's most prized monument," I replied, dryly.

Simon let out a low whistle. "Has anyone ever told you that you seem rather..." he paused.

"Sarcastic. Bitter. Bitchy. Rude. Mean. Angry."

"I was going to say dry," Simon continued, "but if that's what you want to go with.

"Sorry." I took a drag of the joint he passed me. "I'm just used to this place bringing out my lesser qualities."

"Very angst ridden." Simon said quietly.

"Relax, Dr. Drew. I'm not like suicidal or depressed. I'm just honest about my feelings in my current predicament."

Simon nodded. He looked down at the ground and picked up a penny lying heads up. He passed it to me. "Here. Good luck."

"Thanks." I took the penny, placing it in between us. We each took a couple more hits before walking back inside to find Maggie and Miles standing by the bar, talking closely.

"There they are!" Maggie shouted, as we got closer. She scrunched her eyes as she stared at me. She gave me a look, like she was trying to decipher what just happened.

"What?" I mouthed back. She shook her head. The four of us stood there, an awkward silence surrounding us.

"Let's do shots." Simon said, finally breaking the moment. He drummed his hands on the bar. "What'll it be?"

"Anything," we replied. Simon ordered four shots of tequila.

"To new friends," he toasted before we all took the shot.

"So Miles," Maggie began saying in a flirty voice. "Where do you live?"

"I have an apartment in Harris."

She smiled. "It's nice to finally be around someone who also lives on their own." I snarled at her.

"Well, I have a roommate, Tim, but he spends a lot of time on the Internet," he said.

"Okay, I've seen everyone. I'm drunk. I'm home for a week. Let's go to Miles' apartment," Maggie said abruptly.

"I like that idea," Miles said, matter of factly.

"Let me say goodbye to Elliot first, I'll meet you guys outside." I walked back through the crowd that had gotten louder and drunker since my arrival. Elliot was in the middle of a conversation with Dave Lyons about some sort of sustainability project he was working on. I could only hear every fifth word of the conversation. I gave him a subtle wave.

"You're leaving already?" He asked.

"Come on, you know these crowds aren't my thing." It was a cop out, I know. "I'm calling you tomorrow to hang out," I promised as I hugged him.

"Definitely." I waved at Dave and walked away.

I could never bring myself to really say goodbye to people so I always promised to make plans with them for the next day, even if I had no intention of following through. My friends in college used to get so mad at me when we would go out because I would always invite everyone back to our house simply because I couldn't bear to say bye to them and let the party end.

I passed Dad walking in as I was leaving.

"You headed home?" He asked.

"I think I'm going to stay at Maggie's." I didn't mean to lie. I just didn't want to explain the truth. Sometimes a lie is just easier.

"Alright, see you in the morning." He quickly wandered off. I walked outside to find the three of them waiting by Simon's car, Maggie and Miles both smoking a cigarette and Simon looking bored.

"I can drive," Simon announced. I gave him a look. "I've only had three drinks." He walked around the open the passenger's side door.

"Chivalry isn't dead," Maggie added, as she watched him.

"It's not romantic," Simon and I said at the same time.

"The door's jammed and he's the only one who can open it," I defended. Maggie cast me a downward glance. "What?" I questioned. "We've already been through this."

"Hey," Miles spoke up from the backseat. "We're stopping to get beer right?"

"You got money?" Simon questioned.

"Let's use some of those pennies you've got stashed." Miles laughed. I looked at Simon, waiting for him to elaborate on what Miles said but he didn't look over.

"I'll buy the beer," Maggie offered after a moment. "I can expense it." Maggie never used her expense card for actual work expenses.

We walked into the apartment after stopping at the only store between Springhaven and Harris that was still open, and sure enough Miles was right: Tim was sitting on the couch in the dark, the only glow coming from his laptop screen. "Hey," he said, without looking up.

"Tim." Miles called. His low voice carried through the still dark apartment. "Mind throwing on some lights on, dude?" I heard a sharp movement and moments later the room was bathed with light. Tim was sitting proudly in just a pair of Chewbacca underwear.

"What's up?" Tim asked before walking across the living room and down a short hallway to a door on the left. He walked in and shut the door quickly.

Simon led Maggie and I to the couch in the living room. The apartment was sparse. There was a flat screen TV, a tattered tweed couch and a giant coffee table in the room. A few posters of bands I didn't recognize hung on the wall and a couple of amplifiers were stacked on top of each other by the door. Maggie and I sat next to each other leaving Simon and Miles to fight for the last spot.

"Not to worry," Miles said as he walked in holding two canvas camping chairs.

"Well I love what you've done with the place," I said, while standing up to grab a drink. "Anyone else want a drink?" Simon followed me into the kitchen.

"Is this weird?" He asked.

"Yeah it kind of is." I laughed. "Not you or anything," I reassured him.

"Right. Okay." Simon grabbed the beers and started back for the living room. "Let's get drunk," he announced.

We walked back into the living room where Maggie and Miles were already wrapped around each other like a couple of junior high students at a dance.

"I was thinking about your predicament," Simon launched into conversation as we sat in the camping chairs across the room and pretended Miles wasn't two seconds away from latching on and dry humping Maggie's leg right there on the couch.

"Oh yeah? What predicament?"

Simon leaned back in the canvas chair and took a sip from his beer watching my eyes the entire time. "You know, the whole angst-ridden anger you're harboring while you're home."

"Naturally. And what wisdom do you bring to the table?"

"Right now your life is like a layover. Like you know how sometimes when you fly, you have to stop somewhere before you can get to where you need to be? This," he held his arms out wide like he was giving a sermon, "is just your layover."

"Really?"

"I'm just saying," he looked over at me, "it makes sense."

"We're going to bed," Maggie announced. She pulled Miles up by his hand. "You're going to have to lead me there," she instructed to him and Miles jumped up quickly like he'd been set on fire, and just like that they were gone.

I'm not shocked. Maggie was the first person to tell you she was sexually promiscuous. And I was usually the second. I had spent many nights waiting on random couches because Maggie had found someone to fall in love with for the evening. In a way I envied her ability to go after what she wanted; whether it was a guy or a job or a purse, if Maggie wanted it, she would have it. Don't get me wrong, we've all been there, right? My sophomore year of college was like that for me. I was all up in that life style. My day to day was a carousel of dudes circling around me. Okay it was actually five guys over the course of the entire school year, but in the moment I felt like a sexual priestess.

"So do you and Miles do this often?" Simon looked at me, confused. "You know, bring girls back to the bachelor pad and woo them with your charms?"

"You might be surprised to hear this," Simon smirked, "but we don't pick up a lot of girls."

"I'm shocked," I twisted my face in mock surprise.

The muffled sounds of a guitar and Miles' voice singing a John Mayer song from a room down the hall reached the living room. "Oh come on." I started laughing. Simon looked at me for a moment before hearing the same thing I did.

"Hey, Miles has waited a long time to serenade a girl with John Mayer. He usually only gets to practice on me or Tim."

Simon opened a hidden drawer on the inside of the coffee table and took out a joint. "How did you know that was there?"

Simon looked at the table. "I made it."

"The joint or the table?"

"Both."

I looked down at the table. The dark wood had a handcrafted quality that was beautiful, yet still masculine. There were dozens of small tiny triangles carved into the border of the large table and a deeply carved border that separated the triangles from the rest of the wood. I traced my fingers along the edge, feeling the softness. It must have been sanded down at least five times to get such a smooth texture. "This is beautiful," I said, finally.

"Thanks." Simon passed me the joint. "Do you have a lighter?"

"Yeah." I reached into my pocket and felt the penny he had given me earlier. "So what's this thing about you and pennies?" I asked. I pulled out a lighter. "The first night I hung out with you I saw you pick one up in the gas station and then again tonight on the loading dock."

Simon looked down at his shoes. "It's nothing, it's embarrassing."

"My entire life is embarrassing, come on."

"You really are trying to find out all my secrets. If you must know, when my mom and I still lived in Georgia, I used to think that pennies were made of gold. Every time I found one or I got change I would put it away because I thought if I saved up enough, my mom wouldn't have to work all those hours." I was glad Maggie wasn't there to see my face because the only other things to make my heart melt that fast were puppies and chunky babies. Simon inhaled the joint deeply, blowing rings of smoke out of his mouth. "So one day I presented my pennies to my mom and told her to cash my gold in. She laughed and told me that were actually copper and only worth one cent, but that I should still save them and over time they'll be worth more than gold."

"So you're entire life you've saved up all your pennies?"

"Yeah." He said, calmly. He twisted the cap off another beer and took a long sip.

"What are you going to do with all the money?" I asked, intrigued.

"I don't even know why I'm telling you this," he said and then let out a hard laugh.

"Because we're friends and friends tell each other things."

"I want to do my own thing with woodwork and furniture. Eventually I'll see how much money I have and if it's enough for a down payment, I'm going to try and get my own space." I looked at him and saw his face flush. It made the splattering of freckles on his cheeks even more noticeable.

"I think that's pretty great," I whispered, afraid to ruin the moment with a loud voice. Simon slid closer, our bodies skimming next to each other. I had a nervous energy buzzing inside me, but it was a welcomed feeling. Nervousness was something I hadn't felt in a while.

Simon reached out for my hand and I didn't flinch away. His palm felt warm in mine. I couldn't remember the last time I had simply held hands with someone.

We sat there, in the living room, quiet at first, until the Miles' voice spilled out from his bedroom. "One pair of candy lips and your bubblegum tongue," I smirked at the choice of lyrics and an easy silence took over the room.

"Who are you?" He asked after a while.

I knew what he meant. He obviously knew my name, but I think he wanted to know more about how I got to be this way. I could understand that. "I'm the worst kind of person," I whispered back after a pause. "Selfish in all the wrong ways. I'm stubborn to the point of anger. I don't play well with others and I hate country music." I added the last part with a smile. "Who are you?" I repeated his question but he shook his head from side to side, signifying he wouldn't answer so easily.

"Fine." I twisted around so my legs were in between us. "What do you like?" I made my voice warm.

He looked up at me with his eyes half-closed and calmly recited his answer: "I like rooting for the underdog. I like things that are broken. I like messy and complicated."

"You must do well at puzzles," I added thoughtfully.

"I like hearing the sleep in someone's voice when they've just woken up. I like the first sip of a drink when you're thirsty. I like the guitar solo in Layla. I like being on time for things. I like the movie 3 Ninjas. I like holding your hand." He squeezed my hand lightly.

"That was cheesy."

"Did it work?"

"No."

At some point I drifted off because when I woke up the living room was swallowed up in the type of half-light that only seems to exist on Instagram filters. I was lying on the couch with a blanket strewn over me and Simon on the floor below me. My hand was slung over the couch, draping awfully close to his. Good God.

I looked down at him. He slept with one arm resting behind his head, one leg lifted at the knee. It looked uncomfortable. "Hi," I offered as his eyes fluttered open before he closed them again and smiled.

"These are a few of my favorite things," he hummed to himself before falling back asleep.

8

$1,700.16

"I'm the one that got laid last night, so why are you wearing the 'I got some' face?" I shrugged innocently at Maggie's question as we floated on rafts in her pool.

"Can't someone just be happy?"

"Yes, but not you. You don't do happy, you do brooding." Maggie's face lit up. "Oh it's Simon, isn't it?"

"No."

"I just think it's weird," Maggie complained, "I mean you two obviously like each other, so why aren't you doing anything about it?"

I was too hungover to fight with her about it, so instead I flipped off my raft into the water.

I kicked my way to the surface and came up underneath Maggie's raft, tipping her over as well. I waited for her to come up from underneath the water before saying, "Let's talk about you."

"What should we talk about?" She asked as she treaded water. "How I saw Tyler last night and he had on better shoes than I did?" Tyler was Maggie's high school boyfriend who moved to New York City after high school and found his calling in the drag show scene. He's now an out and proud gay man, but Maggie can't help but be permanently convinced she was the one that forced him to switch teams.

"Ha. No, let's talk about Houston." I raised my index finger to the sky. "Texas forever."

Maggie shook her head, "I like Houston. People in the South are different than us. They're nicer."

"Maybe I should move there before I shrivel into a mean old lady."

"You're not going to shrivel into a mean old lady," Maggie scoffed. "You won't shrivel. You'll have good skin when you're old and mean. You've always worn SPF."

"Good point."

I missed days like this with Maggie. Growing up, weekends were our thing. We went out every Friday night and spent every Saturday recovering. Most of the time we were too hungover to get out of bed unless it was for greasy fast food or more drinks. My heart jumped when I thought back to all those mornings, one of us hung over the toilet, the other lying in the bathtub.

When Simon dropped us off at Maggie's house that morning, it was just understood that I was going inside and we were going to lie down in Maggie's bed until we gathered enough energy to continue lying down outside. We walked upstairs into her room, each pulled back our side of the bed and climbed in like we were a couple who had been married for fifty years. It's the kind of friendship you can only have with someone you've known your whole life. The understanding that no matter how much changes, certain traditions withstand the test of time sticks closer to your heart when you get older.

"How was the John Mayer concert anyway?"

"Well, you're a bitch, but I guess a western New York bar tour is still a tour. Check that off the list."

Maggie's list featured quite the eclectic blend of men:

Rodeo Clown

Chef

Pilot

Race Car Driver

Touring musician

Cowboy

Salsa dancer
Doctor
Police Officer
Adult Entertainer
Teacher
Mime
Barista
Mailman
CEO of a Dot Com Corporation

She had no prejudice over any one other profession. These are just the upper echelon. "Did he tell you before or after you had sex?"

She snarled her face and climbed out of the pool. "After, obviously." She answered after a pause. "He was kind of cute in a weird way. Not like Mr. Simon, he's a hunk."

I shook my head. "I'm not even going there. Let's talk about something else."

"Fine," Maggie whined. "Melanie Gorman is still annoying," Maggie announced. She poured two glasses of wine behind the patio bar. She sat down at the edge of the pool and handed me a glass.

"She met Simon."

"Oh God, it probably took all of three minutes before Charlie got a picture message."

I cringed, mostly because she was right. If good news traveled fast, gossip traveled at the speed of light, especially in a small town. "I didn't see him though, so it could have been worse." I sighed. "Mary is convinced that we're getting back together - I'm surprised she hasn't starting booking wedding locations."

"Oh Mar." Maggie shook her head, "If only she knew the not-so-secret feelings you were harboring for your boss." I gave her a warning look. "You not telling me is all the confirmation I need."

"Fuck you. The Charlie situation is never going to happen.

"You two could have had a family together."

"Cute."

She did have a point though. Statistically speaking, either Maggie or I should have a child or be pregnant by now. Okay, not real statistics but after one too many drinks our high school yearbook becomes approved census data. We flipped through page after page and counted how many girls had a kid already. 51. 16 even had two or more. My high school class was 206 people. 104 of them are guys. That leaves 102 girls, 51 over 102 is 50%. ONE IN TWO GIRLS FROM MY HIGH SCHOOL CLASS HAS BIRTHED A HUMAN LIFE. I felt sick. Maggie couldn't stop laughing. "Imagine one of us with a baby slung to us right now." She was near tears.

We spent the rest of the day lounging in and out of consciousness, stealing weed from Dillon's studio and messing around with his recording equipment. I hadn't bothered to check my phone all day. My parents knew that I lived at Maggie's when she was home.

"Why don't you move to Houston?" She asked later that night when we were lying in her bed watching bad TV. "I mean you can stay with me until you find a job and whatever and even then we can look for an apartment together, live the life."

"Wouldn't that be nice," I dreamed.

"Come on what about Texas Forever?"

"In theory it's great, but in reality I couldn't do that."

"Why not? You're always going on about how you hate it here and you want to find out what you're supposed to do with your life. Figure it out with me. I need my best friend."

I knew exactly what she meant. When she came home and we fell back into the comfort of each other, it was almost unbearable to know that it was temporary, that she was leaving and I was staying.

"Give me some time. If I'm still going on about this in six months, then I'm there, but I'm trying to figure this all out."

"Well good luck." She saluted me. "Because it doesn't magically get easier when you get a job. Then you worry about whether you feel like you can grow at this job and if this is the right field. You still question yourself at every turn, some 401K doesn't save you from that."

"You're getting wise in your old age."

"I am two months older than you," she argued back. When we were younger I was so jealous that she got to turn 13 first, then 16, 18 and 21, but after that, I'm glad I have those two extra months.

"And you've held that over my head for years."

I woke up Monday morning with a stiff neck. I had been sleeping on the couch downstairs for the past week because Mom recently started reading *50 Shades of Grey* and I refused to step foot anywhere near my parents' bedroom if they were home. It was bad enough when my roommates in college had sex and I could hear their clumsy movements through the paper-thin walls, but I had a zero tolerance policy for these roommates knocking boots. I still convinced myself that I was dropped on the front porch when I was an infant, like Harry Potter. Only, instead of a giant motorcycle, a stork, straight from the cabbage patch, delivered me.

I figured I'd have a couple solid weeks of sleeping on the couch before the 50 Shades fever died down.

I stood up and rolled my head around my neck to loosen myself up. It was barely 6:00 in the morning but if I went back to sleep now, I wouldn't wake up for work. I grabbed my phone and checked my email as I walked down the hall to the kitchen. Still no replies from any of the jobs I'd applied for in the past two weeks. *Soon enough.*

On the bright side I did have an email from Lizzie inviting me to spend 4th of July weekend her parent's lake house. The email was sent to our other roommates Annie and Kate as well. I emailed them all and told them I planned on being there with bells, whistles and a ton of fireworks. Morning hadn't reached the kitchen yet and the room was blanketed in darkness. I switched on the ceiling light and made a pot of coffee. Part of me hoped the smell from the coffee woke my parents. I wanted them to know what Mom's obsession was costing me. After my second cup there were still no signs of either of them. I left my post in the kitchen and went upstairs to get ready for the day. This early morning could inspire me to actually get ready for work.

I took a shower and I shaved my armpits and my legs. I was not messing around today. My explosion of energy carried over to my outfit as well. I dug a long black cotton skirt out of my closet and matched it with a grey cut off tank top. The outfit was a step up from my usual uniform of ratty shirts and gym shorts. I blew my hair dry and let the brown strands fall strategically in a purposeful mess.

When I got to work there was a large black coffee steaming on my desk. I caught a quick glimpse of Simon who was humming while sculpting a quiche. After a moment of shuffling some order forms and seeing just how far behind I was, a ripped piece of paper fell from the pile.

Reasons working in an art gallery would suck:

-You're selling other people's work instead of making your own

-It's just rich people throwing around words they don't know the meanings to and spending too much money on art they don't really like

-You have to wear ugly outfit's so you never look better than the paintings

-You get a lot of splinters from setting up wooden easels

-A toddler's finger paintings are easier to sell

-It's not based on the art, but what artist can do the most for the gallery

-You can't make fake fruit penises at an art gallery

"Hey." I said. Simon looked up. "Thanks for the coffee and the list." I picked the sheet of paper up. "The last one is dually noted." He put the quiche down and walked over to my desk.

"How was the rest of your weekend?" He asked as he reached down to pull the milk crate closer to my desk.

"It was good. Maggie and I were lazy degenerates all weekend. What about you?"

"On Saturday Tim, Miles and I went fishing and yesterday I worked on a piece of furniture I'm restoring."

I turned my chair towards him and bumped his knee with my leg. I lingered for a moment before crossing my legs. "That makes you sound like a 50 year-old man. I do want to see more of your work."

"Someday," he mused. "I promise."

"Well you'll definitely have a lot of time to work on stuff now that Miles and Tim have hit the open road of the New York State thruway."

"I didn't think they were going to make it," Simon confided. "Miles overslept and Tim went ballistic, screaming about not taking the band seriously and wasting too much time on John Mayer cover songs when he should be writing his own stuff."

"Maggie's breaking up the band, Yoko."

Simon laughed. "She's quite the character," he added. "She invited me to her little brother's graduation party."

"How did she get your phone number?"

"She added me on Facebook, duh."

"We're not even Facebook friends."

"You haven't accepted my request," he volunteered, sheepishly.

"I'll put that on the top of my to do list," I offered. "As a matter of fact, I'll do it right now." I took my phone out and opened the application. Sure enough there it was: Simon Andrews has requested to be my friend. It was a good picture of him. He had a deep tan that made his teeth look a pristine white and his half grin was in full effect. I accepted his request and then looked at his page. "Now we're friends in real life and online."

"Good. Now I can track what moody song lyrics you'll post."

The clock in my car read 6:54 when I pulled into the driveway from work and saw Dad packing his truck. "Going somewhere?" I called.

"Your mother didn't say anything to you?"

"I haven't really seen you guys since Friday."

Dad shook his head. "Well we're going away for the week."

"Why don't I ever get the invites for these vacations? I'm your kid, I live and break bread with you."

Dad clasped his arm around my shoulder. "Q, I love ya, but your mother and I expected an empty nest at this point in our lives. We don't expect our 23 year old to go on vacation with her parents."

"I consider you guys roommates."

We walked into the house.

"Well roommates pick up their own messes, if you get where I'm going with this." My dad couldn't just say he wanted me to clean. He was always subtle in his suggestions of chores, whereas Mom dove right in.

"Yes. I will clean while you're gone and I will finally unpack." I coughed at the last part, hoping he wouldn't hear me.

"Yes. Please unpack," Mom came into the kitchen, interrupting us. "We left some money on the table for groceries, don't spend it all on booze and drugs either, Quinn."

"Mom, come on, what is this…amateur hour? I'm offended. I have a job now. I'll use my paycheck for the drugs, duh."

"Jim let's go before she drives me into an early grave. Goodbye," she kissed my cheek.

"Behave yourself Q." Dad gave me a hug. "Stop and check on the bar too, okay? Your brother should have things under control, but give him a hand if he needs it."

"Okay." I walked them to the door. "Have fun you crazy kids."

"Bye." Dad said.

I looked down at the table next to the front door and saw a copy of the infamous book my mom had been reading. "Mom!" I screamed after her. "Don't forget your book." I held up her bent copy of *Fifty Shades of Grey*. She looked mortified, but stomped across the lawn to retrieve it from me anyway.

"I'm only reading it because everyone won't stop talking about it," she blurted. "I wanted to see what all the fuss was about."

"You don't have to defend yourself to me. Play on player." I raised my fist in solidarity and handed her the book.

"Bye." She grabbed it and headed back to the truck.

I waited for the truck pull off the street before I called Maggie. "My parents just went away for the week. Get wine and come over."

"I'll be there soon, I'm just helping Dillon pick out an outfit for graduation."

I heard Dillon complaining in the background. "Why can't I just wear sneakers and a jersey?"

"It's your fucking high school graduation, not Barbershop 3." Maggie yelled. "Just please wear this for me. Please." I heard him concede in the background. "Quinn, I'll be over in 20. Have something ready for me to smoke."

"Grab some weed from your brother," I shot quickly and hung up.

Logically my next step was to find wine. I paused at the wine glasses in the cabinet. I'm still not fully convinced we should use them in case we broke one.

At what age is it expected that you won't break a wine glass when drinking from it? I knew Maggie and myself well enough to step down to the next cabinet and grab two plastic cups instead.

The front door opened and seconds later Patrick walked in to the kitchen with Nina taped to his side. I was surprised to see that he was still hanging around with her. He was the love 'em and leave 'em type.

"Well hello," I raised my cup in salute. "What brings you to my humble abode?"

"I'm just stopping by to pick some paperwork up from Dad to bring over to the bar. Already breaking into the wine, boozie?" He nodded at the glass in front of me. I took a gulp and kept direct eye contact with him.

"Hello Nina." I sang gleefully.

"Hi," she replied, visibly taken aback by my mood.

"Are you on drugs?" Patrick questioned.

"Not yet, why?"

"I don't know. You're not usually like this. You're usually…"

"Bitchier?" I finished for him.

"Yes," he remarked, fishing through a stack of papers on the table.

"Well what can I say, I'm a changed woman." I cackled, the grin on my face appearing just an inch below sinister.

"Alright, take it easy." He pulled a folder from the pile "If you need anything this week call me, I'm at the firehouse Wednesday through Friday, but other than that I'll be around."

"You betcha."

"Slow down on the wine, will ya?"

"Don't worry, Maggie will be over soon."

"Tell her I said hi." He always had a soft spot for Maggie. Whenever I did something to piss Pat off, like show up at his friend's parties or sneak out past my curfew, which was actually quite often, I always sent Maggie in first to soften him up so by the time he had to deal with me he was at a reasonable level.

"I will. Bye Pat. Byeee Nina."

"Bye Q."

Maggie got to my house and found me sitting out back. I was thinking about what Patrick said. "You don't think we drink too much, right?" I asked as she sat down next to me, placing a bottle of wine on the table between us. I pushed an already filled glass towards her.

"I would be more worried if we didn't drink this much," she concluded. "I mean we're still at an age in our lives where a few drinks means the whole bottle. When we have problems we don't deal with them, we drink with them. Is it the best way to deal with things?" She shook her head and picked up her glass. "No. But it is the most refreshing." We clinked our glasses together.

"So how did Dillon's wardrobe fitting go?"

She took another sip of white wine and pulled her sweater tighter across her body before beginning. "I love my dad, so much, and I know he did the best he could with Patrick after my mom died, but I always wonder how he would have turned out if my mom was still alive. Would he be this little white boy who thinks he has thug appeal or would he have grown up to be an athlete who got a full scholarship to college?"

"You could move back home if you're worried." I suggested after a moment.

"No I couldn't."

"Yes you could. We could get a place together and figure stuff out."

"I have stuff figured out, in Houston. That's where my life is." The tone in her voice told me she was annoyed.

"You could figure it out here, too." I spoke half-heartedly.

"So I'm just supposed to forget about my life and come home because you don't have a job?" The sharpness in her voice surprised me.

"Yes."

"That's a little selfish, don't you think?"

"No." I knew it was the wrong answer.

She took a sip of wine and narrowed her eyes at me. "Of course you don't. The world has to bend itself to your whim or the universe is conspiring against you."

"Whoa. Way harsh, Tai."

She flinched and her face softened slightly. "I'm sorry, Q. But that's a fact. You're selfish sometimes. You want everyone to ride the same emotional wave you do. Up when you're up, down when you're down and that's not how it works."

"That's not true." I instantly said.

"You just asked me to give up my really good job and move home for you."

"Okay. It might be a little true."

"Can you imagine what we would be like if didn't go away to college and we stayed?" Maggie asked later on. It was a game we always played. We called it painting your thoughts. It usually happened when we were drunk or high and we would lie down next to each other and create these glamorous lives that had us making six figures by 25. It didn't matter that none of it would probably happen. All that mattered was in those moments we had something to believe in, something to cling to, even if only for a brief second. "You would be working at the bar, moving into a house with Charlie and I would be probably be pregnant, definitely out of wedlock, most likely with no father in the picture. I would be a cashier at the supermarket and get all the town gossip while asking "paper or plastic" before shoving their meat in the same bag as their produce."

"You've thought about this before." I said.

"It's not really hard. There aren't many options for careers here." She passed me the joint and saw the worried look that had jumped across my face. "You're going to be fine, you know that, right? You're not going to stay here forever. Something is going to come along and you're going to move away and be happy." She put her hand on my arm. "I mean it."

"I know. I just wish I knew what it was going to be."

"There's no fun in knowing. The fun is figuring it out along the way. Nobody ever beats life. We just find ways to deal with whatever it throws at us."

"Even when your little brother is trying to become the next Marshal Mathers?" I questioned.

"Even when your little brother is trying to become the next Marshal Mathers." A smile eased onto her face.

"Paint my thoughts," I begged her.

"Aw come on Quinn."

"Please," I whined. "Just five minutes."

"Fine," she huffed. "If for nothing else than to shut you up." She pretended to be annoyed but I knew she secretly loved it. "You're 29 and you're living near the ocean. You threw out your blow dryer and you only allow your hair to dry naturally. You're painting, mostly small pieces, but you've done a couple murals that have gotten noticed by big Hollywood set builders. You finally got your first tattoo, a tiny pink bow on your wrist and you've met a guy who makes you the happiest person in every room you walk into. You two have so much fun together that you don't even realize other people are around. You come home to visit every so often, stopping in to see your parents at Kelly's. Charlie is there, only thirty pounds heavier with a receding hairline. You smile a polite smile, but don't stop to talk. Melanie Gorman tries to ask for an autograph and you laugh before signing a cocktail napkin. We visit each other once a month because money is no object and we're always planning lavish vacations in tropical places. I started my own events planning company with offices in L.A., New York and Miami where I split my time evenly with my live-in boyfriend. I even planned Diddy's white party."

I closed my eyes and dreamed of her thoughts coming to life. I smiled because even when I wasn't sure of what I was supposed to do, Maggie knew where my true happiness was. Of course she knew all along that I should make my own living, paint my own things, chase my own dreams instead of borrowing someone else's. Maybe that's a start to figuring out what I wanted to do with my life, find whatever makes me happiest and chase it.

"I like that," I purred. "I really like that."

"I knew you would."

My head was pounding at work the next day and a pile of empty water bottles had stacked itself on the floor next to my desk. Managing a hangover was much easier when I only had to sit through two 50-minute classes. Working a 10-hour day in this kind of shape was pure Guantanamo torture.

The majority of the day was spent concentrating on the simple task breathing so I wouldn't vomit on anything.

The office was quiet, Simon was loading deliveries out back with Hector and Gloria had taken the day off. I almost turned on talk radio just to fill the silence. Talk radio? What was this place starting to do to me?

I just finished the top coat of a pineapple when Wade walked across the room from his office. I hadn't even noticed he was here either. Since I had been hired Wade's been around all of three days and most of those were spent in his office on phone calls referring to everyone as 'hey guy.' Did he even know how to do make any of the food?

"How's Quinn today?" He asked standing in front of my desk, another classic Hawaiian barbeque shirt hanging loosely off his frame.

I looked around; hoping anyone else heard how odd referring to me in the third person sounded, but there was no one. "I'm good. How are you, Wade?"

"Couldn't be better, I'm taking the Mrs. on a nice vacation next week. She always likes to get away this time of year."

"That's nice."

"Hey," he continued, barreling over my response. "I wanted to talk to you about the work you've been doing." He looked past me to the windowsill of drying food. "I've gotten some nice feedback about the food recently. My buyers are saying the food looks more natural and authentic." He shifted. "So whatever it is you're doing, keep doing it."

I smiled at him. "No problem."

"Alright, good talk." He was already halfway across the room when he turned back to say, "Tell Simon I had to go out for a while, and I'll probably just go straight home afterwards."

"Okay."

I finished glossing the pineapple and there was still no sign of life anywhere in the room. I had filled all my order forms for the day and I couldn't paint anything if Simon and Gloria weren't around to make anything. I've never been left alone in the production room before. I'd be lying if I said I didn't want to snoop around. Glancing around one last time to make sure nobody was coming, I got up and headed to the front closet.

I don't know what I was expecting to find when I opened the door. I was not Sabrina the Teenage Witch -- there was not a portal to the other realm. It was a closet filled with junk. There was a rickety old floor-standing easel sandwiched between two boxes full of bowling league trophies. Why wouldn't someone want those bad boys on display? I pulled the easel from the mess before diving back in. Further back there was another box, this one filled with broken pieces of fake food. A smashed ear of corn, a shattered bowl and countless other broken pieces littered the box.

"What's going on in the closet, R. Kelly?" I turned and saw Simon, his face bright red and his tee shirt drenched in sweat.

"I was just looking for some more paint thinner."

"Right."

"I finished all my stuff and got bored. When I get bored I snoop." Simon's face broke into a soft grin. "Um, Wade said he had to go out and that he would probably just head home afterwards," I added.

"Well alright then." Simon started walking towards the door leading into the showroom. "Let's get out of here."

"We're just going to leave?"

"There's nothing else for us to do, the order forms have been filled and the deliveries have been picked up. If Wade left for the day, we can too."

I pointed towards the easel. "Do you mind if I take this?"

"I didn't even know that was in there," Simon replied. "Sure you can take it." I picked the easel up, careful not to break the loose ends and followed Simon out of the building.

"Do you want to hang out?" He asked shyly as we got to our cars.

I wanted to. I really wanted to, but I was too hungover to do anything but melt into a soft surface. "Maggie came over last night and we drank too much, the only thing I can concentrate on is driving home and hoping I don't pass out on the way." Simon looked away. "I want to hang out, though."

"Yeah, we'll make plans for something." He got in his car.

"Hey! You're going to the graduation party this Friday, right?"

"Would that be weird?"

"No, I'll be there."

"Alright. Sounds good." He smiled earnestly before his engine roared to life and he sped away.

I woke up from my nap to the sound of bicycles being pedaled noisily up and down the street just as the sky began to turn a fiery shade of pink. It was the type of sunset that deserved to be remembered. I looked down and saw the neighborhood kids laughing and screaming because they'd consumed too much sugar throughout the day. I forgot that school was out for the summer. Screaming children would be the soundtrack to my summer. Shouldn't they all have jobs or something?

My body still ached and I was finding out that hangovers begin to hurt in places you didn't know were possible when you got older. Was I vigorously fist-pumping last night? My arms felt like it.

I went downstairs and stopped halfway to acknowledge the quietness of the house. My heart swelled with anticipation for a full week of silence. My intense joy for silence is probably another sign that I should move out.

At this point, what isn't?

I looked through Dad's music collection and settled on a Beach Boys CD. I brought the wine and the easel I had taken earlier today onto the patio and pulled a stool over to form a workstation. I ran back upstairs for the leftover canvas I had from my last semester at school that was shoved carelessly in the back of my closet. I grabbed the canvas, my toolbox of supplies and a joint off my dresser and went outside.

Painting has always been my release. It is the place I can go to where nobody else can follow. It calms me. A paintbrush in my head gives me purpose and confidence to create. I poured the paint onto an old scrap of fabric from the toolbox. I mixed reds, pinks, yellows, oranges, and purples. I slathered them on the canvas before they quietly disappeared from the sky. I covered the entire surface, blurring the lines between colors with a bright pink ball at the center. The entire yard felt like it was saturated in pink, covering the trees in a slight glow as the sun began to drop from my view.

Painting the sunset was a warm-up. I always started with something universal, like the sun. Something I could stare at. After that I usually smoked a joint and let my mind fan out from there. I worked better with an abstract type of art called color fields. The majority of my paintings are feelings and sensations painted using large planes of color to express the emotions.

It's the only time I am completely focused and serious. Everything else in my head fades out and the only thing that matters is the work in front of me. I missed the block it put on my head. I wasn't worried about Chicago and getting a job—I was completely zoned in on the canvas and the clarity that flooded my bones.

9

$2,382.55

Maggie had me up at 7:00 on Friday morning to start running errands for the party. We picked up the keg, got the decorations, went to the liquor store, picked up the catering. We were at the house when they set the tents up. We had to make sure there was enough ice and that the downstairs bathroom had extra toilet paper. We hid all the expensive glassware from the swarm of teenagers that would fester when graduation parties were thrown.

I wouldn't have thought of half those things, but for Maggie it was second nature. She was in beast mode, running from one thing to the next, checking things off her list. I mostly sat in the passenger seat and controlled the music, trying my hardest to smoke the tiniest clip in the history of clips. "Can you just not be high right now?" Maggie begged when we pulled out of the supermarket for the third time that day.

"I'm sorry, but I am not used to all of this," I mumbled from underneath the giant pair of sunglasses I took off Maggie's visor.

"Sorry I'm being a bitch, this party is stressing me out." She took a drag of her cigarette.

"It's fine," I conceded, "but I'm just telling you now, I'm having wine for dinner."

"There's going to be a lot of people there tonight," she instructed, "My dad really wanted to go all out for Dillon. And I don't want you to be all creepy, but..."

"But what?"

"I just don't want you to get weird and all Quinn-like."

"Please describe Quinn-like."

"Ya know." She turned onto her street. "Bitchy."

"I promise I won't get bitchy."

"Oh great, *everyone* is here," I hissed as I saw Melanie Gorman across the yard. "Maggie throws a party and they all come out of the fucking woods."

"Who cares?" Simon said indifferently. He just got to the party and like usual, his timing couldn't have been more perfect. I had done just about all the small talk I could.

"I don't care," I professed. "I just don't feel like talking to her." I shrugged.

"For someone who thinks she's better than everyone else, you sure seem to care an awful lot about what people think about you."

"I don't think that." I crossed my arms over my chest.

"You act like it."

"Do you always do this?" I asked, rolling my eyes

"Do what?"

"Have an opinion on everything." I took a sip of beer, blowing the foam at Simon. "Even if it doesn't concern you."

"I call it like I see it." He licked the foam off his cheek. "Come on, let's go talk about artsy things that nobody at this party will understand." He grabbed my hand and pulled me to my feet.

"Let's find Dillon and be those cool older young adults smoking pot with the teenagers," I whispered as we waited in line to get more drinks.

"You're a horrible influence." Simon hissed in response. "But I like where your head is at." I laughed as we poured two more beers from the keg. The sun was beginning to set and the party was filling up quickly. People in this town love a good party, especially when there's free booze.

"Quinn!" Someone called my name and I jumped. I looked up and saw Charlie calling my name from across the tent where he was standing with Melissa Gorman's husband, Mike.

I offered a limp wave in response hoping he would take the hint.

"Fuck," I spat. "He's coming over." Simon looked up just in time for Charlie to be standing before us. "Hi Charlie," I said hesitantly as I stepped out to give him a hug.

"You look great," he said as he stepped back and eyed my casual shorts and tank top.

"You too." I heard someone cough beside me and I realized Simon was still standing there. "Charlie, this is my boss, the visionary artist, Simon Andrews."

"Yup that's me," Simon extended his hand. His accent still needed work.

"Nice to meet you, Quinn's told me about you," Charlie replied.

"That's so sweet of her. She is a valuable asset to my production team and she has quite a regal eye for color and detail. If you'll excuse me I'm going to get another drink." Simon chugged the rest of his beer and walked away.

"That's a little odd," Charlie noted.

"What is?"

"That you brought your boss to Dillon's high school graduation party."

"Is that not allowed?" I asked, annoyed. "We're friends."

"No, I mean it's just kind of unprofessional."

"Well things are different in the art world," I defended, stepping away from him. "We have real modern relationships with our superiors." I drank the rest of my beer.

"It was good to see you, I'm going to find Simon."

"Sorry." He choked out. "I'm not used to seeing you out at places with another guy."

I rolled my eyes. "Charlie he's just my friend and we broke up four years ago." I turned around to walk away just as Simon reappeared with two more drinks.

"Thank you," I said, grabbing the beer. "See you later, Charlie."

"Well that was awkward," Simon announced. We settled in a pair of chairs along the tree line of the backyard.

"That's Charlie for ya."

"Am I going to have to defend your honor?"

"You just might."

"Good. There is nothing I love more than a good ol' fashioned bare-knuckled brawl."

"That makes two of us."

He put his fist out and I bumped it with mine.

"Look at Dillon." I pointed to where he was posing with his friends for a picture, trying to spell out a gang name with their fingers, none of them smiling. "The poor kid. He's got no idea what's about to happen to him. His whole life is going shrink from a huge open field of choices down to a single patch of grass. All those promises people made to him about chasing dreams are going to break."

Simon looked me up and down, "You do know you're 23, right?" He was only half-joking. "There are a lot of people who would say the same thing about you, that there's still this whole world of opportunity awaiting you."

"If anyone else had told me that, I would have said something really rude."

"I'll take that as a compliment," Simon triumphantly proclaimed. "I've got a theory about you," he began, leaning back in his chair like he was getting ready to tell me a bedtime story. "You are like a cake."

"Excuse me?"

"Listen," he continued. "You are like a cake in the oven and the top looks all cooked and hard and ready to eat, but then you stick a toothpick in and the inside is still gooey and needs more time to bake."

"You're comparing me to cake." I gave him a warning glance.

"What I mean, is that you try to be all tough and act like you don't care, but underneath the hard exterior, you're mush. You're not really a bitch; it's just easier for you to act like one so people won't want to get close to you. You act tough so people don't see how good of a person you actually are underneath." He semmed pleased with himself.

"Do you watch a lot of Dr. Phil?" I swatted at a mosquito that landed on my neck.

"Intelligence does not always correlate with education," he said smoothly. He had a bulletproof smile etched on his face with a mind that was probably full of nothing but bad ideas.

"Good to know. Come on." I stood up, pulling Simon up as well.

We walked back towards the tent and the unwavering noise that came with it. I caught sight of Maggie across the yard, deep in conversation with her neighbors, Mr. and Mrs. Rich. She looked up and smirked when she saw Simon close behind me. I rolled my eyes, but kept walking towards her.

"Hi, Mr. and Mrs. Rich." I greeted each of them with a hug.

"Oh, Quinn." Mrs. Rich put her hand on her chest. "How are you sweetheart?"

"I'm good, how are you?" Good was a relative term nowadays.

"I'm fine. How are you making out with the job hunt?" She leaned in, interested.

"Well I just graduated in May. After a small break from the working world, I took a job as an assistant to a successful designer."

"Oh that's wonderful!" She cheered. "I saw your mother in the market a few weeks ago and she was worried about you. I told her my cousin's daughter works as an appraiser if you needed any help."

"Oh that's so nice of you. If you'll excuse me," I looked up and pretended to wave to someone on the other side of the tent. "It was great to see you."

"You too hon, if you need anything at all, let me know." I pulled Simon's hand hurriedly, trying to get as far away from any adult as possible.

This party was like a game of minesweeper; one wrong move and I would be blown up.

We found Dillon sitting at one of the tables, his equally thugged-out friends surrounding him. "Pssst." Dillon looked over. I pretended to take a drag from a joint in between my fingers. "Let's smoke." He nodded and stood up before telling his gang of merry men that he'd be right back. We went down to the basement, checking both ways to make sure nobody saw us.

"I just picked up some new stuff." He pulled out a sandwich bag full of weed. "We should smoke it out of the bong." He reached behind the desk and pulled out a green, glass bong at least two feet tall.

"What the fuck?" Simon gasped.

"Here, I'll pack it." I reached for the piece while Dillon fumbled with something on his computer.

"You've got to hear this new mix I made," Dillon said as I took a hit. Simon looked on, confused.

"Dillon is an aspiring musician." I said, exhaling a mouthful of smoke.

"That's cool, man," Simon croaked. I passed him the bong and waited for the musical snack to fill the air.

It was surreal sitting down in this basement smoking pot with Dillon. I remember how much time Maggie and I spent down here playing house, always making Dillon the baby. We took turns carrying him on our hip and pretended to cook dinner at the Fischer Price kitchen Maggie got for her 7th birthday. It was hard for me to be thrust back into a place that brought on so much nostalgia. I don t know if it was the alcohol or the massive bong hit, but I was suddenly bordering on tears. There was a part of me that wished I could have been brought back to those moments of naïve innocence, when I still believed religiously in fairytales and pinky promises.

Simon nudged me with the bong, but I passed on hitting it. He looked at me, his eyes tinted with worry. "I've never known you to pass on smoking," he half-joked. I gave him a pained look and he didn't push it.

"I'm going to go back upstairs," I announced quickly. Simon stood up to follow but I urged him to stay. There was suddenly heaviness in the air that I needed to shake.

It was crazy to think about how much time had actually passed since those days spent playing make believe. It felt like yesterday but it was lifetimes ago.

These thoughts of childhood ambushed my mind and I wished so badly there was a switch to turn it off, but suddenly I was paralyzed with knowing. I came back to a town that only ever knew me as a child. It was hard to convince myself I was becoming an adult when my past coiled itself around my present so tightly that I could no longer see my future.

There was no one in the kitchen when I got upstairs and I took the empty room as my cue to sit and embrace the quiet. I sat for a few moments before the door to the basement opened and Dillon and Simon climbed out, their eyes red-rimmed and squinted. "Cheech. Chong." I nodded at them. "Nice of you to make it out of your van."

Dillon walked back outside but Simon came around the table to sit next to me. "Are you okay?" He asked before taking a long sip of his beer.

"Yeah I'm good." The words had rolled off my tongue before I could give them a second thought. "Let's go outside."

There was a small sliver of moon hanging in the sky that illuminated the faces of everyone around us as we stepped outside. The crowd had grown in size, mostly young people soaking up the humidity.

"You want to hustle some high school kids in beer pong?" Simon asked as we approached a table full of teens clutching solo cups tightly in their sweaty palms.

"Oh but of course."

"We've got next," Simon croaked, loudly to a group of teenage boys.

"You can't drive home. You're drunk," I told Simon a few hours later. "You can sleep on my couch."

We were both pretty drunk. The graduation party was well over and had turned into the after party where Dillon and his high school friends drank the rest of the keg and gave the girls a maximum of three wine coolers in hopes it would increase their chances of getting laid. *The Glory Days* as some call it. Somewhere Bruce Springsteen was smiling to himself knowing that song would never run out of people who related to it. Our time at high school parties had passed and the longer we stayed at this one, the more desperate we would have appeared. "Maggie I think we're leaving," I said to her as she stood over the sink washing dishes, a cigarette in her mouth.

"Already? You suck."

"Call me tomorrow, we can hang out before you leave," I hugged her.

"Hey Simon!" Maggie called out as we were walking towards the door. "Do you need a ride?"

"That's alright, I'm going to stay at Quinn's, but thank you," he replied, much too loudly.

"I know." She smirked. "I just knew that Quinn would have never told me." She turned the sink off. "Wanted to hear it myself." She winked. "Bye guys."

"I hope you don't mind walking," I said as we started down the driveway. "It won't take that long."

"What was that about?" Simon asked as he pointed at Maggie's house.

"Oh, that's just how she always is," I shot back quickly. "She's always trying to embarrass me because she thinks I don't tell her enough about my life, which I don't," I pointed out. "But she makes everything about sex and it's not always about sex." I was rambling.

"Well my ears definitely perked up at sex." Simon exhaled.

"Okay."

"Okay what?"

"Okay let's have sex."

"Are you serious?"

We stopped in the middle of the road in front of Mrs. Snygg's house. She was a horribly mean old lady. She once threatened Pat with a shotgun when he was 13 because she said he was loitering in front of her house. He was the paperboy.

"Are you serious?" He repeated.

I squeezed his hand, ready to respond when Mrs. Snygg turned her front light on and walked towards the front door. "Come on." I pulled his hand closer and started running.

"For someone who smokes a lot of weed, you're really fast." Simon gasped for air as we slowed down in front of my house.

"I'm a runner." I tried to shake it off like I always sprint two miles, but it was probably me being drunk. I would be sore tomorrow.

"I'm starting to think your parents don't actually live here," Simon noted as we walked into the once again empty house.

"They're on vacation."

"Oh okay."

I took my shoes off. "Okay so there's the couch." I pointed, jokingly. "Let me grab you some pillows and blankets." I walked towards the stairs.

"Come on," Simon whined from the bottom of the stairs. "Give me a tour of the palace."

"You just want to see my room."

"Well you've got me there," Simon said, honestly.

"Okay."

"I thought that every girl had to have a Johnny Depp poster in her bedroom?" Simon stared at the large willow tree painted on my bedroom wall. "A willow tree seems like an odd choice, no?"

"A willow tree is often used to symbolize rebirth." I stood next to him. "Even if a willow tree is cut down it can still re-grow itself as long as it's roots are unharmed." I ran my fingers along the tree. "I painted it the summer I left for college."

"Tsk-tsk," Simon chided. "Full of rebellious teen angst, weren't we?" Simon continued to walk around my room, picking up random trophies and pictures and inspecting them. He picked up a picture of Maggie and I from when we were five, wearing matching overalls and bowl cuts. "Only you could manage a face like this," he said as he pointed to the death glare I gave the camera.

"If you had that hair cut you'd be pouting too." I grabbed the frame from his hands and put it back on my shelf. Simon reached for another picture, but I grabbed it before he could reach it.

"That must be a good one." He reached around my back to grab the frame. I switched it into my other hand but Simon grabbed me by my waist and pulled me into his body. "Let me see it." He peeled the frame from my hand. "Oh my God," His eyes raked over the picture. "This is the best picture ever." I grabbed it from him and looked down at the mess of teased hair and the cheap sequined ball gown on me as I stood in front of a polyester backdrop.

"My mom made me do a beauty pageant when I was 14." I cringed. "I wore Delaney's old prom dress. It was a last minute thing. I hated the pageant thing."

"You hate a lot of things," Simon observed. "Hating things doesn't give you a chance to see them beauty in them."

"Spoken like a true artist." I put the frame down. "I don't hate *you*."

I didn't rush to untangle myself his hold around my waist. We stood pressed together at a stalemate, both of us hesitant to make the next move. The only noise between us was the steady hum of the air conditioner.

"I think I like you," he whispered into my ear. I closed my eyes and breathed in the mix of beer and pot on his breath. "There's something about you, and I'm still not sure what it is, but I think I like you."

"That's a dumb idea." I said. I pressed my face into his neck. "You're my only friend here. Don't fuck it up."

He moved his hand from my waist up my arms, leaving a trail of heat from his touch along the way. He ran his fingers across my throat and his thumb pad traced circles on my pulse point. His light touch sent a chill up my spine. "I want to kiss you," he whispered into my ear. I pressed my body further into his, leaving no space between us.

"Friends can kiss," I countered and nudged him with my hips.

He leaned down, still tracing circles on my throat and let his lips rest inches away from mine, waiting to see if I would budge first. I kept my lips still. My eyes were closed and my whole body buzzed.

I couldn't take it anymore. I started to lean into him when his plump lips crashed into mine.

The moon was still hanging in the sky when I woke up. The glow from my clock told me it was 5:08. I knew three things: I already had a hangover; I needed water in the worst way; and those were Simon's arms wrapped around me and his body spooning me in my twin-sized bed. I lifted the covers. No pants on. Typical for me, but then I noticed that Simon still had his shorts on. That was interesting. I untangled myself from him and went downstairs to get water.

We didn't have sex. I'm pretty sure we didn't have sex. The last thing I remembered were his lips doing some vacuum cleaner level sucking on mine. Then I blacked out.

I stopped at the medicine cabinet in the kitchen and took two aspirin, something I would thank myself for later, and frantically gulped down two glasses of water before lazily climbing the stairs back to my bed.

I took a moment to glance over the boy sleeping in my bed. Was he a boy? When can you stop calling people boys and girls?

Simon rolled from his side onto his back. He now took over the majority of the bed. I had two choices: get back into bed with him, or go sleep on the couch.

I crawled back into bed, wrapping my arm around his stomach and resting my head on his chest. Instinctively his arm wrapped around me pulling me close.

I will regret this moment later.

When I opened my eyes again, the first thing I saw was a protruding baby bump standing over my bed. "Good morning, sunshine," Delaney's voice dripped with contempt. I looked over and saw that Simon was still asleep, unaffected by the fire breathing dragon that stood over us.

"Morning."

"Would you care to explain to me who this boy is?" She managed to sound both intimidating and concerned. Once again her mom mode was on point.

"This is Simon."

"Ooh, Simon your coworker?" Delaney cooed, intrigued all of a sudden.

"What's it going to be?" I questioned.

That's how it worked with us, if you caught someone else doing something you knew they would get in trouble for, you didn't tell, you bartered. Blackmail was common for us growing up. The prices varied depending on the act. One summer I caught Delaney and Corliss in enough compromising positions for Maggie and I to get concert tickets to Britney Spears and 'N Sync.

"You're going to paint the nursery," she whispered, quickly. "I can't stand painting."

I felt Simon begin to stir under the sheets and I prayed that even if he were awake he would pretend to stay asleep for thirty more seconds.

No such luck.

"Good morning," he whispered, wrapping his arms around me. I let out a hard cough. He looked up and his eyes grew wide "Shit." He moved away from me at lightning speed, pushing himself against the wall.

"Hello Simon," Delaney broke in. "I'm Quinn's sister, Delaney, but I bet you guys don't spend a lot of time talking about things like that."

"Actually," Simon said, "We spend a lot of time talking. Until last night all we ever did was talk. "Congratulations, by the way." He pointed at her ever-growing stomach.

"Thank you." She looked shocked at his honesty. "Well maybe you two can talk some more when you paint the nursery." She turned on her heels to walk out of the room. "Q, your paintings look good. I saw them on the table downstairs."

"Thanks. I'll call you later."

Delaney began her waddle down the hallway. I put my finger to Simon's lip, quieting him until I heard the front door shut. He climbed over me and brought his feet to the floor.

"Where are you going?"

"You know all my secrets," he confessed. "I want to know yours." He disappeared from the doorway. I took my time going after him, pulling on a pair of shorts.

When I got downstairs, Simon was standing over the dining room table, focused on a painting I did. He traced his fingers along the black canvas that was covered in yellowish orbs fanning out from a single point in the middle. He looked up, pop-eyed, like he was in a trance. "What is this?"

"Those are phosphenes."

"What?"

"Phosphenes." I repeated, leaning my head against the wall. "The colors and shapes you see when you rub your eyes."

"How do you even think to paint stuff like this?"

"I never took much to painting people and regular objects," I walked over to stand next to him. "I liked the idea that nobody else on this earth would ever create the same exact interpretation of something that I did. I paint phosphenes, illusions, emotions." I pointed to another painting. "This is the electricity you feel in your body when you're excited. That one," I picked up the red canvas across the table, "is the pulsating in your heart when you're nervous."

"And you're painting fake food for a living?" Simon asked, shocked.

I shrugged my shoulders. "Abstracts are better for me. I've always fallen in love with the *idea* of things rather than their physical parts. I've been like that since I was a kid."

"I knew you were good at painting, but this," he walked around the table. "This is what you need to be doing."

"What I need is money, and painting fake food is going to give it to me."

"Yeah but this stuff makes you happy and being happy is more important than having money."

"This is coming from the person with a lifetime supply of pennies stashed away in his house? Come on," I started for the kitchen. "I'll cook breakfast."

"What are your thoughts on painting nurseries?" I asked as we sat at the kitchen counter eating eggs.

"I've haven't put my thoughts into a specific box regarding painting nurseries, why?" He asked, skeptical.

"See, the thing about having siblings is that they're always trying to tell on you, even when they're 29 and pregnant. So in order for our secret little sleepover to stay our secret little sleepover, I have to paint the nursery and since we were both in the bed, I thought it would only be right that you helped." I batted my eyelashes for dramatic effect.

"I don't think I really have a choice in the matter."

"As cute as this fuck fest is," Maggie's voice broke through as she appeared in the kitchen, "I'm leaving today so let's make these last few hours about me." She plopped down on the other side of the table and pulled my plate of eggs towards her, helping herself to a heaping spoonful. "I'm hungover."

"Oh, well please, by all means." I pushed my coffee cup in her direction. "Help yourself."

"So," Maggie said looking back and forth between Simon and I. "It smells like sex in here."

"It's probably your upper lip," I said jokingly.

"Well the party was a raging success because at 5:00 a.m. I got to escort two teenage girls from my basement," Maggie began. "Apparently they gave up the goods too quick and then they got booted."

"That's disgusting," I grimaced. "Were we like that when we were their age?" I questioned, standing up to load the dishwasher.

"You weren't." Maggie pointed to me. "I was." She added with a shrug of indifference.

"I'm going to go get my car, but I'll call you later and we'll do this whole painting a nursery thing." Simon said.

"I can't wait."

"Alright." He walked towards Maggie. "It's always a pleasure seeing you, Maggie." He pulled her into a hug. "I'm sure I'll see you again."

"Your car's out front by the way. I drove it over." She tossed Simon the keys. "That thing is a beast."

Simon laughed. "See you guys later."

Maggie immediately turned towards me after the front door shut. "So about last night."

"Yeah things are little unresolved there."

Sending Maggie back to Texas sucked as usual, but at least she would be back for Elliot's wedding at the end of summer.

I had one more night to myself before Jim and Mary came home and I wanted to hang out with Simon.

It's my last night of freedom in my house before my roommates come home. Let's do something.

Oh yeah.

I mean unless you're too busy.

I'm not.

Well I'll be here so come over whenever.

I'll be there soon.

This could work out good. Simon was a good kisser and if I felt what I thought I felt this morning, he had a pretty impressive dick too. Sex would be cool but I want to avoid things getting to that weird friend or lover stage. As long as I was honest with him about my intentions to use him for his body then we would be good to go on the issue.

I went to my room, pausing to take my hair out of a knot and make it somewhat presentable. It was easier to manage since I cut it, but sometimes I missed the length. I pinched my cheeks trying to bring life to them and changed out of a tee shirt, instead opting for a sundress that skimmed leisurely above my knee. It was a little too housewife for my usual penchant of tee shirts and underwear, but there are certain times in a girl's life where she just has to suck it up and cave to the annoyances of being a female.

I'm not very good at being a girl. I mean that in the most honest way possible. Girls are so often viewed as these porcelain dolls full of grace and humility and I'm just, not. I'm a mess. I wipe up spilled coffee with my sock. I swear too much and my friends and I devote a lot of our time to talking about pooping. I don't know how to sew or knit and on most days I can barely put on make-up without feeling like a moron. I'm clumsy. No, like really. I trip and fall over everything, high heels aren't an option in my life. I don't have this magic wand in my purse to turn me into an angelic person -- I think we should worry more about being strong than angelic. If girls are viewed as fragile, shouldn't it be more important to be strong and prove everyone wrong?

One swipe of mascara and I was tapped out from giving a shit. I looked around the room for any more embarrassing childhood mementoes and shoved a spelling bee trophy and three beanie babies under my bed never to be seen again.

I sat on my bed and Marlowe attached herself to my side. I leaned back and before I knew it, my eyes were closed.

I didn't meant to fall asleep, but when I opened my eyes again Simon was sitting at the foot of my bed. "You should lock your doors," he instructed sternly. "Any random psycho could just walk right in and start giving your guard dog belly rubs." He nodded at Marlowe who was lapping up the affection.

"She's useless." I shrugged. "How long have you been sitting there?" I sat up, wiping the sleep from my eyes.

"10 minutes, tops." He smiled, placing his hand on my knee. "Was this the big plan you had for tonight? Because I could use a nap myself?" He climbed over my body, lying down next to me.

"I wore a dress," I noted meekly.

"You wore a dress," he repeated. "You wanted to impress me?" His usual smug grin appeared across his face.

"I did."

"I didn't even think you had thighs until this morning," he joked and placed his hand on the outside of my leg. "You should bring them around more often, I like them."

"Hey, about last night."

"You know," Simon whispered, propping himself up on one arm, "you were so good. I didn't peg you for such a screamer."

My face dropped, eyes rich with concern. He noticed immediately and placed a reassuring hang on my forearm. "I'm kidding."

"What?"

"We made out and then you were too drunk."

"Thank you so much for being so chivalrous." I sat up "But really, about last night, I don't want to make it big deal. It happened and that's fine. I like you and you're basically my only friend around here, but I'm not going to be around here much longer and the whole relationship thing isn't really my style."

"That's fine. I'm not asking to marry you." He said.

"Right."

"We're friends." He wiggled his eyebrows at me.

"Friends who occasionally kiss and have sex?" I asked.

"Yeah, friends who can occasionally have sex."

"But also friends who hang out and smoke weed?" I specified.

"Exactly."

"Okay great. Let's smoke weed or drink something."

We cooked hamburgers on the grill. Okay, Simon cooked hamburgers on the grill and I drank two glasses of wine.

"You put mayonnaise on your hamburgers?" I asked in disgust. Simon smeared the bun with the gooey condiment.

"It tastes delicious."

"It's disgusting." I sat on the patio chair dousing my own burger in ketchup. "This," I pointed at the bottle in my hand, "is the American dressing, the upper echelon of condiments. You probably like movies where the dog dies too."

"Those are some strong opinions about such a joyous condiment."

"It's a texture thing and really, what does mayonnaise even mean?"

"It means deliciousness," Simon spoke, a bite of hamburger in his mouth.

"Ketchup or mustard?" I questioned.

"Ketchup," he answered instinctively. "Breakfast or dinner?" He countered

"Dinner. I'm never up for breakfast." I shrugged. "Friday or Sunday?"

"Friday. The whole anticipation of the weekend thing." He opened another beer, taking a long pull before speaking again. "TV or movies."

"TV. I have an addictive personality, one movie won't satisfy me." I took a sip of wine. "The book or the movie?"

"The movie." Simon said.

"Oh God. No."

"What?" He asked, confused.

"There's just something better about the way the story happens in our minds when we read books that makes it better." I said. "They mess that shit up when they make movies. They always cut out the little scenes and the moments that make you feel like you really understand the characters. Not to be a bragger, but I do have all the Harry Potter books. You should give them a gander."

"You're really convincing me to buy into this Harry Potter stuff."

I shrugged my shoulders. "It's a lifestyle." I took a sip from my wine. "Okay," I said, "What's one thing about yourself that you've never told anyone else?"

"I made it to the third round of auditions for "The Real World" when I was 20." I stared at him, curiosity etching across my face in the growing evening light.

"Um."

"But they decided I wasn't chemically imbalanced enough to be filmed non-stop for four months."

"You could have made a killing on the challenges."

"Your turn." He leaned back in his chair, a cocky smile on his face.

"Well I guess it's only fair. I was arrested my freshman year of college." Simon's eyes grew wide. "Hey, all the charges were dropped," I defended. "My friends and I were doing a bar crawl and I may have gone to the bathroom behind one of the buildings. You know how it is when you're drunk, it's like the whole world is your toilet."

"The whole world is your toilet?" Simon questioned. "That's some Shakespearian shit right there.

"It was so embarrassing. What's the best advice you've ever gotten?" I interrogated, tucking my leg under my body.

"Don't ever let a girl with daddy issues give you a boner," he said thoughtfully.

"Wow. Some real shit."

Simon's cheeks blushed slightly at his declaration. "Uncle Rodney gave me that advice when I was 13."

"Well, he sounds like an insightful man."

"He's not," Simon offered. "He's been married four times, couldn't take his own advice."

"Ah."

"Let's get back to talking about your paintings." He leaned forward in the chair.

"What is there to talk about?" I asked.

"You're good."

"Well thank you, but there's a little more to it than that."

"Then tell me. I tell you stuff all the time."

"You're right." I took a sip of my drink. "In high school it was easy because everyone had to take an art class and I was painting next to people who could butcher a stick figure. My teachers wanted me to pursue it and up until then it was just something I kind of did. They entered one of my paintings in a state-wide competition and it did well."

"How well?" He leaned in closer.

"Well." I shook my head. "It doesn't matter. It didn't seem logical to go to college for painting so I became a business major and then halfway through my junior year I was sitting in my accounting class and I just stopped taking notes. I still went to all my classes but I wouldn't pay attention to the lessons. My notes became these blank pages and I would go home and paint the pages instead. At first it was a lot of muted tones, bland shit because that's how I felt about things, but eventually they got better. So I talked with my advisor and did all the necessary paperwork to change my major, but then I found out it would take an extra year and my parents couldn't float that, I didn't expect them to. So I took everything I had saved and paid my extra year's tuition. I spent the next two years taking art classes year round to makeup for the lost time. I used my accounting notebook as my portfolio to get into the program." I looked over at Simon who was fixated on something he was reading on his cell phone. The bright light from his screen illuminated his face.

"You won," he croaked so quiet I almost didn't hear him. "You won that competition."

"Did you just search me on the Internet?"

"Yeah, because you wouldn't tell me," he reasoned. "That's awesome. You're like some artistic genius moonlighting as a food painter."

"That's one way to look at it."

Simon shook his head. "No way. You can't short-change yourself like that. You've got to be your biggest believer. If you don't think you're good, why should anyone else?"

"Do you give inspirational talks or something? You're more positive than a pregnancy test on an episode of Maury."

"I mean it's pretty simple. You've just got to think about things as if they aren't your problem. Give yourself advice like you would give it to Maggie. You would always tell her to go after what she wants, why should you be different?"

"That's a good question." I stood up and began to blow the Tiki Torches out one by one. "This friends with benefits thing, does it start tonight?" I looked at Simon for an answer.

"One hundred percent."

Simon left early the next morning, saying something about having to help Wade with yard work. I spent the day painting and washing my sheets to eliminate the lingering stench of sex and alcohol from the previous night.

I kept waiting to feel some sort of feeling about sleeping with Simon, but it never came. I took that as a good sign because it meant that emotions had yet to be compromised. This arrangement could only survive if emotions weren't on the table. That's when things get ugly.

It's not that I didn't like Simon. I just really don't have the emotional energy to go there. I had other stuff to deal with, like the fact that I was still in this goddamn town.

The shrilling buzz signaled the end of the wash cycle and shook me from my momentary stupor. I switched the laundry into the dryer. I planned on having my sheets back on my bed before my parents came home. It would lead to too many questions if they saw me actually washing my own linens.

The front door opened and seconds later Mom's voice flooded the house. "Quinn." She called my name like I was Marlowe. "We're home."

I hurried out of the laundry room to meet her in the front hall. "Hi mom." I leaned in to hug her. "How was your trip?"

"It was good." She looked passed me into the house. "Did you have a party while we were gone?"

I stepped back. "No. I don't have friends to throw a party for, mom."

"Why is the house so clean?" She walked further into the house, stopping to inspect each room along the way.

"Because I wanted to clean it."

She turned back to me and pursed her lips. "Really?" She questioned.

"Yes." I walked into the laundry room. "See." I held up my clothes hamper. "I even washed all my sheets and laundry."

"Wow." She was shocked.

"I'm so much more adjusted than I was before you left."

She smiled at me. "Good for you, Quinn."

"I know, right." I followed her back through the house where Dad was carrying too much luggage for one person.

"Quinn." He greeted me as best he could with no hands. I pulled the straps to two of the bags off his shoulder and dropped them to the floor.

"Hi dad." I hugged him. "How was your trip?"

"It was good." We stepped apart and he stared into the house. "Did you have a party, the house is clean."

"No dad."

"She's just well adjusted now." Mom chimed in.

"Completely well adjusted." I looked between my two parents. "I'm so well-adjusted that I'm going away for the 4th of July weekend."

"Oh really." Dad said. "Where are you going?" He dropped the rest of the bags he was carrying.

"Lizzie's lake house."

"Who's going?" Mom asked.

"Lizzie, Kate, Annie and me."

"Are her parents going to be there?"

"I don't know, mom. We're 23. We'll be fine either way."

"I know how you girls get, that's all. You're going to be hammered drunk all weekend. One of you should be sober at all times."

"Yeah. Okay mom."

10

$2,300.56

July slapped me right in the face with its sweaty, humidity-laced palm. Thankfully a body of water was in my immediate future. The morning I left for the lake house, Lizzie's horn hadn't even finished beeping before I was out the door. My ride to temporary freedom was mere feet away.

"Quinn." I froze at Mom's voice in the driveway.

"Yes mom."

"Were you going to leave without saying goodbye?"

Yes. "No. I was just going out to say hi to Lizzie. I was coming back inside."

"Okay." I followed her towards the house, stopping short of the door. "Bye mom. Bye dad. I'll be home Sunday."

"Wait a second." Mom yelled from inside.

"What's up?"

She opened the door and handed me her copy of *Fifty Shades of Grey*. "Here. Just in case you want to read something while you're gone."

"Thanks mom." I grabbed the book and shoved it in my purse. "Alright, bye. Love you guys."

"Love you too. Have fun."

Seeing Lizzie's car parked at the end of the driveway and her mop of dark hair sticking out the driver's side window was like a mirage of water in the desert. Was it real? Was I just dehydrated?

She popped her trunk open as I neared and I threw my bags in before I climbed into the passenger seat. "Hi Q." She reached over and hugged me.

"Lizzie. You're a savior. Lets get the fuck out of here." She smiled and backed out of the driveway.

We were on our way to a weekend filled with drugs, alcohol, and immature decisions. My favorite kind of weekend. Our other roommates, Annie and Kate were driving from the opposite end of the state and would meet us there. Lizzie's parents were away on some weird Colonial Fourth of July Independence cruise in the Bahamas, which doesn't make a lot of sense, but whatever, it freed the house up for us to be reckless.

"When was the last time you talked to Annie?" Lizzie asked about twenty minutes into the drive.

"We've texted here and there, why?"

"She called me last week and said she had something to tell us."

I sighed because when Annie said stuff like that it usually meant she had a new show on TV she wanted us to watch. "Maybe she finally dumped Mark."

Annie's college boyfriend Mark was nice enough, but we all kept waiting for the moment she would outgrow him like she outgrew her phase of being obsessed with Justin Bieber sophomore year.

"Maybe."

"Do you want to smoke a joint?" I pulled out a sandwich bag of joints I rolled the night before with my grandfather's old cigarette roller. Technically he left it to Pat but Pat never took it when he moved out so I figured it was only right that I take it and make use of it.

"Always."

"So how's work?" I asked. Lizzie worked as a data analyst for a tech start up company that made a quarter of a billion dollars last year. She's doing pretty well in her post-graduate life.

"It's good. Busy, but good. How's...Wait a second, what are you doing again?" She pinched the joint in between her fingers when I passed it to her.

"Officially or unofficially?"

"What is it like some secret agent job? You'd never pass a drug test."

"No. Nothing like that. I told everyone I work for this successful artist."

"Okay so what are you officially doing?" She took a hit of the joint.

"I paint fake food for a living." I sighed and Lizzie let out a cloud of smoke followed by a string of forceful coughs.

"That's not terrible," she said after a moment.

"Not to you."

"So what. Who cares what people think about you?"

I took a hit of the joint before speaking. "Says the girl who made six figures her first year out of college."

"I got lucky."

"Maybe I'll get lucky too."

It could have been because I was high, but the two-hour drive flew by and soon we were driving down the main strip of the small lakeside town.

A quarter mile in we got stuck in standstill traffic. Most of the traffic consisted of minivans with rooftops full of luggage and pickup trucks towing boats, families coming to enjoy the holiday weekend.

After thirty minutes of driving at eight miles an hour, Lizzie turned off the main street onto a narrow stone roadway. We drove for another five minutes before we pulled up to the back of a two-story lake house. The wooden structure had a wrap around porch that led to a lake front view on the other side. A dozen pine trees stood on either side of the yard shielding the house from neighbors. The front of the house looked out onto a private dock with a speedboat and two kayaks.

I don't know what Lizzie's parents do for a living, but that shit pays well.

"The girls should be here soon," Lizzie said. We were sitting on the deck after unpacking the car. "They won't mind if we have a drink before they get here." She nodded at the wet bar across the deck. We stood up and walked over.

"No of course not." I agreed, sitting on a bar stool. She mixed herself vodka with pineapple juice and then looked up. "Do you still drink liquor like my Uncle Dennis?"

"Yes. I still drink whiskey."

"That's aggressive." She poured me a glass.

"I'm a real go getter."

"Any cute guys at this job of yours?" Lizzie wiggled her eyebrows suggestively.

"Yeah. I guess. I recently slept with one of my coworkers."

"What? Really? Do you have feelings for him?" Lizzie couldn't resist asking questions.

"No. It's not even like that."

"Come on. You two could fall in love."

Lizzie was a hopeless romantic. She believed the true love of her life was going to reveal himself at the most cinematically appealing moment. When she travels she pretends to struggle with her luggage so some Romeo will swoop in and whisk her away to a better life.

Her words, not mine.

"Why does everything have to be a fucking love story?"

Lizzie sighed and took a sip of her drink. "It doesn't. I just thought that maybe…"

"I'm not going to be home long Lizzie. This is simply a sexually beneficial situation for the two of us."

"Will you at least tell me his name?"

"Simon."

"Fine. Simon says will you please at least tell me his name."

"No you dick. His name is Simon."

She didn't get a chance to respond. A car horn blew repeatedly letting us know that Annie and Kate had arrived. We ran out back to see the girls climbing out of Annie's SUV. A belligerent round of screams and hugs ensued.

"Okay." Kate spoke once we were sitting out back after Lizzie gave us a tour of the house. "Are you guys drinking because I need a drink?" Lizzie and I nodded, sitting back down in our seats while Kate made herself a drink. "Annie do you want a drink?" She asked.

"No I'm good." Annie looked across the bar to Lizzie and I. "But I do need to tell you guys something." She ran a hand through her auburn curls.

"Okay." We said in unison.

Annie shifted on her feel and ran her bottom lip through her teeth.

"Just say it." Kate instructed.

"I'm pregnant."

"Fuck." I said instantly.

"Shit." Kate coughed.

"Congratulations?" Lizzie tried to sound supportive.

A moment of silence washed over the four of us.

"I'll take you to the appointment to get it taken care of." I said, finally.

"Holy shit, Quinn. I'm not 19 years old. I'm going to keep it."

My eyes went wide in shock. "Oh Annie, I'm so sorry. I didn't mean it like that. I just meant that like, I would be there for you, if you needed me to. This is totally a your body, your choice moment happening right now." I finished the rest of my drink.

Annie tried to smile sympathetically but I could tell she was pissed.

"No. I get it." She finally spoke. "Marc and I talked about it and decided that we're going to spend the rest of our lives together anyway, our family is just starting sooner than expected."

Kate cleared her throat and finished her drink as well.

"Alright." Lizzie stood up. "Lets get you something nonalcoholic to drink and unpack the car." She started for the screen door and Annie followed leaving Kate and I alone at the bar.

"Dude." Kate said.

"Yeah."

"So."

"Wow."

"This is happening."

"I guess it is."

"Let's do a shot."

"I feel bad." Lizzie looked at Annie like an animal in captivity through the screen door later that day. Kate, Lizzie and I were smoking a joint on the front porch while Annie sat on the couch.

"She's pregnant not dead." Kate said.

"Plus it's not like she can't stand outside, its weed, not crack." I added.

"That's a little extreme." Lizzie cast me a sideways glance. "Maybe we should tone down how fucked up we get."

"Seriously?" I questioned.

"She's our best friend, Quinn." Lizzie defended.

"That's why she would want us to get fucked up." I passed the joint to Kate. "You've been pretty quiet Kate." I glanced at her.

"I don't know guys, she's a grownup. She can handle us drinking a little bit and smoking some pot. Until she had a bun in her oven that's what she did too. She'll be fine"

"Can we just try to enjoy our time together?" Lizzie asked dully. "Let's grab Annie and go for a boat ride."

"I'll get her." I volunteered and walked inside.

"Banana." I called out and Annie came into the living room from the kitchen. "Hey." I reached out for her. "I'm sorry if I reacted badly. I'm happy for you. If this is what you want, then this is what we'll support."

"It's okay." She leaned into my hug, her short frame tucked into my side. "I expect you to react this way to things."

"What does that mean?"

She sighed into my shoulder. "Just that you're Quinn and you like when things go your way and me having a baby and starting a family doesn't bode well for your plans for everyone."

"Okay now that's just not true. I'm always supportive of my friends and their life plans."

"Sure you are." She stepped back from the embrace. "It's not a bad thing, it's cute like Lizzie and her quest for true love."

"What does that mean?"

"It's not a big deal." She tilted her head to the side. "You just have all these things planned out in your head that you want to come true because you believe that's how it has to be for all of us. Sometimes those plans get in the way of actually living and seeing where life takes you."

Am I really this self-absorbed? I hadn't noticed. My friends certainly had. Annie wasn't the first person to comment on my asshole ways recently.

"You're right." I agreed

"Come on lets go outside." She started for the front door.

"Does this mean you'll be our designated boat driver?" I flashed her a smile.

"Fine, but only because I packed a captain's hat."

"Fair enough."

On the 4th of July we acted as any civilized American would. We shotgunned beer and lit fireworks. We kept Annie at a safe distance the entire time.

The more we talked about her being pregnant and I saw how happy she was, the more I had to deal with the fact that my friends were right. I call myself selfish all the time, but hearing it from the people I love cracked me a bit more than I cared to admit.

It's not their fault that we're all growing in different ways. It wasn't practical of me to believe that we would always be this close, this young and this in tune with that the other one was going through. Our lives are no longer the same. We're not standing on the platform of college life together anymore. We've all shifted and we're on entirely different levels now. I shouldn't expect them to leave theirs because I'm lost in my own. They're good friends though. They don't hold it against me.

"Quinn fucked her coworker." Lizzie announced by the fireside that night. "She's not in love with him though, just sleeping with him."

"Thank you for the clarification and for taking care of my public relations, Lizzie. Yes. I have slept with someone I work with."

"Is sophomore year Quinn going to make a comeback?" Kate asked from across the fire.

"No. It's just someone for me to have sex with while I'm home."

"That's cool. Regular sex is good for you." Annie spoke up next to me.

"Annie you may not be the best spokesperson for regular sex right now." I said. I pointed to her stomach. "You know, the whole pregnancy thing."

"Obviously use protection, but regular sex is good for you."

"Is there anyone else besides Annie and I that is currently getting laid?" I asked the group.

The openness I have with my friends from college was harvested over many drunken Friday nights and hung over Saturday mornings. The foundation of our friendship was laid out over all-nighters spent finishing projects during midterms and smoothed down with reassuring hugs and shoulders to lean on when something so stupid, yet so incredibly important at the time, happened.

"I recently had sex with a guy in the unit next to me." Kate confessed. Kate was a nurse at a hospital near New York City. "He did two tours in Afghanistan as an army nurse and we're going out to dinner next week."

"Everyone's getting laid but me." Lizzie said with a whine.

"You're just waiting for the right guy, Liz." Annie said in a soft voice. She smiled at our friend.

"I'm beginning to think that idea is a crock of shit." Lizzie said.

We woke up early the next morning for one last boat ride before we left. Lizzie drove the boat out to a bay and we floated for a while as the sun peaked over the hills on the south side of the lake. "When is the next time we'll see each other?" Kate asked. She took a sip of her coffee.

"The baby shower." Annie smiled. "I'll give you guys the details when it happens, but obviously I want you all there."

"I'm helping with Delaney's shower. I'll send you all the good stuff to register for." I offered.

"That would be really cool, Quinn. Thank you."

"No problem."

"Cheers to a great weekend." Lizzie said. She held up her coffee cup. "I love you guys." We all reached our mugs up and clinked them with hers.

This weekend was far from what I expected.

I almost liked it better that way.

11

$2,200.56

The first heat wave in July was upon us and Simon and I were spending our time in a room with no air conditioning. We were sacrificing our weekend to paint the nursery with one lousy box fan as a form of relief from the humidity.

"Just let me finish marking the thing before you start painting," Simon instructed. I sensed the annoyance in his rushed tone. I didn't blame him. It was hot.

"Sorry master."

After a long conversation with Delaney and Corliss, they decided they wanted the nursery theme to be classic literary characters. I drew out all these classic children's book characters at a picnic on a sheet of paper and Delaney instantly knew that's what she wanted. We were going to paint it as a mural. The Berenstain Bears, Peter Rabbit, Curious George, Velveteen Rabbit, and Babar the Elephant were all mingling together across one of the walls. The other walls were going to be painted a light shade of green. Delaney also convinced my parents that I was doing this out of the goodness of my heart as a baby shower gift.

Simon took a bunch of stuff from the warehouse and we used the money Delaney and Corliss left us to get more acrylic paint.

They were out of the house for the weekend, claiming they needed to get away one last time before the baby came. It was fine by me. Now we didn't have to pretend it wasn't at least a little weird that she found us in bed together last weekend.

"So am I supposed to sit here and just wait for you to be done or are there other ways I could be making myself useful?" I asked quietly.

"I'm thirsty. Maybe you could get me a cold drink if you really want something to do," Simon answered, his voice hopeful.

"You should let me make you a sandwich as well," I teased. "After all, as a woman, my one true destiny is the kitchen."

"Good," he said, jokingly. "And no crusts either, wench." I laughed and I opened the door to the cool rush of air conditioning while Simon stayed inside to fight the heat alone.

Delaney's refrigerator was filled with mostly health food, a lot of green juices. Mom must have filled Delaney's head with her juicing propaganda and Delaney being the nice person she was couldn't refuse. I settled on two beers and was halfway down the hall when I heard my Mom's voice outside.

"Hello!" she called and let herself in the front door.

"Mom?" I questioned.

"Hey hon," she waved. "Just stopping by to check on you."

"Here I am. Just being a 23-year-old adult."

Mom pursed her lips. "Adult is questionable." She continued walking through the house. "Really?" She pointed to the two beers in my hand. "You're doing this drunk?"

"As someone who owns a bar I hope you would understand that drinking one beer does not get you drunk."

"Right, but two is a whole new game."

I tried to save myself. "My boss is here."

"Oh Christ." She ran a hand through her hair. "That's professional."

"Once again, as someone who owns a bar," I began to say before the bedroom door opened and Simon appeared in the hallway. He couldn't see Mom from where he was standing and even as I shook my head towards him the words were already leaving his mouth.

"Hey woman, where's my sandwich?" He yelled in mock authority.

Mom's face grew wide with panic. "Is that how he speaks to you? Because I know a lot about the rules of the workplace and he can't talk to you like that."

"Mom, relax," I tried to calm her down, "He was joking."

"Does he tell you to say that?" She lowered her voice. "Quinn, blink twice if he's hurt you."

"Mom, I'm fine."

Simon walked down the hall and for his own protection I pushed him behind me.

"I'm calling your father," she reached for her phone.

"Mom, please don't do that." I grabbed the phone out of her hand. "There is nothing wrong."

"Mrs. Kelly." Simon finally spoke still standing behind me.

"Shut up you little prick," my mom shot back, fire in her eyes.

"Okay." Simon brought his fingers across his lips like a zipper pulling against the teeth.

"Jesus, Mom. Calm down. He's not my fucking boss." I finally exploded, the words leaving my mouth before I even realized. "I made it up."

Confusion spread over her face. "What do you mean?"

"Here," I handed her a beer. "Let's sit down for this conversation." I opened the other beer and took a long sip. "Simon will you grab a couple more beers?"

"Yes." Simon sprung towards the kitchen, probably just relieved to be out of Mom's line of sight.

"Okay," I began once we were sitting down on the couch in the living room. "I sort of lied to you about my job. I mean technically I am Simon's assistant, but he's not my boss and we don't design art."

I gave her a second to process.

"Surprise! I paint fake food for a living." Mom didn't make a sound. Instead she raised her eyebrows like I had just told her I was an alien and not her daughter.

Simon walked back into the room carrying more beer. "Here you go," he said heroically when replaced my now-empty beer with a new one. He sat down hesitantly on the other side of the couch.

"He's my coworker," I repeated to my mom. "We just work together."

She took a long sip of her beer before speaking. "Well this was just an absolute mess. Simon, I apologize, but you understand why I reacted the way I did."

"Don't worry about apologizing," he said. "It's fine, I would have done the same thing. You're a good mom," he added.

"Wouldn't it be nice if we all thought that?" Mom responded. She stood up and started walking to the front door.

"Mom," I followed her to the door. "I'm sorry I didn't tell you, but sometimes it's hard to explain things to you."

"We'll talk later." Her tone was cold. "Goodbye Simon, it was nice meeting you," she said before walking out the door.

"Fuck." I covered my face in my hands. "That could have gone way better."

"Or worse," Simon added.

I had to laugh, because if I didn't I would have cried.

It's hard trying to navigate living at home with Mom. The last time I lived at home with her I was 18 and trying my hardest to get out. For so long she's been able to have a say in everything I've done, from my jobs, clothes, even my boyfriend. She's always imparted her two cents even when it wasn't wanted.

Parents always say they want better for their children, but really they just want their children to be better versions of themselves. I think it made Mom anxious to know that I was living my life well off the beaten path of hers before me.

"So any chance I could still grab that sandwich?" Simon joked.

"You're a dick."

"It's fine, we can just stay here all weekend and pretend we both don't live with our parents," he offered in support

"We might as well get drunk." I raised my beer to his. "Cheers."

I couldn't sleep that night. Simon was passed out beside me and even the steady metronome of his breathing wasn't enough to lull me into sleep.

I found myself sitting on the ladder in the nursery; a joint between my lips, painting the crown on Babar well into the night, pausing only to mix more colors. I had finished drawing half the mural before we both agreed it was too hot to stay in that room any longer, but now with the moon at my back, a cool breeze ushered through the open windows and I felt like I could stay doing this for hours.

The darkness outside began to give way to the soft morning sun by the time I had moved on to painting the red and white-checkered blanket that sat on top of the hill.

"There you are," Simon spoke from the doorway.

"Did I wake you up?" I asked, still checkering the blanket.

"The smell of your pot did," he responded as he walked across the room, grabbing the joint from my hands and he stood in between my legs.

"Sorry." I offered meekly. "I couldn't sleep."

He held the joint between his fingers as he took a deep hit. "As long as you're not sick of me yet." He said through his exhale of smoke.

"Nah. Give me a couple more days, then I'll be bored of you."

"You say the sweetest things."

"Your vagina is going to dry up like the Grand Canyon. That whole thing used to be full of water you know." Maggie's voice cascaded

through the receiver as I sat on the toilet in my bathroom, the water running to muffle the conversation from my parents. I had gotten home from work and immediately ran to the bathroom. "But then it didn't have sex with the hot guy and poof, it dried right up."

"My vagina is not going to dry up because I am neither a canyon nor a 70-year-old woman." I reassured her.

"It's weird that you guys haven't boned yet," she pressed on.

"First of all, my sex life is not the most important thing in my life right now. Secondly I say sex life because we have had sex. I repeat. We have boned." I said at last.

"Thank god. Does he have a nice dick? I bet he does."

"A very nick dick."

"You're a lucky girl."

"What's going on with you?"

"Ugh, nothing at all. Literally. Nothing. We just got a new summer intern and believe me; I've put the feelers out there and nothing. Cold, not a drop."

"I'm assuming you're referring to his desire to sleep with you."

"Yeah what the hell else would I be talking about?"

"Never mind." I said as I turned the water off. "Alright I hate to cut this short and make it all about me, but I've got to go. Simon and I still have to finish painting some of the nursery."

"Good luck," she shouted in the phone before hanging up.

I looked both ways for signs of my parents as I walked out of my bathroom. Things were pretty icy in the Kelly household with Mom refusing to speak to me since the incident over the weekend.

Like usual, Dad had no idea what was going on. He just chalked everything up to one of us having our periods. It was better that way.

I tiptoed downstairs, making sure to stay on the outside of each step. Sneaking out when I was younger taught me that the middle of the stair is where the creak comes from. I was on the last step when my foot got caught on a shoe that was laying on the stair and I flew into the closet door. "Fuck!" I yelled as my hip jabbed into the doorknob.

"Hello." Mom called from the kitchen. My whole body froze. I closed my eyes, pretending I didn't hear her. She yelled again, "Hellooooooo."

I could either go into the kitchen where I would calmly rationalize my reasoning for lying to Mom like an adult, or I could run out of the house and away from my problems like a child.

I made sure to shut the front door quietly.

I ran hurriedly up the street and out of view from my house quickly in case she saw me from the front windows. I knew she wouldn't come outside. She was too scared to make a scene in front of the neighbors.

My head was turned, watching my house fade from view when I ran straight into a solid surface that knocked me back a few steps. I knew from the feel of his body who it was before I looked up.

I lifted my head and stared straight into Simon's eyes. "Don't ask." He nodded. "Come on, let's finish this." I pulled him towards Delaney's house.

The walls in the nursery had sprung to life. Gone was the mute shade of beige that once adorned the nursery walls. The light shade of green made the nursery stand out from the typical pinks and blues. The mural on the north side of the room drew your eyes immediately. The characters came to life on the mural. Some of them sat on the blanket while the Velveteen Rabbit carried the picnic basket. The Berenstain Bears were intertwined with Peter the Rabbit and Babar.

We didn't use brassy paints, which would make it look too cartoon like and cheap. We chose softer shades that would bounce off the mural and give the room a timeless look when natural light seeped in through the windows. The only thing we had left to do was paint the trim on the other three walls.

We just finished cleaning up the sheets we put down to cover the carpeting when Delaney and Corliss came bounding into the nursery, well Corliss came bounding, Delaney gave more of a waddle.

"Wow!" Delaney put her hands on either side of her face. "This looks so much better than I ever imagined it would." I coughed. "Not that I thought it would look bad, I just didn't think it would be this good."

"We get it." I quickly added.

"And to think, all of this was possible because Delaney caught you guys in bed together," Corliss said casually as he draped his arms around Simon and I.

"Corliss!" Delaney screamed, still taking pictures. "I told you not to say anything."

"I'm sorry," he said. He stared ahead at the floor.

I heard my phone buzz from across the room. I walked over to it and saw that I had been tagged in a photo on Facebook, a life or death moment for any person, especially if they don't remember taking any pictures. I opened the notification to see Delaney had already posted pictures of the Nursery and tagged me in them. *"My baby sister painted this for my baby"* was the caption on the picture of the mural.

"Aw Delaney," I put a hand to my chest.

"Don't," she pushed. "I'm already overly emotional as a Cancer and that mixed with the pregnancy emotions and the baby shower this weekend." She let out a soft whine, "it's just I can't believe it's happening, this makes it so real." I nudged Corliss who snapped out of a momentary trance and rushed to wrap a protective arm around Delaney. I nodded to Simon and then made eyes for the door. We took the chance to slip out of the nursery quietly, leaving the family to enjoy their moment alone.

We stood awkwardly in front of Simon's car that was parked in front of the house, unsure of what to do next. "Hey, if you don't want to go home, you can come stay with me," he offered quietly.

I shook my head, "I want to, but."

"But? There's always a but with you," he grimaced, rubbing a hand over his face.

"But," I continued, "I don't have any clothes and it's a Tuesday night and we have to work tomorrow and I don't want to sneak into the basement of your house to avoid my boss."

"None of those are really good enough reasons."

"Oh, I'm not saying they are."

"But, they're yours," Simon finished.

"Now you're getting it." I smiled, rubbing my thumb over his hand to makeup for my refusal. "Besides, I think I have to go take care of something at home." I nodded down the street.

"Yeah. You should go take care of that." He reached for his door handle.

"One joint wouldn't hurt?" I suggested. "You know, just to ease up my nerves."

His ears perked up. "Right." Simon walked around to wiggle open the passenger door. "This time I'm being a little romantic."

"I could sense that in your strut."

He drove to the orchard and parked his car between two rows of growing apple trees. He turned his lights off and looked over at me. "Ready for that joint?" He asked. I looked at him and nodded slowly. I took the joint from his hand and stuck it between his lips. My fingers fumbled for the lighter and I sparked. He inhaled and I pulled the joint away from his lips and kissed him hard on the mouth.

"I might have something else in mind." I said after we pulled apart. I turned and climbed over the center console to the back seat.

It was a blur of body parts and clothes flying, his lips attacking mine the whole time.

One of the best parts about sex with Simon, besides his Thor hammer of a penis, was that we never took ourselves too seriously.

"I thought having sex in my car would only happen when I was a teenager." Simon said. We were still lying in the backseat, sweaty and half on top of each other.

"It's fun every once in a while. It keeps you young." I laughed.

"We should probably go soon." He lifted me off his chest gingerly. I climbed out of the car, grabbing my clothes along the way. I stood outside and put my clothes back on. Simon stepped out a moment later only dressed from the waist down.

"How do I look?" I grinned at him.

"Thoroughly fucked." He winked and pulled his shirt over his head. We got back in the car and shared a joint on the ride home before Simon dropped my off in front of my dark house.

"Don't worry." He said and patted my knee in encouragement. "You'll be fine."

"Thanks." I climbed out of the car and walked up the driveway. I felt like I was 16 years old again, coming home hours after my curfew. I used to walk inside and get the, 'We're not mad, we're just disappointed' talk.

I braced myself and turned the door handle. The hallway light was still on. She was downstairs still. I tiptoed down the hall and peeked my head into the living room.

There was no need to be scared because Mom was asleep on the couch. Her hand was still clutching the remote in a death grip. I pulled a blanket off the back of the couch and draped it over her small frame. She moved a little but settled back into the couch.

She looked so young when she slept. It reminded me that when she was my age, she already had two kids with a third on the way.

I had the chance to leave and go to college, but she never got that same chance. What would she have done? Who would she have become? It was almost as if she was frozen in time at 18 because she became a mother and suddenly her life wasn't her own anymore. She lived for her children. Whether or not that will be my choice is not important. The fact is her choices are why I'm here today and that's what matters.

I pried the remote from her hand and turned the TV off. She stirred again and I moved quickly from the room. I sprinted down the hall and up the stairs at full speed into my room before she had a chance to wake up.

"We're going to Mickey's for dinner tonight, you should come," Mom said the next day when I got home.

I pulled my head out of the refrigerator. Was she talking to Dad? I presumed he was already on the guest list. I looked around the room to see if Delaney or Patrick had walked into without me noticing. Nope. It was only the three of us.

"I have to work be at the bar until 8:00," Dad spoke to no one in particular. "I'll be over after."

"I could go in for you so that you can go earlier." I offered quickly. They both turned their heads to me at once. "What? I can help out."

"That would be great. I'll head down to the bar, unload the delivery then come home." Dad said as he pressed a quick kiss on my head. "Thanks for working for me, Q."

I inched myself towards the stairs, using the sudden traffic to escape. "Not so fast," Mom called after me after Dad left the room. "Why don't you and I have a little chat?" I knew it wasn't optional so I followed behind her onto the patio.

"Can I have a drink for this, or possibly smoke something?" I added lightheartedly. The stern look on Mom's face told me no.

"What happened Quinn?"

"Nothing happened," I shot back defensively.

"Don't catch that tone with me, I'm not asking to punish you. You're 23, I can't just send you to your room and take away your phone. I really want to know what happened." She patted the empty space next to her on the couch. "Come sit down."

I sighed heavily but sat down next to her.

"I know you love me," I said. "And I know you want the best for me, but sometimes you make it hard for me to live outside what your goals are for me." She shook her head like she was confused. "We knew I was going to be different when I decided to go away to school, we all knew that my dreams lay somewhere else, but we didn't know where. And when I came back here with my tail between my legs, I felt like such a failure, like I didn't live up to these impossibly high standards."

"We have never set standards for you to live by," she interrupted. "From a young age you were very open about your plans and goals and we knew that even if we tried to tell you no, you wouldn't listen." Her voice was calm.

"You may have never said the words, but your opinion on my life choices are still known."

"I can't help that, I'm your mother. I'm always going to worry about you and want the best for you."

"When I came home and I didn't have a job, I panicked. I panicked because I thought that everything I fought so hard for meant nothing, that I was back to the place I started and nothing had changed."

"That's not true." She said. She took my hand and placed it in her own.

"I got the job painting fake food." I paused, choosing my words carefully. "And when I thought about trying to tell everyone that I painted fake food for a living it sounded ridiculous, so I made it seem like I had this chic art job."

It sounded so dumb when I said it out loud.

"Quinn," She spoke softly. She squeezed my hand and smiled. "My sweet girl who has always been so stubborn and defiant. You have always craved a type of freedom we didn't know how to give you, especially when you were young. It made things a little harder with you. Delaney and Patrick were so compliant, but you pushed and pushed and pushed. You didn't like hearing the word no. You've never been the type of girl to do what is practical. That's why you're so special. You always took what you wanted and you didn't care what anyone else thought. Don't start now." She leaned in and kissed my forehead.

"You're right," I said sheepishly.

"That's because I'm your mother." She stood up. "Go get ready for work. Your shift starts in twenty minutes and I don't pay you to sit around."

"Roger that."

The bar was pretty empty when I got there. Dad must have just left because he was nowhere to be seen. There were a few singles sitting at separate ends of the bar, half-filled glasses in front of them. They would be easy to take care of. I wasn't too worried about a busy crowd. It was a weekday afternoon, how wild could things get at the bar?

I took my time wiping down the counters behind the bar. I washed an entire rack full of dishes before one of the guys cleared his throat with a soft grunt to let me know he wanted another drink. "What are you drinking?" I asked politely. The man pointed to the lager on tap. "Anything else I can get for you?" I added, forcing a smile out of politeness.

"I'll take a wad of hundreds if you got 'em," he smirked, laughing at his own joke.

Ah, customer service humor, the worst type.

"Ha," I laughed once. "Right, well if I had that I probably wouldn't be serving drafts on a Tuesday afternoon." I pursed my lips in a tight smile. "Is there anything else I can get you…in this bar…right now?"

"I'm good, sweetie." Gross.

I should be used to it by now, the horrible back and forth between a server and the customer, but I could never get used to the pervy tone that accompanied most requests.

The afternoon carried on like this, people stopping in quick for a beer, never staying too long, just enough time to forget their day-to-day lives, never more than five people in the bar at the same time. I stocked the juices and cut up two trays of lemons and limes, anything to avoid making small talk with the customers. Most bartenders excel at pretending to give a shit about the customer's sad tales of loneliness and financial strife. Not me. It makes me a horrible person who probably gets smaller tips, but for my own sanity and theirs I just can't deal with it. I always end up saying something snarky or offending them so I just avoid conversation altogether.

The door opened and four girls I went to high school with walked in. Not just any four girls, four girls who prided themselves on being young moms. The type of moms who post countless to-do lists on social media as if we're responsible for their 1:30 PM baby check up. Audrey Munn, Keri Wilson, Jennifer Mitchell, and Bridgette Meyer. They referred to themselves as J-KAB, because you're never really friends with someone unless you have an acronym group based off the first letter of your name. Maggie and I never had enough girlfriends for that and while at the time I may have been a little remorseful, looking back I'm thankful.

"We'll have three chardonnays and a seltzer water," Audrey barked, not looking up. Kid or not, she peaked in high school. I'll say that up front. "What?" Audrey responded to the annoyed look Bridgette gave her. "I'm still breast feeding."

"Pump and dump," Keri whined, "it's mommy time."

Fuck me. Who orders chardonnay besides an old man at the early bird special?

"Okay, fine. Make it four," Audrey said, finally looking up. "Oh my gosh! Hi," she squealed, her voice mimicking the sound a pig makes. "Quinn!"

"Hey guys," I replied, springing my head back and forth like a bobble head. "Girls night, huh?"

"It's our one night a week to let loose, have some wine, talk about what's going on," Jennifer spoke, flipping a piece of her auburn hair to the side of her face.

"Tuesday nights at 6:00 are perfect for that." I nodded sourly.

"So how are you?" Audrey said. She wasn't even looking at me. She pretended to smooth an imaginary wrinkle out of her shirt.

"I'm pretty good." I skirted around the question, knowing she didn't care for the answer. "And you guys," I pointed to the quartet, "are quite the fertile myrtles."

They laughed, happy the conversation was headed towards the only subject they were capable of talking about. "I know," Bridgette cooed. "We already have enough for a basketball team."

I wish I had a dollar for the amount of times one of them has inevitably said that to someone. I could have probably given Pervy Patron #76 his coveted wad of hundreds.

"Yeah. Wow."

"What about you?" Keri questioned. "Any baby plans?"

"Um," I poured wine into each of their glasses. "Yeah, I'm going to let you guys ride that one out for a while, I've got a lot going on between drinking copious amounts of alcohol and staying awake past 11:00 pm."

"It's the most rewarding experience," Jennifer chimed in.

"Yeah, so is getting your period after a questionable pull out." I bit back. On cue a look that can only be compared to serious constipation came over their collective faces.

"We'll keep a tab open," Bridgette said before they walked over to a table in the corner to no doubt discuss collecting a sample of my hair for the homemade voodoo dolls they just found on Pinterest.

I know there is a special place for me in hell. Maybe one day I'll bite my tongue and be one of them, but one of us should be enjoying their 20's and if it's not going to be them, I've got no problem volunteering as tribute.

If we're being honest here, none of their marriages will last and I'm willing to put down a serious chunk of cash that at least one of them poked a hole in the condom to trap their boyfriends forever. Which is cool I guess, if you're into that type of stuff.

You would not believe who's in the bar right now. I had to text Maggie. She's the only one who would fully understand how funny this was.

Mara Harris. She answered, referring to the girl a year ahead of us who moved to Los Angeles after she graduated and got deep into fetish porn. Literally.

Better. J-KAB.

GET A PICTURE.

They still move as one person.

Don't they all have 18 children?

Pretty much.

They remind me of a cult.

I'm still not ruling that out.

I looked up to see the four girls ogling something on Keri's phone. "And Elijah would be such a good pumpkin for his first Halloween, but he would also make a really good cat."

"Not a pumpkin. Sadie was a pumpkin last year," Audrey whined.

Tackling the issues one day at a time.

The rest of my shift was spent keeping a tally on the number of times one of them muttered 'breast is best' (14) and the number of contagious diseases they were worried about their children getting, even though they were vaccinated (7). If I had to make it a drinking game, I would have been hammered.

I know where I won't be next Tuesday.

Nora couldn't have come in at a more perfect time. It was just before 9:00 and I was ready to get out of the bar before anyone else came in. "Oh I see the Mom Squad is here and all riled up on chardonnay," she noted when she put her purse under the bar.

"Yeah they're intense." I walked around the bar. "Do you need anything? Everything is pretty much done."

"No, I'm good. I should be able to deal with them as long as one of them doesn't start lactating like she did last week."

"Ew," I snorted. "I'll see you later." I walked to my car quickly, but not before seeing the minivan parked next to me with the stick figure family stickers on the back. A mom, dad and two stick figure babies were stuck to the let side of the window. I laughed to myself, knowing if I had one of those it would be one person with a dozen liquor bottles surrounding her.

Maybe I'll invest in some.

My roommates were sitting on the couch when I walked in. "How was the bar?" Dad asked.

"Pretty slow, saw a couple people from high school, nothing too major."

"Who?" Mom asked, her gossipy nature spilling over.

"Just my good friends J-KAB. The young mother order."

"Ooh," Dad winced and made a sour face. "Yeah I forgot they come in on Tuesdays."

"How was Mickey's?"

"Good. Quinn, can you take the dog out?" Mom asked without taking her eyes off the television.

"Yeah, just let me change." I went upstairs and changed into my go to choice of an oversized tee shirt with no pants. I grabbed a joint from my underwear drawer and tucked it inside my bra for safekeeping.

"Really?" Mom questioned me when I reappeared downstairs. "Again with the no pants."

"Mom," I began, "we all came into this world naked, I'm simply paying homage to my humble beginnings." She shook her head at Dad, as if this was his fault.

"She's your daughter," he shrugged.

I grabbed the leash from the hook near the door and Marlowe's head jerked up at the jingle.

It was dark enough on the street that if anyone did see me they would think I was wearing a pair of shorts under my shirt. I passed Delaney's house and kept going until I hit the deserted lot three yards up. Feeling safe enough that nobody would bother us, I let Marlowe off her leash and lit the joint. My phone vibrated. It was a text from Maggie asking me what I was wearing to Elliot's wedding. I answered quickly.

I looked up and couldn't see Marlowe anywhere. I glanced in all directions and checked for any movement behind bushes. "Marlowe,"

I hissed. “Now is not the time.” I walked further back into the lot and was calling out for her when I heard a voice behind me.

“I’ve got her,” My next-door neighbor, Mr. Lanigan, said proudly.

I turned to face him slowly, joint still in my hand and froze. “Thanks,” I said, pressing my legs closed together.

And that is exactly how Mr. Lanigan caught me smoking a joint with no pants on. He pretended not to notice my attire and set the dog down gingerly. She ran over to me, excited and peed on a patch of dandelions by my left foot.

“Just out for my nightly walk.” He saluted me.

“Have a good night.” I said.

I did the responsible thing.

I waited for him to get past Delaney’s house before relighting the joint and inhaling deeply.

12

$2,776.43

I was already annoyed from a busy day at work when I walked in the door that night.

Simon decided today was the best day to give me all the backlogged foods and Wade wanted them all done for a display he was making for a convention. I'm not sure. I stopped paying attention once I saw five crates of clay that needed to be painted.

The last thing I wanted to do when I got home was apply for jobs, but my routine of applying for jobs every night had slipped in the past few weeks and I needed to get back on track.

My parents were still at the bar. Marlowe and I had full reign over our kingdom and we planned on taking full advantage of it. I unbuttoned my shorts and kicked them off. First, I needed a glass of wine. I pulled the box from the refrigerator. I could make a drinking game out of the job search. Drink every time a job requires at least two years of experience for an entry-level position. Just kidding, I would end up getting my stomach pumped before sunset.

I sat down at the counter and turned my laptop on. I was curious to see what new jobs awaited me.

Gallery Assistant. Posted six hours ago.

Interesting. I clicked the link. It lead me to the gallery's homepage. West End Gallery was fairly new, but had already experienced mild success when some actress mentioned them in an Instagram post. The owners were two guys with ridiculously well manicured beards. The position was listed like most other gallery jobs, except this one didn't require two years experience, just a personal statement and portfolio.

I finished the rest of my wine and copied down the gallery's address. I could manage a personal statement and my portfolio had seriously grown in the past few weeks.

I spent the rest of my night gathering my portfolio and using all of my parent's printer ink to print pictures of my work. I printed an 8x10 of the nursery as well. It wouldn't hurt to throw that in.

The hard part was going to be the personal statement.

Fuck it. I was just going to be honest. This was the only position I was qualified for and I would do whatever it took to get it. People lie about stuff like this all the time. I'm living proof of that.

I opened a blank word document and started typing. I sort of zoned out and when I came back around, it was written.

Art is interpretation so you might not understand the things I say, but you understand the passion behind my words. My experience pales in comparison to my work ethic and my willingness to learn.

I chose to study art because I believe the freedom to express ourselves is the most important freedom. Without it we are nothing. Art allows us to be something.

Working at your art gallery would give me a chance to find myself.

(And I could finally move out of my parent's house.)

Attached are copies of my portfolio. Actual copies can be sent upon request.

Quinn Kelly
qkelly@globalmail.com

Mornings started to suck less.

By the end of July I hardly groaned anymore when I got out of bed in the morning. Flashy Foods became less of a task and more of a warm-up. Painting every day at work, even though it was fake food, kept me in a nice rhythm to paint for myself at night. I was growing more confident in different techniques. A few days ago I used spray paint instead of my usual acrylic paint. The spray forced me to practice steadying my hand better and the color left a stronger hue on the canvas than the acrylic.

If I hadn't spent all day painting I wouldn't have considered using spray paint. It also gave me an odd sense of satisfaction because it felt like I was vandalizing someone's property.

Dare I say that my days were even floating along quite nicely?

Which is why I almost forgot about the gallery assistant position.

I applied for dozens more jobs since that night. I was almost confused when my phone buzzed with an email from West End Gallery asking for me to fly out for an interview the following week. The email said they liked my raw sense of self.

I wanted to reply immediately.

This was what I'd been waiting for all summer. This could be my ticket out. This could be the start to my story. In ten years I could look back at this moment and remember the summer I spent at my parents house dicking around before I became someone.

My finger lingered over the button. What was my hold up? I had nothing to be unsure about? I probably just needed to hear someone else tell me I should take the interview.

I put the phone down, climbed out of bed and went in search of my parents. They were my best shot at having hype men pump me up for the opportunity.

I found them across the hall in their bedroom. Their bedside lamps were still on and my parents were sitting up on either side of their bed.

"I've got an interview in Chicago." I walked in and sat on the edge of their bed. "I should take it, right?"

"Yes." They said at the same time.

"That settles it. Thanks." I stood up.

"Wait a second," my mom said. She put her book down. "This isn't like the job you found on Craigslist, right?"

"Nothing like the job I found on Craigslist."

"And you're sure this is what you want?" She asked and she narrowed her head in my direction like she didn't believe me.

"Yeah. This was the plan all along." I lingered in the doorway.

"If this is what you want, we support you." Dad said.

"This is what I want." I repeated. "It's finally happening like it's supposed to. Goodnight guys." I shut their door and went back to my room.

My parents didn't exactly raise the bar on my excitement. Maggie would. She would be so excited for me. I couldn't call her though. This had to be my journey alone. Everyone else had their shit to deal with. I needed to buck up and handle mine.

I replied to the email telling them I was thrilled for the opportunity to interview and would see them in a week and put my phone on my nightstand.

Even when I closed my eyes to sleep my mind wouldn't stop thinking about the interview. There was so much to be done and no time to do it. This wasn't a cute montage sequence either. There would be no synthetic pop music in the background of my life for the next seven days. My week was going to be long and ugly.

Delaney's baby shower was next weekend and I already took the Friday before off work to get stuff ready for that. There was no way I could take another day off without staying late everyday next week. I needed new paintings to show them in addition to what I sent. They'd want to see my work, right? I had to buy a plane ticket and an outfit and a suitcase on wheels. A duffle bag wouldn't cut it this time.

It's fine. I had a week before the interview to get ahead at work and most of the stuff for the shower was done already.

I'll be fine.

13

$2,174.76

Airfare is even more expensive when you purchase it six days before your flight. Luckily I don't spend money on much, but it was still a blow to my bank account to drop $500 to fly to Chicago and back in one day.

I drove myself to the airport the morning of my interview and paid an obscene amount of money to leave my car in the parking garage for single day parking. It was barely 5:00 AM. My flight wasn't for another two hours but my dad insisted I get there early in case going through security took a long time.

It didn't.

Actually it took me all of twelve minutes to get my boarding pass, go through security and find my gate. It was so early that most of the shops in the terminals hadn't opened yet. I sat down at empty loading gate and put my headphones in. A few moments later I was sound asleep.

After a quick wake up to board, I continued to sleep for the two-hour plane ride. We landed safely and I waited patiently to get off the plane.

The airport was crowded. It made me enjoy the luxury of being able to travel alone. It was much easier navigating through a busy terminal without toting kids in strollers or worse leashes with nine bags of luggage between everyone. Not for me. I brought one carryon suitcase, a messenger bag with more paintings and a backpack. I watched Meet the Fockers enough to know not to check a bag if you absolutely didn't have to.

Businessmen and women in power suits walked leisurely throughout the airport and I power walked passed all of them in search of caffeine, only stopping when I saw a neon sign illuminating the word coffee.

The good news was that my interview was scheduled for noon and I still had plenty of time to get ready for it. The bad news was that I had to get ready for my interview in a public restroom, but we would cross that bridge when we got there.

I got my coffee and followed the signs for the taxi stand outside. My armpits started sweating as soon as the automatic sliding doors opened. So much for Chicago being the windy city. It was midmorning and it was easily 90 degrees. Not to worry because I have no sense of decency and traveled in gym shorts and flip-flops for comfort.

The sidewalk was flooded with people hailing cabs and trying to navigate their luggage through the small strip of cement walkway. I stepped off the curb and gave my best hail a cab stance, my arm and leg stuck out towards traffic.

Within a minute a cab pulled in front of me and stopped. An older man stepped out and opened the trunk. "No that's okay." I clutched my bags tighter. "I'll keep them with me."

"Suit yourself." He slammed the trunk shut and climbed back in the car. "Where are you headed?" He asked me once I was seated in the back. I repeated the address from the email and he peeled away from the curb.

Twenty minutes later we drove through what had to be a younger Chicago neighborhood. The storefront mannequins were dressed in contemporary summer dresses and most restaurants had chalkboard drawings on the signs outside. The cab pulled up to the modern gallery.

The black awnings on the door made the building stand out against other businesses on the block. There were several paintings drenched in light hanging in the window displays on either side of the door. West End Gallery was printed in plain bold text across the French styled doors.

"Here we are." The cab driver slapped his palm on the meter to stop it. I stared back at the building.

"Actually, can you drop me off at the coffee shop down the block?"

"No problem." He drove away from the gallery and down five buildings before stopping again.

I handed him money and climbed out of the bags. "Thank you." I shut the door and stood on the sidewalk. I adjusted the messenger bag across my chest. There was still three hours to kill before my interview. I couldn't go to a bar and get a drink. I didn't have marijuana in any form. I was headed into this day stone sober and I was not pleased.

If I couldn't have an illegal buzz, I would have to settle for a caffeinated one. I hauled my bags inside the small coffee shop. Aside from a few customers by the counter, the place was empty. It had a small sitting area with a couple shabby couches that were obvious rejects from the coffee shop on Friends. Not that I minded the empty place, the less people that see me get ready in a public bathroom, the better.

I ordered an iced coffee and sat down on one of the couches. Traveling all morning and sleeping the entire plane ride hadn't given me the chance to focus on the actual interview.

I should be more excited. I should have an electric force field protecting my optimism and joy.

Maybe I was still adjusting to the time change. Sure it's only an hour, but that's still sixty whole minutes that went away somewhere.

I took my laptop out of my bag and searched the gallery again. Now seemed like a good time to do some interview preparation.

Two hours of stalking and two more coffees later, I felt like I knew the entire history of the gallery. The gallery was run by two cousins, Matt and Mike, who opened it with family money. They mostly do weeklong exhibits featuring one artist. Those artists all seem to be

Chicago natives. Once each season though, they host exhibits by artists from all over the country. The gallery opened two years ago. For three years prior they did pop up exhibits throughout the city before they finally settled in one place.

Matt and Mike really crammed culture down my throat with their extensive biographies on the gallery's website. They mainly highlighted their semesters studying abroad and the summer they spent traveling through Europe, but never touched on their authority on art.

The pictures on the website focused more on photo filters than the art itself. This gallery was the belly of a very big hipster beast.

That's fine. I'm used to the stereotypes of artists. My friends and I joked about them all the time in college. Art majors bled irony and isn't that what hipsters cherish most?

Looking beyond their chin stubble and plaid suits, I thought about the greater good of art and the greater good of myself.

There was still an hour before the interview but I needed to get out of my clothes and hopefully my mindset.

I shut my computer and put it back in my bag. I picked up my bags and wheeled my carryon to the single, unisex stall in the back of the coffee shop. The wheels made a small whistle on the hardwood floor and a few employees turned to look at me. I hope they didn't need to use the bathroom anytime soon.

The light in the small room was bright enough that my makeup wouldn't look like I was getting ready to sing backup at a seedy jazz club.

Not wanting to get too dressed up because dressing down for an important interview is ironic and who loves irony most? Artists and hipsters.

I wanted to look like I still put thought into my appearance, but still look organic and effortless. When artists can't express themselves through their art, they express themselves through their personal style. Some artists have a signature accessory they wear with everything. It could be a pin, or they always wear a flower. One girl at school wore all white, every day. Their signature style is anything that alludes to how original they are.

As I myself am an artist, I too have a signature style. I think it's important to dress for comfort. My wardrobe contains a lot of soft cottons with elastic waistbands. They make professional sweatpants now. It's the best invention in a while if you ask me. They hang loosely on your thighs and get tighter around the knee until the pant cuts off above the ankle. I just put on a pair of those pants and I'm instantly artsy.

Taking my clothes off in a public bathroom is up there on my list of gross things I never want to encounter. It slides right in between finding a maggot-filled dead animal in my basement and opening a Twix bar with only one Twix inside.

I broke records with my speed change, even hopping on one foot to put on a pair of flat sandals without touching the floor. I threw on a basic black tank top and black blazer over the white cotton pants. I looked sophisticated and well read. I started brushing my teeth when a pair of knuckles tapped on the bathroom door. "Miss. Are you okay?" A voice asked.

"Be right out." I answered with the toothbrush still in my mouth. I still needed to put deodorant on. I fished my hand through my bag but didn't find it. It's summertime. Of course I packed it. I dumped the bag into the sink. There was no sign of it anywhere. The closest thing I had was foot deodorizer. I took the top off and sprayed under my armpits. An instant tingle ran through my arm. I sprayed my other armpit anyway. It had the word deodorize in the name, I'd be fine.

"Miss." The voice was back.

I swept everything in the sink into my bag and hawked a monster chunk of toothpaste into the sink. I zipped my bags and opened the door. The cashier from earlier scowled at me with her arms folded across her chest.

"Sorry about that. I needed a minute." I tried to disarm her stance with politeness.

"We're not a homeless shelter."

"I'm not homeless."

"Bathrooms are for customers only." She scrunched her face and the deep lines on her forehead stuck out.

"Oh fuck off." I said without thinking twice. "I bought three shitty iced coffees from you. I'm a patron of this establishment." My voice had risen steadily.

"Calm down ma'am." She uncrossed her arms.

"Don't call ma'am me. I'm 23." I walked to the front of the shop while the cashier hovered behind me until I made it to the door.

Ideally that scene would have taken longer because I still had a half hour to walk 500 feet. I'll go early and check out the art. There were probably dozens of other people interviewing.

The sun still beat down at an unhealthy rate and I could smell the shoe deodorizer through the sleeves of my blazer. Thankfully it was only a short walk because three or more blocks of that would not be cool.

I paused outside the gallery doors. This moment needed background music, an 80s rock song to set the stage. I wanted to walk in there and set it off like a quarterback breaking through those paper posters at the beginning of football games.

The gallery was smaller than I imagined based on pictures alone. The one story building narrowly stretched back with art hung on either wall. The pieces started small and gradually got bigger. There were a few sculptures and couple installations in front of a high top receptionist desk at the back of the gallery.

A young girl sat in a chair behind the desk, thick-rimmed glasses covering most of her face.

"Hello." I greeted and approached her. "I'm Quinn Kelly. I have an interview at noon."

"Marvelous." She cooed. "Wait here." She hopped down from the chair and disappeared through a large door behind her.

Hipsters or not, the art is here was good. There were a healthy variety of pieces in the exhibit. Pop art blended nicely with conceptual pieces and minimalist paintings were scattered throughout the otherwise clean space. Crisp white walls and plenty of lighting allowed the art to take center stage. A dish of business cards sat on the desk. Remy Torres. I remember that name from the website. This was the big leagues. This was not Flashy Foods and Gloria, though spirited in her own right, was no Remy Torres.

The door opened and Matt and Mike appeared without the receptionist. "Hello, Quinn. I'm Matt." Hipster Thing One stretched his hand out in greeting. He looked different from his picture. The real version of him was shorter and paler.

"Nice to meet you." I said, extending my own hand.

"Quinn. Mike. Really zen to meet you." Hipster Thing Two extended a tattoo-covered arm.

"It's a pleasure. Thank you for having me." I shook his hand. "Chicago is a beautiful city." My mouth went on autopilot and released charming phrases without much work from my brain.

"Let's take a walk." Thing One said. He turned on his heel and started in the direction of the art. Thing Two was hot on his trail. I dropped my bags and followed them.

"We've read your personal statement, very spirited by the way. What really caught our eye was your portfolio. You're quite uninhibited with a paint brush." Thing Two spoke casually.

"Thank you." I said. Nobody has ever called me that before. I'm not even sure I know what that word means.

"You have potential." Thing One said. He paused in front on the installation. "Why take an assistant job?"

"It's always been a dream to work in this environment and I imagine being an assistant is the first step in the right direction."

The two men glanced at each other and then back at me. "Where do you see yourself in two years?" Thing Two asked.

The question didn't surprise me. It was a normal interview question. "If I'm fortunate enough, in two years I'll be working towards running a gallery."

Thing One's eyes widened. "Maybe you are the ambitious type."

"Your personal statement said art is interpretation." Thing Two recalled. "What do you think this piece represents?" He pointed at the installation in front of us.

I stared at the three dimensional piece. The top was a flat, stormy sky suspended in the open air. There was a hole in the middle and hundreds of small golden specs floated in air below the opening. The easy thing to say would have been something literal like we are born from stardust, but I was a little less profound.

"I think it's all your childhood dreams floating into a black hole never to be seen again leaving you with a false sense of everything you've ever known to be true." I stretched it out in one breath.

"You're dark." Thing One said. "We need more of your dark realness."

"Yeah." I said in a short tone.

"We appreciate you flying out on such short notice." Thing Two said abruptly. "If you'll give us a minute."

"Of course. Take your time." I said.

The pair walked back through the door behind the desk and I was alone in the gallery once again.

Was that the whole interview? I heard stories in college about how strange the interview process could be sometimes. They were probably just grabbing coupons to give me before they sent me back to New York. I spent $500 on airfare for a ten-minute interview; I better get some fucking coupons.

The door opened again the beard cousins walked towards me with purposeful strides. "We don't know what it is about you Quinn, you're certainly not the most qualified or experienced, but there is something about your aura we really like." Thing One said. He clapped his hands together.

"We'd like to offer you the position," Thing Two cut in.

My body tensed at his words. I waited for instant relief or joy to flood through me, for my body to finally exhale. "Yes." My autopilot responded. "I would love to work here."

"Let's go in back and talk." Thing One said. I nodded and followed them through the door behind the desk into a small room. There was a wide table with bench seating in the middle of the room and two desks on either side of the back wall. We sat at the wide table and talked about my pay, start date, expectations, and the crushing announcement that I would not be offered health insurance. I planned on leaving that part out when I call my parents later.

My start date was the day after Labor Day. Matt said art comes more alive with the changing of the seasons. All that meant to me was four short weeks separated me from Chicago.

I kept waiting for the joy to come.

I waited in the cab ride to the airport. I waited in the full body scan by TSA. They probably saw a hint of jubilation in my x-ray. I waited while I ate two slices of expensive airport Chicago-style pizza and still nothing.

I was bored out of my mind and there was still 20 minutes until my plane boarded. Napping right now was out of the question due to the four iced coffees I drank. I needed something to knock me out for the flight so I found a small drugstore near my gate and bought a tube of Dramamine.

I reached for my wallet to pay and grabbed my phone by accident. The screen lit up and showed I had a missed call from Simon.

He thinks I've been at a doctor's appointment all day because I didn't tell anyone at Flashy Foods that I had an interview.

I overpaid for my Dramamine and called Simon on my walk back to the gate. It rang twice before he picked up.

"Hey." He greeted.

"Hi. What's up?"

"Nothing really. I wanted to see how your day spent at the doctors went."

A voice came over the loud speaker in the airport. "Flight 902 nonstop to Philadelphia is now boarding."

"What was that?" Simon asked.

"That was just my dad watching TV. He loves that shows from the 90s about the airport." I got to my gate.

"Wings." He said.

"Yeah. That's the one."

"You want to hang out tonight or are you tired?"

I forced a yawn into the phone. "I'm kind of tired tonight." It wasn't a lie. It had been a long day. "We'll do something this weekend."

"Like what?" He asked.

Passengers were beginning to line up at my gate. "I don't know, something good. I've got to go. I'll see you tomorrow."

"See you tomorrow."

I hung up the phone, swallowed two Dramamine and got in line for my flight.

14

$2,753.65

The rest of the week I tried, and successfully failed, at putting my two weeks in at my job.

My plan was to quit immediately and have a little bit of time off before Chicago. There was a lot of shit that was happening before I left. Delaney was a ticking time bomb with that baby inside of her. I thought she was a maniac for wanting to have her baby shower this late into her pregnancy.

There was also Elliot's wedding coming up. Labor Day weekend actually. I could spend my last hours in Springhaven with all my old pals. At least Maggie was my date. We told Elliot not to give us plus ones if we didn't have boyfriends at the time of invitations being sent out. It's awkward bringing a date to a wedding that is not your lover. Plus Maggie and I will have way more fun with each other.

I also had the small task of finding an affordable place to live in Chicago via the Internet. Not really easy.

On Thursday I almost told him. I had him cornered by the coffee pot, which was a rare occasion in itself. The man was never around. The words were dancing on my tongue, ready to leap out. "That's just not the way I care to run my business." Wade was talking about a phone call he got earlier. My lips stared moving, I swear. My back was straight and my eyes were staring straight ahead, but he kept rolling along about the phone call and I didn't have the heart to do it. I poured a cup of coffee and walked back to my desk.

Simon walked over and stood in front of my desk, his eyebrows raised in a curious manner. "What were you and Wade talking about?"

"Nothing." I said quickly.

He couldn't know about the job. There was no way he could, only my family and Maggie knew about it so far. I was acting paranoid. I picked up the unpainted pumpkin on my desk and started sponging mixed paint onto it. "He had a weird phone call today."

"Oh." Even if he didn't know, I had to tell him soon, just not at work.

He started picking at a spot of dried paint on the corner of my desk. "We're still going to hang out this weekend, right?"

"Yeah. Delaney's baby shower is on Saturday but we can do something after."

"We can go out for drinks." He suggested.

"Can we go somewhere on your side of the tracks?"

"We can do that." He said.

"Good."

I was in hell.

It was hot and there was so much high-pitched noise and general over reaction about everything that in that exact moment I knew this is exactly what hell will feel like when I get there in 60 to 80 years.

The bar was filled with smiling women all wearing the same type of bright sundress. Most of them sipped mimosas and cooed obligingly at every present Delaney unwrapped. Under normal circumstances I would have been bored to death by the eighth bath towel, but Delaney opening presents helped me dodge my family's opinions on my new job.

My grandmother didn't think it was safe for me to go to a big city alone. Mom's sister, Rita, agreed and said that my body type was the prime body type to mug. "You're not meaty enough to put up a fight." She reasoned when we stood by the bar.

"Have you seen her ass lately? She's meaty enough." My grandmother said as she lightly slapped my butt. At least their opinions about my job were better than their usual opinions on my dating life.

Volunteering to work behind the bar was a welcome break. It offered the perfect view of the room draped entirely in blue decorations, most of them store bought. I painted a bunch of small pictures of baby animals on brown paper and hung them with clothespins on a thin wire.

Mom sat next to Delaney, writing down every gift and who gave it like a courtroom clerk in the heat of a cross-examination. I offered to write them down, but she shooed me away. I think she mostly wanted to be in the background of all the pictures that were taken of Delaney.

"Quinn everything looks so great," Delaney's high school best friend Jessie walked up to the bar and complimented me. "By the way, the nursery is awesome, I didn't know you were so talented."

"Thanks Jessie." There wasn't much more to say.

"If you're looking for more work, Dan and I are looking to paint our living room. We'd love to see what you think of the space."

"I'm not sure. I took a job in Chicago. I'm leaving in a few weeks."

"Good for you." She clinked her champagne glass against mine.

We looked at Delaney who was unwrapping a gigantic diaper genie, her face covered in utter joy. "She's super pregnant." I said. I poured her another mimosa from the pitcher below me. Jessie hummed in agreement. "Like, she's going to be a mom soon." Jessie just nodded knowingly.

My phone buzzed with a text from Simon. *What time do you want to hang out?*

She's still opening presents. I'll meet you in an hour?

Ok. See you soon.

I looked at the small pile of presents still left to open on the table. The end was so close, yet so far. Jessie thanked me for the drink and walked back to her seat.

Now that the baby shower was basically done, it was one less thing I had to worry about, which meant I could now direct my full attention to telling Simon about my job.

It annoyed me that telling Simon warranted a bullet point on my to do list. He's my friend and he'll be happy for me. If not then he's a dick and at least I figured that out. It's not going to end like a romantic comedy where he follows me to Chicago and pines for my heart. In all likelihood he would follow me to the airport and pine for my vagina. That one I'd be okay with.

A bed bumper, three more football jerseys and 30 packs of diapers later, the presents were finally done being open.

Delaney thanked everyone and some people lingered for a little while, but most of the shower guests left after she finished opening presents. I volunteered to load the stuff into the cars. Mostly so I wouldn't have to talk to anyone anymore and if I loaded the car I would be able to leave without feeling bad.

The presents were separated into categorized piles and I tried my best to keep that in mind when I packed the cars but there was a pile of bigger stuff I left by the door for Corliss to lift later.

I poked my head through the open door when I finished. "Hey if you guys don't need me anymore, I'm going to head out." I said with a silvery tone in my voice.

Mom and sister both looked up from the table. "No. Go ahead." Mom said. Then added, "Wait, where are you going?"

"Out with some friends."

"Have fun." She went back to listening to whatever Delaney was saying. Delaney looked over Mom's shoulder and winked at me. I threw up my middle finger and shut the door.

His disheveled hair was the first thing I saw when I walked into the bar. He was talking on his phone and he ran his other hand through his hair. He looked up and saw me, then waved me over. When I was close enough, I could hear his words over the baseball game that was playing on the screen behind him. "No shit." He said into the receiver. "I'm hanging out with Quinn tonight. One night. Really? Let me call you back." He hung up the phone and looked at me. "Hey. Tim and Miles are back. The bar they were supposed to play at tonight got shut down for health code violations. They're home and they've got a bunch of mushrooms. They want to know if we want to go to their apartment and take them."

"That's one way to spend our night." I said. Telling him would be better if he was on psychedelics.

"It could be fun." He said. He sipped his beer.

"Let's do it." I said.

Mushrooms were a horrible idea. These boys consumed drugs in the same way they picked up girls: awkwardly, with reckless abandon and with far too much hip gyration.

Miles decided it would be best to make a peanut butter and mushroom sandwich to ease digestion and obtain *maximum trippage.* Tim and Simon pureed their mushrooms in a blender with orange juice and ice to get it all down in one shot. I opted out, figuring at least one of us should be relatively sober.

Things were going okay for the first hour of their trip. Miles sat in the corner, thoroughly consumed by an Etch-A-Sketch. Tim kept watching magical illusion videos on YouTube; and Simon talked an awful lot, which isn't very different from non-mushroom Simon. His thoughts were erratic with most of his sentences starting and ending with "It may just be me."

We were almost an hour in when Simon started to sweat far too much. His face was red with blotchy patches appearing on his forehead. "Have you ever done mushrooms before?" I asked. We stood outside because I thought fresh air would help him, but it didn't.

"Nope."

"Yeah, fuck this." I grabbed his hand and pulled him towards his car. "Give me your keys." He slapped them in my hand dramatically.

We walked along the road until we stood in front of his car, Simon pacing back and forth. "Get in the back seat." Simon looked offended but did as he was told. "I'm not a doctor, but I spend a lot of my time on WedMD and I think you're having an allergic reaction to the mushrooms. So I'm going to get some Benadryl, okay?" Simon made a mewing sound and smacked his gums together as he threw his body across the back seat of the car.

I left him in the car when I went into the drug store. It's fine, I cracked the window so he had steady air flow, but I took the keys so he couldn't go anywhere. I didn't think taking him out of the car was my best option at the moment. I came back with Benadryl, two bottles of water and rolling papers because I believed that weed could cure anything, including an allergic reaction to hallucinogens.

"Hey." Simon looked up at me, his pupils blown up. "Take this and drink some of this." I handed him the pills and water before I started driving. I didn't want to take him back to the apartment. He needed fresh air. The apartment. I left the other two there to take on the rest of their trip solo.

"You know what?"

"What?" I looked in the rearview mirror and Simon was leaning up against the window.

"Headrests are so weird." He took the headrest out of his backseat and spun the rods back and forth between his fingers. "These aren't even comfortable." He rubbed the itchy fabric against his face. "Let's go clean my car." He said, suddenly.

I rolled my eyes slightly but then realized it was one of the better ideas he could have had at a time like this. "Okay, but you're going to vacuum and I'm going to sit on the trunk with my arms crossed in annoyance the whole time."

"We could have been having sex right now." He marveled.

"Yup." I pulled into the car wash and turned the car off. "I'll go get quarters."

When I came back to the car Simon had the floor mats arranged on the ground and was jumping back and forth, playing hopscotch on them. "I was always really good at this when I was a kid," he half-smiled and after a beat added, " Which is actually pretty weird."

"No." I walked towards him. "It's not. I used to be really good at tetherball. Probably because I could play it by myself."

I deposited the quarters in the machine and as soon as the first sign of noise protruded from the hose Simon recoiled back behind me like something had bit him. "Oh no. Oh no." He pressed his face to my shoulder. "You don't even see this right now." He wiped his brow. "Beetlejuice, Beetlejuice, Beetlejuice!" he screamed. I tried to stop myself from laughing, but he was definitely entering a different level of his trip. "The vacuum, it has the tiniest head, like a voodoo doll." Simon's voice was so small.

"No, it's cool," I turned around, rubbing his arms soothingly. "You're just tripping, it's not real."

"It is," he argued. "Shake, shake, shake, senora," he started to sing. "Shake it all around." I debated getting my phone and taking a video to show him later, but I couldn't stop laughing long enough to get it out.

"Just keep singing it's working. He's going away." I played along.

"Work, work, work," he kept humming to himself while I began to vacuum the car. After the longest five verses of that song ever sang, the vacuum finally shut off.

Simon sat on the trunk of the car with his knees pressed against his chest, rocking back and forth. I rolled a joint on the hood of the car and sparked it before offering him the first hit. "Here." I pushed the joint in his hand. "Smoke this." He inhaled deeply, letting his mouth fill to the brim with smoke before exhaling. "Thanks." He passed it back to me after another hit. "I don't think mushrooms are for me."

"I'd agree with that."

"We could have had sex tonight."

"Indeed we could have, but alas here we are, not having sex."

"Stupid health code violations."

"Mmhmm."

"Did you ever just stare up at the sky and wonder if the stars talk to each other?" He asked. Simon leaned his upper body against the back window.

"I don't know if it works like that." I slid up next to him.

"No it definitely does. Think of all the Greek Gods, they're up there somewhere. Apollo is cueing up a soundtrack for everyone to dance to while Poseidon makes sure the hot tub is warm enough for everyone to chill in."

"Dionysus' got a keg and some ecstasy," I added.

"Exactly." He wrapped an arm around my shoulder and puffed the joint. "Just lie back and think about all that's going on up there."

"You're so fucked up," I laughed into his shoulder.

"I don't know, I think I might be onto something." He handed me the clip.

"You are onto something." I patted his knee. "Too many psychedelics for one night." He smiled dopily, his eyes completely glazed over. "You're pretty fucked up. You might not remember this. I still feel like I have to tell you." I said.

"I bet you I'll remember." He said. A chuckle erupted from his throat that made him laugh harder.

"I got a job in Chicago."

"The place?"

"Yes."

"Doing what?"

"I'm going to be an assistant at West End Gallery."

"What does that mean?" His words were slurred.

"I'll help the owners with booking exhibits, running openings, stuff like that."

He shrugged his shoulders and turned his mouth into a scowl. "That sounds boring."

"It's necessary to move up. Everyone that ever became successful started from the bottom of somewhere."

"When do you leave?"

"Labor Day."

"Shit." He touched his fingers together. "That's three weeks."

"Yeah."

We grew quiet and sat content in our own thoughts on the trunk of the car for a moment.

"I'll miss you when I go." I spoke some time later. "Not because I want you to be my boyfriend. You were the only friend I had this summer. Our friendship is important to me. And I like your dick."

"Yeah I'll miss you too, but I get it."

I drove Simon back to Miles and Tim's apartment around the same time the sun came up. He fell asleep leaning against the back window for an hour and I felt too bad to wake him. We smoked another joint when he woke up and then he decided he was sober enough to get in a moving vehicle again. I didn't want to make him drive me, but I left my car at the bar yesterday and I didn't want to hang around their apartment. Simon flicked on the radio I realized someone else could take me to my car.

"That's right, ya'll, it's me DJ Beast Mode taking you from your Saturday night into your Sunday morning. I hope you're all going to sleep with a good story to tell in the morning. I'm headed home now, but I'm going to leave you with one last jam that'll leave you feeling full. One." Dillon's voice flowed through the car. Anyone who listened could tell that the DJ was a 150 lb white boy but I had to admit—he sounded good. It was a natural fit. I texted him to see if he could pick me up on his way home and he answered yes right away. I sent him the address and he said he would be there soon.

"Do you want to come inside?" Simon asked when we pulled up outside of Tim and Eric's apartment, the sun brightly lit in the sky now. I got out of the car and handed him the car keys.

"No. I'm going to wait for Dillon to pick me up then I'm going home to sleep until forever."

"Yeah, me too. I'll wait with you."

"No. Go to sleep, I'll see you later."

"You sure?"

"Yeah. I'll see you at work tomorrow."

He turned for the door. "Just so you know," he spoke without turning around, "I would go to a party in the stars with you any day. Mushrooms or not."

"I know."

I heard a car pull up. "Hey," Dillon said as rolled the window down. "Someone stay out a little too late?"

"I could ask you the same thing. I heard you on the radio." I got in and shut the car door. "You were great."

"Thanks." He pulled away from the sidewalk. "They might play some of my mixes next week."

"That's awesome."

"Yeah, the morning's show producer really liked my last mix tape."

"You're doing so well."

"I hear you are too. Maggie told me about the job in Chicago. Congratulations, Q."

"Thanks. You think you'll be okay without the Spanish lessons?"

He laughed. "I'll be good. My days of selling are over. I've got a real job now."

"Wow. Look at you. You're growing up right before my eyes."

"Am I taking you home?" He asked when we pulled onto a main roadway.

"My car's parked at the bar over on Oneida."

"I know where that is." He turned his blinker on to cut across the back streets.

"Rough night?" He asked while we drove. He eyed the teal sundress I'd been wearing for almost 24 hours. I ditched the shoes I failed to keep on during the baby shower. The bottoms of my feet were completely black from walking barefoot.

"It was a long night."

"I guess."

He pulled the car into the parking lot and parked alongside my jeep. "Thanks for picking me up. I owe you one."

"No problem. I always got time for my day ones." He honked the horn twice and drove away. He's an odd kid, that's for sure and Maggie might beat herself up over it, but Dillon turned out well.

The rest of my day alternated between napping and looking at much too expensive apartments. Even with the money saved all summer, financially there was no way I could afford a decent one-bedroom apartment. Finding roommates on the Internet scared me. My only viable option for living alone was to rent out a finished basement turned apartment in an elderly couple's house. We exchanged emails back and forth, I'm assuming for them to flesh out if I was an axe murderer. It was a two-way street and I did my research on them as well. I made sure their email address was legitimate and their street address matched property taxes. Previous tenants came up in the search as well and they were all still very much alive. You really can find anything on the Internet.

My bulleted list was getting smaller.

15

$2,730.04

"Wade can I talk to you for a minute." I stood determined in the open doorway to his office Monday morning.

"Sure." He said casually. He looked up from the paperwork on his desk. "Have a sit." He gestured to the metal folding chair in front of his desk.

I sat down, adjusting myself in the chair before I made eye contact again.

"What's up?"

"I'm sorry to do this on such short notice. I'm truly thankful for the job you've given me and my time spent here."

Wade raised his hands to stop me from talking. "But you got a job somewhere else."

My shoulders loosened immediately. "How did you know?"

"I've been in this business a long time. By now I know when someone is just passing through quickly, like yourself, and when someone is going to be here a while." He nodded in the direction of the production room. "You have nothing to apologize for."

"Thank you. I feel so much better now."

"Where's the job?" He asked. He seemed legitimately interested.

"Chicago."

He let out a whistle of approval. "The windy city, huh? Better bring some hairspray." He chuckled to himself.

"I'll remember that. Thanks again." I stood up.

"We'll have to get a lot of work done in these next two weeks now, won't we?" His tone was joking, but I knew that's how he got his point across.

"Yes sir." I nodded and walked back to my desk.

Wade wasn't fucking around. He made sure my last two weeks at Flashy Foods were my busiest. He pushed up orders that didn't need to be filled until the middle of October. He didn't want to fall behind with orders while he searched for a new painter.

Simon and Gloria were annoyed. I could tell. Talk radio played louder than normal and cups of coffee appeared on my desk less frequently. I didn't blame them. I was leaving them high and dry.

We were finishing up the last of our work Friday afternoon when Simon walked towards my desk. "Want to hang out this weekend?" Simon said.

He'd barely spoken to me all week and now all of a sudden he wanted to hang out. I wanted to call him out on that but I was too tired, my fingers were cramped from holding my paintbrushes too tightly and the air was so thick and humid I swear I could've choked on it.

"Are you talking to me?" I said dryly. I continued painting the carrot in front of me.

"Yeah. Who else?" He rested one foot on the milk crate.

"I assumed when you ignored me all week that meant you didn't want to hang out."

"Not ignoring you." He said. I looked up and he pushed his shoulders back and puffed his chest out a little. "We were all busy."

"Mmhmm." I smudged a final dab of orange on a bare spot. "I can't. I need to pack." That much was true. I was leaving in two weeks and I hadn't sorted through anything yet. I just unpacked from school and the thought of repeating that task again made my stomach lurch.

"Right."

As someone who normally prides herself on being immature, I refrained from saying anything to him while he retreated to the other side of the room. I shook my head to myself and rolled my eyes.

Did we just have a passive aggressive fight?

No. First of all we are not a *we*. I am a me and he is a he. Secondly, he's got nothing to be mad about when he knew this was my plan the entire summer. He was acting stupid.

Now seemed as good a time as ever to be done for the day. I turned my desk light off and gathered my things. Neither Simon nor Gloria acknowledged me when I walked by them on my way out.

"Five days." Maggie cheered into my ear. "Five more days of that place and you're free."

I was barely a minute into my drive when I called her to complain about work. "It shouldn't bother me. I gave them two weeks notice. Why are they acting like this?"

"Because he's obviously upset. From what you've told me, Gloria sounds like a mute anyway and Simon is just mad you're leaving and he won't be able to penetrate you anymore."

"You're right." I sighed and leaned back in the driver's seat. As always Maggie brought some much needed perspective into my thinking.

"Something like this happened at my job last year. This girl Amy was high up in the human resources department and one random day she put her two weeks notice in. She had the opportunity to partner up in some consulting firm in Atlanta. Obviously she had to take the job. She would have been bat shit crazy not to. That still didn't make it suck less for the rest of us when we spent extra hours picking up the slack while they interviewed her replacements."

"Was that supposed to make me feel better?" I asked. "Because I feel like you wanted to make me feel better but there was a plot twist at the end."

"Yes it's supposed to make you feel better." She groaned into the phone. "The point is even though she annoyed some people, she made herself the priority and made the best choice for her. Don't feel bad for making decisions that further your life, even if it pisses some people off."

"Lead with that next time."

"Will do. Sorry to let you go, I have a staff meeting to get to."

"No that's fine. Thanks for picking up."

"Anytime. I'll see you soon."

"See you soon." I hung up.

The thing with Flashy Foods would blow over, but if it didn't, then it didn't. I couldn't let a couple of disgruntled employees rattle me about what was going on in my life.

"What about this shirt?" Mom asked. She held up a green, long-sleeved turtleneck I wore in 5th grade.

The clock on my nightstand hadn't reached 10:00 am on Saturday morning and Mom had already gone through half of my wardrobe throwing things in random piles on my floor.

"I don't know."

"Chicago is cold and windy. An exposed neck is not something to be messed with."

"I understand that, but that's why I have scarves and jackets. Turtlenecks are a little outdated for anyone not over 40 or an avid skier."

"Fine." She said in a way that meant it was anything but. She folded it and threw it in the donation pile.

Finding compromise and balance with Mom was something I was working on, like when I agreed to pack a fedora hat she bought me because she thought it made me look more artsy. There were however some things that I could not budge on and a ninja turtle foreskin colored turtleneck was one of them.

She checked her phone for the fourth time in as many minutes. "Mom." I called to her sharply. "She's fine. Delaney said she would call us if anything happens."

"I know." She put the phone down but kept her eyes on the screen. "Her due date is tomorrow, she could go into labor at any time."

I folded a pair of jeans and put them in the pile of clothes to bring with me. "Isn't she the one that's supposed to be nervous?" I asked innocently.

"A mother does not ever stop worrying about her children." Mom was talking about Delaney, but the way her eyes were staring at me with such intent I knew she meant those words for me as well.

I didn't push the subject further and said nothing else when she checked her phone for a notification of some sort every second like a narcissistic teenager for the rest of the afternoon.

By Sunday night Delaney still hadn't had gone into labor.

My parents spent the weekend leaping at any vibration or sound thinking it was their phone going off to let them know it was time. They would have been over at the house if Delaney hadn't banished them after she caught both of them stopping by unannounced every hour "just to check on her."

My time was best spent in my room, packing. Piles of boxes were stacked neatly at the foot of my bed, towels and linens to be shipped ahead of time. The apartment had furniture already and that was one less thing I had to worry (spend money) about.

Cleaning and packing my room revealed that I was still in possession of an unhealthy amount of slap bracelets from elementary school, I did not dust my electronics nearly enough and it made me slightly sad for a moment.

It happened when a stack of sketchbooks from college fell from a shelf in my closet. I picked them up and flipped one open, pausing to look over some of the drawings.

Out of all the classes I took in college, drawing was my least favorite. Each semester I avoided drawing classes at all costs, taking only the minimal requirements for my major. I leafed through the smudged pages of the sketchbook and remembered each drawing well enough. As much as I hated drawing classes, I would take four years of them just to be able to go back to college again.

I threw the book on my floor.

No.

That's not true. I'm about to start my first real job in a big, new city. I'm going to have my own apartment where I can store kitchen spatulas I will never use. The American Dream has dropped itself right into my lap and it made no sense for me to waste my time longing for things that would never be anymore.

I picked up the notebook and put it in my throwaway pile.

I hated my drawing classes anyway.

The next morning was the first time all summer I dreaded the idea of work. As soon as my feet hit the floor from my bed, a pit swelled in my stomach.

I took my time showering and getting ready. I even drank a cup of coffee with my parents on the patio before I left to kill more time.

I was still early. The parking lot was empty when I pulled in and I used my set of keys to unlock the front door, flipping on the lights on my way through the showroom.

My mood took an immediate nosedive when I walked into the production room. Rows and rows of dried fake food lined the space in front of my desk. The long table where Gloria and Simon sat was covered in unwashed tools and chunks of discarded clay.

I grabbed the wastebasket under my desk and swept tiny chunks into the trash.

The clay wasn't dry which meant whoever made this mess, most likely Simon, hadn't made it too long ago. I looked over to the kiln and even though it was turned off, the faint smell of drying clay still clung to the room.

I turned when the knob on the door to the loading area twisted. Instinctively, I crouched behind the table and clutched the detailing tool with the sharpest point. The handle jiggled again and the door swung open.

I peeked up at a disheveled looking Simon coming through the door. "Jesus." I stood and dropped the tool on the table. "Where the fuck did you come from?"

He rubbed his eyes and walked over slowly. "I worked all night. I pulled my car into the loading area and slept in there for an hour." He sat down in the chair next to me. The bags under his eyes made his whole face look swollen.

"The couch not working out too good for you?"

Simon sat up straight and leaned forward to crack his back. "No." He sighed. "The car didn't work out well, either."

"Weren't you awfully busy?" I turned my head and nodded in the direction of my desk.

"Yeah actually," Simon began. He scratched the top of his head. "Wade wanted me to get it all done for you." His voice was tight. "He said once you paint this last batch of stuff you're good to leave."

His words caught me off-guard. I assumed the workload this week would be like last week. I braced myself for twelve-hour days and endless silence. Now the food by my desk didn't seem like a lot at all. It would take me a day and a half at most. I could probably get it all done today if I stayed late tonight.

"Oh. Okay."

"Don't worry about the money, either. Wade said he'll pay you for the full week for all the extra work you've done."

"Thanks." The word fell flatly off my tongue.

What else was there to say? I stood and picked up the first row of food from the line, loaves of sandwich bread for a lunch display, and put them on my desk. I grabbed roughly for the brown paint on the shelf and missed, hitting the row of gloss finish below. Two tubes of paint tumbled onto the desk. Simon looked over at the noise and I turned away from his stare. I picked up the tubes and continued my morning in silence.

I know it makes me a hypocrite to expect a grand good-bye from anyone at Flashy Foods. Okay fine, it makes me a hypocrite to expect a grand good-bye from Simon. I spent the whole summer telling him that I couldn't wait to leave and that my life belonged somewhere else. He probably thinks he did me a favor by getting all the food done. Now I had extra time to spend with everyone before I left.

We continued to tip toe around one another with a silence that suffocated the room. I worked at mach speed to get everything done and Simon moped around the production room with a coffee in his hand for most of the morning, his eyes completely bloodshot. He probably should have gone home, but we both knew he wouldn't.

It wasn't until early evening, after Gloria left for the day, that he came over to talk. "Wow." He said. He stared at the painted pieces along the windowsill. They needed to be glossed still, but even Megan could handle glossing them throughout the week without fucking them up.

"Yeah. Five apples left and that's it."

"Are you excited?" He picked up an unpainted apple and threw it into the air.

"For what?"

"Your last day. Chicago."

"I am. What's with the face, though?"

"Nothing."

"Oh yeah."

He let out a single, hard laugh. "It's funny, that's all."

"What's so funny?" I tried not to scowl.

"You."

I sighed and put the apple down. I didn't want to play this stupid game. At this point I just wanted to finish these five apples and leave Flashy Foods for good. "Why are you doing this?" I asked finally.

"I think it's funny. Because you're selfish in every part of your life except your career."

Where the fuck was this coming from? "Taking this job is being selfish with my career." I bit down on my lip, waiting for his response.

"You think you're making a career move. You're taking some cool sounding job in a big city, but you're not even doing what you love." He put the apple on the table and folded his arms across his chest.

"This is what I want to do. Working in a gallery has always been my plan." I could hear how defensive I sounded.

"Whatever you say." He said casually and walked back to his desk.

I wanted to throw an apple at the back of his head. I wanted to tell him how he was just being immature, and even though he thinks he does, he doesn't know the answers to everything, but my phone buzzed on my desk. It was Mom calling. I picked it up immediately.

"Hey."

"Your sister's water broke. The baby's coming."

"Okay. Are you on your way to the hospital? Is she like crowning right now or do I have some time to finish stuff up at work?"

"She's dilated five centimeters. You have a little while."

"Okay."

"Your father and I are going now, though. Just in case."

"I'll be there soon."

"Okay, bye."

I hung up the phone and picked up the half-finished apple. I painted the rest of it in quick, rushed strokes, not stopping to check if it was fully covered. It wasn't my best work but did I really care anymore? The baby was coming, I was done with this job—let there be light.

Simon looked over when I stood up to put the apple on the windowsill. "Don't worry about the last ones. I'll finish them. You should go." He offered with a tired voice.

Normally I would have said no and told him to fuck off, but I just wanted to be done. "Are you sure?"

By the time he replied that yes, he was sure, I stood in front of him with my bag hanging off my shoulder and my car keys in my hand. "Thanks, I appreciate it." I gave him a quick hug and kiss on his cheek. "I'm sure I'll talk to you before I leave."

"Yeah. Give me a call." He stepped out of the embrace and I hurried out of the door without looking back.

Julian Christian Thompson was born at 3:37 in the morning on August 23. He came in weighing an alarming 9 lbs. 12 oz. and was 21 inches long. He was a big guy from his very first breath. The first millisecond I laid eyes on him I fell in love. A completely different kind of love that wraps your entire heart in sugar and puts it in the oven to melt.

I wanted to hold him in my arms and protect him from the world, wrap his tiny hands in mine and never let go. He was so snuggly. Each time I held him in the hospital, he nestled further into me and my heart melted yet again. I never thought I would love someone so instantly, but here I was wiping happy tears from my eyes and falling in love with this beautiful baby.

"How do you feel?" I asked Delaney. She was lying in her hospital bed, the baby swaddled protectively into her chest. Corliss sat on the edge of the bed and stared adoringly at them both. The three of them looked so happy in that moment. The emotion was evident by their loopy grins. It reminded me of the cheesy pictures of the family that comes inside the picture frames when you buy them.

"I feel like everything has changed. The moment he came out, my life became bigger than just me. He makes me never want to break a promise to anyone, ever again. He makes me want to do everything better because he deserves it." I wanted to gag at her statement, but she's Delaney and she deserves this more than anyone in the world.

She's perfect.

Julian's perfect.

This is perfect.

Motherhood really did suit her.

16

$3,201.59

"We're going to be late." Maggie said before she applied another coat of mascara to her lashes. "You can't be late for weddings."

Elliot's wedding was finally here.

I spent the past week and a half cuddling Julian as much as I could while I promisng Mom I wouldn't take the subway in Chicago after midnight.

Despite our earlier conversation stating otherwise, I hadn't called Simon since I left Flashy Foods. Part of me was annoyed with how he acted during my last day, but it was mostly because I had more important things to do. My last days at home weren't going to be spent on a random friend I sometimes fornicated with. They were going to be spent on my family.

"Relax. When is the last time one of those things started on time?" I grabbed for her deodorant and put some under both armpits.

"Did you just use my deodorant?" She looked at me through her vanity mirror.

"Yes. Don't be weird. I just took a shower." I looked in the mirror and wiped lip-gloss from the side of my mouth. "Come on. We're going to be late." I walked out of her room.

"You're an asshole." She called after me.

"Are you nervous?" she asked me on our drive to the ceremony.

"I'm not the one getting married. Why would I be nervous?"

"Because you're armpits are already starting to sweat."

I looked down and saw the beginnings of a stain in the shape of Hawaii on my dress under my right armpit. "Shit. I'm not even nervous about today."

"You're nervous about something."

"I'm starting to get anxious about Chicago." I turned the air conditioning up and pointed the blower at my armpit.

Chicago was starting to worry me a bit.

Mike and Matt both emailed me multiple times a day now. The subject of the emails ranged from work attire (nothing patterned, black is preferred) to their coffee preferences they want me to bring on my first morning (two large soy bean lattes served from a French press). They told me the coffee shop down the block sold them. I should probably find another place though after my last run in with them.

The two of them also want me to be available to open and close the gallery if they need me to due to their weekly 'socialite obligations.' This job was starting to sound more like a personal assistant and not a gallery one.

Okay yes, I had to start somewhere and yes, this was the opportunity that I very much wanted, but what would this job teach me and what would this job cost me?

"You're just nervous because it's a big change." Maggie reached across the center console and patted my knee. "I felt the same way when I moved to Houston. You just need a little time to adjust to it. By the end of your first month you'll love it so much you won't ever come home."

Part of me believed her and that my new life simply needed some getting used to, but part of me couldn't help but pump the breaks at the thought of it all.

Now wasn't the time for this discussion. We pulled into the orchard and followed the line of cars to park on the grass on the far right side of the property. "Right. You're right." I settled on saying.

Maggie flipped the passenger seat visor down and checked her reflection in the mirror. "Of course I'm right."

I pulled in a spot and turned the car off. "Ready to be the best looking dates here?" I asked and stared at my reflection in the rear-view mirror. The light yellow maxi dress I wore, courtesy of Maggie's closet, made me look like an ethereal sun child. That's how my personal style worked, I was either dressed like a fashion messiah at the top of my game or homeless beggar—there was no in between.

"Let's make this wedding epic." She said.

The ceremony was beautiful. They were married on the edge of the orchards under a flowered trellis. Elliot beamed from ear to ear the entire time. Michelle's white lace dress looked beautiful in front of the flowers and she skipped the traditional veil for a flower crown. The ceremony wasn't too long, not too much religion, but there was Corinthians. There's always Corinthians.

Maggie and I sat in the back next to the flower shop owners, Mr. and Mrs. West and I'd be lying if I said I didn't dab at my eyes slightly when they exchanged vows they wrote to each other.

The cocktail hour was in the barn next to the orchards. The theme was country with an eco-friendly, hipster flare. The doors of the barn were open and both doors were wrapped in burlap-covered wildflowers. The cocktail area was filled with barrels of hay and drinks were served out of mason jars. The theme was very in your face, but they served moonshine and it was open bar so I tried to keep quiet about the décor.

We walked from the barn to a large, string light covered tent for the sit down dinner. "I'll get us a drink. You find our table." Maggie instructed..

The tent was filled with a happy buzz, a little from the nuptials, but mostly from the cocktail hour. Weddings had the tendency to do that. Tonight would turn into a shit show, but so far everyone seemed to be keeping it in check, for now. I did see a couple guys from high school funneling beers in the parking lot. We had an hour, tops, before someone spilled a drink on the dance floor.

The place cards were folded on a long, decorated table in the back on the tent. I scanned for our names and plucked them from beneath table twelve. Also at our table were Melanie and Mike, Charlie, Taylor Danahy and two of the Elliot's third cousins, a guy and girl close to our age.

Maggie walked up behind me with an entire mason jar of moonshine in her hand. "Put this in your purse. I swiped it from behind the bar. They only have one bartender for dinner service. I'm not waiting in a long line for drinks all night."

I stuffed it in my bag. "We're going to need it." I pointed to our table number. "Look who's at our table."

She ran her eyes over the table. "Well," she said when she saw who it was, "I'll take that moonshine again."

A nice combination of earthy folk and country music played throughout dinner. The moonshine proved to be the perfect social lubricant for table twelve.

Maggie was right. The line for drinks during dinner service was awful. Charlie and Taylor stood in line for fifteen minutes to get a round of beers for the table. We felt bad and passed the jar around to everyone. We finished it before the salads were cleared and Maggie volunteered to poach another one.

Melanie was surprisingly more fun with a bunch of moonshine coursing through her veins. "I smoke weed every once in a while." She confessed and slapped her hand over her mouth. She giggled hysterically. "Mike loves it because it makes me horny." I closed my eyes and started laughing, my body shaking lightly with each chuckle.

Even Elliot's cousins were drinking some of the hooch. Lauren and Drew were the perfect addition to the table. They were both 30. Twin brother and sister and looking to get completely hammered to take away from the judging vibe their family gave them because their younger cousin got married before them.

Lauren and I went shot for shot after the second bottle of moonshine arrived at the table.

"This is really fun." I said to Maggie.

"What?" She tried to talk over the DJ coming on to announce dancing had begun.

"This is so much fun." I said louder. I took another sip of moonshine. She arched her eyebrow. "Seriously. I'm having a lot of fun."

"You should tell everyone about your job." Maggie said loudly during the .3 seconds of silence in between songs. Six sets of eyes turned towards me at once.

"I got a job in Chicago. I leave Monday." I took another sip of moonshine.

"That's awesome." Charlie said instantly.

A chorus of congratulations from the table followed.

"Thanks." I smiled awkwardly. "Who wants to dance?" I stood up and walked towards the dance floor not looking back to see if anyone was following me.

Maggie caught up to me a moment later. "Do you want to talk about something?"

"I'm good. Let's dance." I said.

She tilted her head at an angle and pursed her lips. "Let's go outside and talk."

"Okay." I moved to the entrance to the tent.

Maggie turned around and walked back to the table. "I'm grabbing the moonshine. I'll meet you outside by your car."

The sun was barely peeking out from the horizon when I got outside. The wedding didn't end until midnight, either. I would most likely transform back into a pumpkin by then because my drunk hit me full force on the walk to my car. My head was engulfed in a sheet of fog and my brain felt heavy. I needed water and marijuana immediately.

Once I got to my car, Maggie wasn't far behind with the moonshine and my keys. I pushed the moonshine away when she offered it to me and climbed in the backseat of my jeep to unearth a forgotten full bottle of water under the passenger's seat. I drank half the bottle in one sloppy gulp. "Grab that joint from my console, please." Maggie walked around and came back with the joint already lit between her fingers.

"You're being weird." She took a hit and passed the J to me.

"I'm drunk."

"Not that. You've been like this since before the ceremony."

I took the joint in between my fingers and sucked in a deep hit. "I'm scared." I said after I exhaled a milky cloud of smoke. "I'm scared that the choice I made was wrong and it's going to lead me to a miserable life." I took a sip of water.

"That's a pretty big conclusion to come a few days before you're supposed to start a new job across the country." she said. Her tone wasn't accusing or rude, it was matter of fact. Maggie took the joint from my hands.

"What do I do?"

"No." she squealed. "I can't answer that. You can't do this anymore, Quinn. You can't make other people in charge of your own life. We're only getting older. It's only going to get harder."

I braced my hands on my legs to steady myself from her words more than the alcohol. "I've wanted this job for so long," I said after a minute. "And now that I have it, I'm confused. The whole thing looks good on paper, but is it really a good move for me to make?"

Maggie opened her mouth to speak but I raised both my hands to signal her to stop.

"Don't say anything yet." I hiccupped, and knew it was only moments before I puked. "I know I owe it to myself to go and try. If not, the whole lifetime full of regret thing, yadda, yadda, yadda." My words slurred together and I stared at the ground for something to focus on. "What if it sucks?" I hiccupped again.

"You're not going to be held there against your will. You're 23 and allowed to have more than one job for the rest of your life. If it sucks, leave," she answered flatly.

"Yeah." My eyes fluttered up in her direction and the feeling of nausea stirred once more in my stomach. "That's true. But I think I'm going to puke real quick. I'll meet you back inside."

"You good?"

"Yeah. I just need a couple minutes. Leave the joint," I said before my body started to heave, all of my limbs convulsing at the sheer force of puke coming out of my mouth. It sounded like someone dumped a bucket of water onto the ground when it hit the grass.

I felt better instantly.

"I'll stay right here." Maggie rubbed soothing circles into my back with one hand and held back my hair with her other as my body emptied itself again and again on the grass.

"Thanks."

It subsided after a few more minutes and Maggie produced hand sanitizer, gum and a comb from her purse.

"You carry all of this?"

"It's my job to be prepared," she said.

"Just light that joint." I ran the brush through my knotted hair.

Ten minutes and another dry heave later, I walked into the bathroom, praying for a moment alone to collect myself. There was no point in trying to pretend that I was sober, but I felt a little better.

I splashed water on my face and tried to wipe off the make-up that pooled under my eyes. The comb helped my hair and if you squinted slightly, I still looked like a solid eight.

The whirling sound of a toilet flush filled the room and a moment later Melanie appeared, every single blond hair on her head was still pinned straight. Even drunk she still looked every bit the model wife. I let out a sharp laugh.

Melanie made no attempts to make a smart-ass comment when she washed her hands and I continued to collect myself on the other side of the sink. I looked rough and she could have been a bitch about it. I was at her mercy. It's not like I would see her after today so what did it matter. Now seemed like the perfect time to ask her the question she had been waiting fifteen years for me to ask.

"How do you do it?" I asked.

"What?"

"God. It seems like you all have your shit together. I mean look at yours and Mike's fucking jobs." I wiped my nose.

"You're not serious," Melanie spoke as she reapplied her lipstick. "That is not true at all."

"Look at you and Mike. You're married and you both have good jobs. He works at the college," I slurred.

She laughed so hard she snorted. "Mike is a groundskeeper at the college. He power washes the sidewalks in the spring when the geese come back and shit all over the place."

"He made it seem..."

"He made it seem like he was the fucking dean, right? Even my parents don't know." She hoisted herself onto the sink. "They would never let me marry him if they knew we weren't financially responsible as they like to call it."

I swallowed thickly. "I had no idea."

"Does anyone really have their shit together?" She lifted her head back and let out a laugh. "We're in so much credit card debt. Mike yells at me all the time because I can't stop shopping at Target. Those assholes get me. Every time I walk in there I know I'm down $100."

"Me too." Nothing brings two girls together more than their mutual love/hate relationship with that store.

We were quiet for a moment before Melanie spoke again. "What ever happened to that guy I saw you with?"

"Simon," I replied. I hoisted myself on the sink next to her.

"Right. Simon. I liked him, he was good for you."

"You met him once."

"Yeah, but he like, really made you happy," she said in a serious tone. "You laughed a lot with him. You didn't laugh with Charlie."

"Simon's just a friend."

Melanie went on as if she didn't hear me. "Don't get me wrong, I love Charlie. He's Mike's best friend, but I never saw the two of you together." She put her hand on my shoulder and I forced a polite smile. "You were too much for him." I couldn't tell if the conversation was going somewhere or she was trying to give me a compliment. "Charlie likes things simple and you're anything but." She hopped off the sink, straightening her dress and fluffing her hair in the mirror before walking to the door. "But hey, I'm just a small town girl who never went to college. What do I know, right?"

"Yeah," I said more out of confusion than agreement. She smiled at me and walked out of the bathroom. In all the years I've known Melanie that was the best conversation I had with her.

Simon.

I suppose I could call him to pick me up and we could have one last sexual tryst, but at this point I'd already puked, I was tired and I was leaving in two days. I wanted to go home and sleep in my bed.

Maggie found me in the barn on my way out of the bathroom. "Don't worry about throwing up. At least you did it in the parking lot. Elliot's cousin Lauren just puked in the bushes on her way out of the reception right in front of Michelle's grandparents." She laughed sharply.

Poor Lauren.

"Can we go home?" I asked once we got back to the table. "I'm partied out." I took a sip of water.

"Yeah. It's about to get real sloppy in here anyway. Charlie and Taylor just funneled the rest of the moonshine. We should probably head out. I'll text Dillon."

"Let's find Elliot and Michelle and say our farewells." I grabbed my purse off my chair. "We can Irish good-bye everyone else."

"I like your style."

We found the happy couple standing by the entrance to the tent. Elliot had his arm draped around Michelle's waist and they looked so effortlessly in love in made my drunken heart swell, or maybe I was going to puke again.

"The wedding was beautiful," I said, wrapping each of them in a hug. "We're going to head out though."

"Quinn puked," Maggie confessed dramatically when she leaned over to hug them.

"That too. Plus I'm leaving for Chicago on Monday." I know it was their special day, but it was time to become familiar with the fact that in 48 hours, Chicago would be my home.

"Good luck with the new job." Elliot patted my shoulder.

"Have fun on the honeymoon." I waved at them and Maggie and I walked back to my car to meet her brother.

The next morning I woke up with an earth-shattering hangover. My lips were swollen and cracked from dehydration and the inside of my mouth could sand a fucking coffee table it was so dry.

The whole family was coming over for a good-bye brunch but all I wanted to do was lay in my bed. Obviously that wasn't an option so I dragged myself to the bathroom to shower.

The euphoric feeling of being bathed staved off my hangover for about twenty minutes before I felt like shit again.

I went to the kitchen and drank two cups of coffee in rapid succession. I'd just coast off a caffeine buzz.

Mom stood over the stove flipping bacon in the kitchen. I took a seat at the counter, nursing my third cup of coffee. "How was the wedding?" She asked.

"It was good."

"Did you say all your goodbyes?"

"Yeah. Got 'em all taken care of."

"That's good."

Patrick was the first to arrive for brunch. He walked into the kitchen carrying a box of donuts in one hand and a can of pepper spray in the other. "Here." He tossed me the pepper spray. "This is for protection and shit."

"Aw. Thanks Pat." I stood and gave him a hug, reaching around him to take the donuts out of his hand before plucking a glazed one from the box.

Delaney, Corliss and the baby arrived soon after. In between more coffee and too much breakfast food, everyone fussed over Julian and I slumped on the couch trying to get a handle on my shit. My thoughts were still jumbled from yesterday. I passed right out when Dillon dropped me off last night.

I didn't have sober time to process everything I'd finally said out loud. It's too late to back out of the job. That option is off the table completely seeing as most of my underwear and other belongings have already been shipped to Chicago, but at the moment that's all I wanted to do.

I'm being stupid.

Everyone feels like this before they move, right? Maybe it's my hormones fucking with me before my period this month. Everyone else always chalks it up to PMS, it's definitely just that.

"Are you okay?" Delaney asked when we washed dishes after brunch. I told her to sit down and that I'd do them, but she refused.

"Yeah I'm good."

"Are you ready for tomorrow?"

"Yeah. Definitely. I'm so excited. I'm going to miss you guys though."

"We'll send you pictures everyday and we'll video chat all the time."

"Yeah."

The baby cried from the other room. "Go. I'll finish up here," I said.

"Thanks." She turned and walked out of the kitchen and reappeared a few minutes later with a diaper bag over her shoulder. "Hey we're going to go, the baby needs to go down for his nap."

I turned the sink off and followed her back into the living room where Corliss was cradling the baby in his arms and Patrick was inching closer to the door for his exit as well.

"Alright. This is good-bye." I smiled and kissed Julian's forehead. "I love you sweet baby boy."

"I love you too," Corliss said and leaned down to kiss the top of my head.

"Ha. Ha."

"Be safe," he said. "Good luck, you'll do great."

"Thanks."

"Call us when you get settled. We'll send pictures every day." Delaney said as she wrapped her arms around me. "I love you."

"Love you too and I will."

Patrick walked over to me while my parents continued to fuss over the baby down the hall to the front door. "Don't be stupid and go out by yourself or get so drunk you lose shit." He looked me sternly in my eye.

"Yes, captain."

"I'm serious. Don't be stupid. Good luck with the job." He hugged me and tapped my back twice before letting go.

"Love you too, Pat." I called to him.

"Love you, Q." He turned around and smiled.

"Now you're sure you have everything packed?" Mom asked later on that day.

"Yes. Everything."

"Nothing else needs to be done?"

"No. Everything is done."

"You're sure."

"HIV Positive."

"Quinn."

I smirked and rolled back over to press my face against the couch and take a nap.

At 6:00 my parents both told me to just go to bed. My flight was early anyway. At least this way I could 'sleep off my alcohol' as they so lovingly put it.

You think for two people who own a bar, they'd be a little more understanding of my suffering. I didn't fight them and trudged quietly up the stairs into my bed. It was probably better for me to be asleep anyway. At least when I was unconscious I couldn't feel the pit slowly starting to grow in my stomach.

I woke up in the middle of the night. The neon red numbers on my clock said it was 1:23 and suddenly I was wired. I crawled out of bed, grabbed my last joint and shimmied out my bedroom window to sit on the roof.

Lighting the j and taking a long drag got me thinking that finding a weed dealer in Chicago will have be top billing for me once I get settled. Until then I would have to rely on copious amounts of alcohol to see me through.

I leaned back on my elbows and continued leisurely smoking the joint, soaking up my last hours of quietness. The apartment I was renting in Chicago was directly underneath the L train. I'm not envisioning much quiet, even if I am living in the basement. I took another hit and my lips curved upward slightly because the crackling of weed was the only sound in the night. Maybe I would just need to be high a lot.

I pinched the clip of the joint and threw it off the roof into Mr. Lanigan's shrubs and crawled back inside to my bed. I closed my eyes and waited to fall asleep but I slept too much during the day and now I couldn't fall back asleep.

I watched the clock get closer to my wake up time of 4:00, the less confident I became. At 3:45 I finally just got up and took a shower. It was time.

Marlowe and I sat on my bed while my parents showered and got ready. Her little dog body curled itself against mine and it made me way sadder than I thought it would. She was my road dog this summer and I was going to miss the pooch, no doubt about it. Dogs can totally sense when you're about to abandon them too, she's been giving me Sarah McLaughlin dog commercial eyes for a week now.

"Ready?" My dad poked his head in my door.

"Yeah."

"We'll be downstairs."

I stood up and gave Marlowe one last kiss. I walked to the door and she stayed sprawled out on my bed looking like an actual angel with her tail wagging at warp speed.

We were out of the house in record time, partly because I've already been up for three hours and partly because before my final nap of the day yesterday my mother forced me to pack all my stuff in the car so she could make sure I had everything I needed. I guess she didn't believe me when I told her I did.

My stomach began the familiar lurch on the ride to the airport. By the time my parents were hugging me goodbye after I checked in and telling me they love me, my mind was somewhere else completely. I remember squeezing them tight and whispering that I loved them too, but I was completely detached from the moment.

I reached the top of the escalator, still in a daze. How I made it to my gate I'm still not sure, but I did. I sat down in the seat closest to the gate and closed my eyes. The uncomfortable plastic of the chair did nothing to soothe me before the flight and there was no more denying it—I was completely shitting my pants over this entire thing.

17

$6,340.43

I arrived in Chicago on a bright Monday morning in September.

I left Chicago on a dark Monday night in March.

I lasted six months. Which, when looking back on the experience, is five more months than I thought I would.

I departed the windy city for a multitude of reasons. The main one being that my job sucked because it turns out, Hipster Thing One and Hipster Thing Two were not qualified to run a gallery. They grew restless and realized their passion wasn't in art and they wanted to open a vegan food truck.

Being a personal bitch to two pussy-ass rich boys spending their parent's money was no longer a dream of mine. I say personal bitch because the only time I was actually in the gallery was when I had to run it because those two ass hats were recovering from a bender of some sort. I made sure everything ran smoothly while they popped molly and river danced across the entire city of Chicago.

It wasn't just that specific gallery job either. Sure those two guys are complete dick heads, but the idea of working in a gallery didn't complete me like I thought it would. Being exposed to what the job really was threw everything off balance for me.

My living conditions were less than stellar. The basement had a tiny bathroom that ran along side a kitchenette. When the listing said the apartment came with furniture, it meant there was a coffee table and couch that pulled out into a bed. The whole place had a real minimalist vibe going on.

On the off chance I wasn't being an errand boy at work I was home painting. The good thing about your bed coming out of your couch is that it's a real space saver and there was plenty of room to set up an area to paint at. That probably sounds really sad, but I don't think it was. There were some nights when I would stay up well into the next day trying new techniques, getting familiar with different surfaces. Even though my days were spent miserable, my nights were filled with vibrant shades of color and solitude and probably too much weed. Those nights were some of my best memories of Chicago.

The gallery made me hungry.

Seeing others people's work on display made me crave that for myself. Helping other people make their dreams come true wouldn't satisfy me anymore. I wanted to make my own dream comes true. So I kept painting. Every few weeks I would send some off to Maggie and my parents. Delaney and Corliss loved the stuff I sent them. I even sent one out to Flashy Foods.

It's good that I left Chicago though. I didn't appreciate the city enough to struggle in it. I probably didn't give it the full chance it deserved and that's on me, but there was no point staying in a place that no longer held the key to my dreams.

Sometimes it's better that it doesn't work out. At least that's what Maggie told me when she picked me up from the airport with a suitcase full of winter clothes for the warm Houston spring.

I did agree to move in with her if my plans fell apart. I stayed with her from March until May. Maggie got me a temporary job working as a caterer but I mostly painted in her living room when she went to work each morning and worked two nights a week catering.

Maggie even got one of her regular business clients to buy two paintings I made. My first commissioned work. They completely overpaid, but I wasn't complaining. That money will keep me comfortable for a while.

Texas was fun.

Not the kind of fun you have at a birthday party when you're six, but the kind of fun you have with an aunt or uncle that you could have sworn was boring. Maggie and I spent three months in a constant fit of laughter. I formed abdominals that spring, but I didn't stay in Texas.

For the first time in my life I didn't have a plan and I was high off the freedom that came with that.

My heart kept beating all the same even though I wasn't working in an art gallery.

I came home to Springhaven a few days before Memorial Day. My parents picked me up at the airport just before midnight and the first thing I did when I got home, besides cuddle Marlowe, was crawl into my twin-sized bed. The familiar smell of dryer sheets engulfed my senses when my head hit the pillow and my heart settled. I was home.

The funniest part of that moment was just a little over a year ago I spent days moping in this bed because I didn't have a job, *I wasn't adult enough.*

That's so fucking stupid.

I'm beginning to understand things I tried to ignore last year. I realized that I'm not going to wake up one day and start acting like an adult. Adults don't even act like adults. Everyone is scared to let go and scared to grow up and scared they aren't doing it right. There is no such thing as adults. It's just a word thrown around to describe people who've let their dreams die.

This experience hasn't enlightened me to some higher calling of what I want to do with my life.

I'm 24 and it would be dumb to think that I get to ride off into the sunset this early because I've figured it all out and that's all there is. I'm simply saying that now at least I know what I don't want to do. Figuring out what you don't want is sometimes more important than figuring out what you do want.

"I'll baby sit Julian until I figured something else out. I submitted myself to a couple statewide contests when I was still in Texas," I told mom the next morning.

"But what will you do for money?"

"I'll be fine for a little bit. I have some money saved." I hadn't told her about being commissioned for two paintings. The conversation would go somewhere along the lines of my mom thinking that because I sold two paintings I thought I could make a living of selling my art. Even if that was the case, she would still panic because it's not a reliable profession no matter how good I may or may not be. The passive aggressive war between us would rage on once again. I'm smart enough to avoid that now.

"What kind of contest?"

"A few art ones. Just something to keep me busy."

"That sounds nice. What are the prizes?"

"One of the contests gives the winner their own exhibit at the Albany Institute of History and Art. The other one is money and an introduction to a board member from the Museum of Modern Art in New York City."

"Those sound like major things."

"They kind of are."

"I hope you win them both."

"Thanks, mom."

"What are your plans for the day?"

"I'm going to see Delaney and Julian. That's as far as I've thought."

"That's nice. I'm going down to the bar. I'll be home later tonight."

"Maybe I'll stop down and see you."

"I'll hold you to your words."

"That's why I added the maybe."

"Smart ass."

I made it as far as Delaney's couch because once she brought the chunk monster that is now my nephew out of his room from his nap -- nothing else could hold my attention ever again.

He's crawling all over the place now. His stubby legs are trying so hard to walk. He still hasn't gotten the hang of it though because each time he tries to take a step, he topples over and closes his eyes for a moment before getting up to try again. It's the cutest thing and now most of the videos on my phone are comprised of that exact sequence.

Sitting on Delaney's couch everyday has been the only thing penciled in on my agenda for two whole weeks. It gave her a nice break and gave me a reason to stare at her adorable baby all day, which I was currently doing.

"Hi sweet boy," I cooed into Julian's ear as he climbed on me. "You are the best baby." I giggled at him and he squealed in delight and his tiny body teetered back and forth for a moment before settling in my lap.

My phone buzzed on the table and I picked it up before Julian could notice. "Hello."

"Hello is this Quinn Kelly?"

"Yes it is. May I ask who's calling?"

"This is Angie Labella from The Albany Institute of History and Art." I motioned for my sister to grab the baby and she plucked Julian from my lap in one quick swoop.

"Hi Angie. How are you?" I stood up and walked into the kitchen.

"I'm well and yourself."

"Good."

"I'm calling to let you know that your work's been selected as the winner of this year's Norman Fielder competition. A selection of your work will be featured in a one night exhibit on Tuesday June 24th."

My mouth went dry. I swallowed thickly. What? I submitted my work to this contest on a complete whim after too much wine at dinner one night in Houston. One of those 'ah, fuck it' moments. It was nothing I actually banked on. "Thank you," I finally managed to choke out.

"My assistant will contact you with further details, but you can choose whatever thirty pieces you'd like. We'd like to see them beforehand, preferably with a description of each piece, though it does not really matter."

"That's not a problem."

"Good. You'll hear from her later this week. Congratulations, Quinn."

"Thank you, Angie."

Delaney came into the kitchen, Julian slung on her hip as soon as the conversation was over. "What happened?"

"I won."

"Won what?"

"This art competition. I'm getting a one-night exhibit in Albany."

"Ah." Delaney shrieked and Julian mimicked her sound with his own. "This is so cool. You're going to become famous."

"One step at a time."

"Call mom."

"Yeah. I will."

"I'm calling everyone." She bounced out of the room with the baby giggling wildly in her arms.

I spent the next whole week making moves. I finalized my pieces for the exhibit and sent them to Angie's assistant for approval. I decided against giving them descriptions for a few reasons. One being that some of the paintings I chose were painted in various states of inebriation and I couldn't remember what they really meant. The second reason being that it's not up to me to decide what people should get out of my work. I'd be a shitty artist if I didn't support the whole art is interpretation thing.

The day of my exhibit was finally here and what felt like everyone I had ever met in my life planned on driving the 60 miles to Albany to see it. I told my family I had to set up the exhibit two hours early and drove myself. It worked out because I would have been too nervous to force small talk for an hour in the car anyway.

The Albany Institute of History and Art was smaller than I remembered from when I was here in high school. I parked my car and walked up the sidewalk inside the front of the building. The heavy thwacks of my sandals echoing in the empty glass atrium did nothing to soothe my nerves. I found the main staircase easy enough and took the marble stairs up to the third floor, with a bag full of paintings on either shoulder.

Angela and her assistant, a chipper young woman in lime green gaucho pants, greeted me and helped me set up.

"Do you have a specific order in mind?" Angela's tone was as serious as the shoulder pads in her blazer.

"Yeah. I have them in order." I spent last night ordering them by date from earliest to the most recent paintings. The later ones were a cluster of light blues and greens with accents of yellow, a peaceful picture compared to the more violent reds and oranges that took up the first dozen paintings. "I don't mind setting them up alone." Those two were giving off a cold vibe and I wanted to be by myself for a little while longer. "It helps me get into the mindset of my work, you know becoming one with my creations."

Hot pants nodded her head like a Jesus bobble head doll on a souped up Lincoln and Angela pursed her lips and fled from the room.

It turns out I'm good at this whole artist thing because I excel at spewing bullshit and lies at every opportune moment. Art, in a sense, is getting people to buy into your bullshit. Let them interpret that the green and red painting means warmth and holiday traditions. I'm almost positive I painted that on Cinco de Mayo after Maggie and I drank $20 worth of margaritas at $2 drink night.

It took twenty minutes for me to set the paintings up in order. There was still plenty of time to kill before anyone showed up. Angela and her assistant would be good for awkward small talk, but I wanted to wait as long as I could to walk back out there with them.

"Who would have thought you would get your very own art exhibit?" A voice from behind startled me. I turned and Simon standing on my right. His tone was casual like we were mid conversation. He looked pretty good, dressed simply in a white tee shirt and jeans.

"Hey." My voice was laced with surprise. "How are you?" I quickly recovered, throwing my arms around him before I could stop myself.

"I'm good and apparently early." He nodded in the embrace and pointed his head to the paintings on the wall. "Man, this is impressive. You painted all of this?"

"Sure did."

"That's crazy. Hey I remember that one," he pointed at the phosphene painting I made last summer.

"Oh yeah, you did see that." I smiled lightly.

Silence hung in the air and I knew this was my chance to say what had I should have said a year ago. "I'm sorry for things not working out last summer. I wasn't a very good person then. Not that I'm an amazing person now, but I was mad at everything last year, mostly myself. And when I'm with someone I want to be really be there with them as the best version of myself. It was more important for me to find myself before I went looking for someone else, you know."

"Hey I get it." He rubbed his head. "Things wouldn't have worked out for us anyway last year."

"Yeah."

"So you're better now?" He said softly. There was hopefulness in his voice.

"Well now I know more of who I am and what I want."

"How'd you find that out?"

"Pushing myself to go to Chicago, even though it was scary. I think being scared and doing it anyway is the only way we'll ever learn who we are."

"Are you going to be around for a while?"

"Yeah, maybe. I'm not sure what my plans are."

"No plan. That's risky."

"Plans get too fucked up. Better to just go where life takes you." I laughed slightly hoping he would recognize I was making a joke. His crooked smile at my words told me he did. "And for the record it's Solsbury Hill."

"What?"

"My end credit song. It'd be Solsbury Hill."

"Interesting choice. That song is about coming home and you couldn't shut up about how much you hated it here last summer."

"Eh. Sometimes you've got to come back to your roots."

"So where have you been for the past year?" he asked after a moment.

"Well I lasted six months at my job in Chicago. I hated it. I quit and moved down to Texas with Maggie for a couple months. Then I came back here and who knows where I'll go next."

"Oh, so you traveled?" He didn't hide the smugness in his voice.

"Yeah some dude I met a while ago said it's better to move around a lot, get a taste for all that life has to offer, or some bull shit like that."

"Sounds like something I would say." He smirked.

"Yeah. I guess I should thank you." I shifted on my feet slightly.

"Nah. Don't thank me, you did this all on your own, I just opened up a part of yourself you hadn't seen in a while. It was all there. You just needed to be seen again."

"That's a nice way to put it."

"Some girl told me I had a way with words," he said quietly.

"She seems smart." I laughed.

"She is."